C000149980

Robert Edward Myhill Peach

The life and times of Ralph Allen

Robert Edward Myhill Peach

The life and times of Ralph Allen

ISBN/EAN: 9783337802202

Printed in Europe, USA, Canada, Australia, Japan

Cover: Foto ©Raphael Reischuk / pixelio.de

More available books at **www.hansebooks.com**

RALPH ALLEN.

THE

LIFE AND TIMES OF RALPH ALLEN

OF PRIOR PARK, BATH, INTRODUCED BY

A Short Account of Lyncombe and Widcombe,

WITH NOTICES OF HIS CONTEMPORARIES, INCLUDING
BISHOP WARBURTON, BENNET OF WIDCOMBE
HOUSE, BEAU NASH, Etc.

WITH NUMEROUS ILLUSTRATIONS.

BY

R. E. M. PEACH,

Author of *Bath, Old and New; Historic Houses in Bath; History of the Bath Abbey Church;
The Hospital of St. John Baptist; Street-Lore of Bath; Annals of Swainswick;
Rambles about Bath; History of Freemasonry in Bath; &c.*

"Quick and improved correspondence is the life of trade."

LONDON:
D. NUTT, 270-271, STRAND.
CHAS. J. CLARK, 4, LINCOLN'S INN FIELDS, W.C.
—
1895.

" I would the great world grew like thee ;
Who growest not alone in power
And knowledge, but by year and hour
In reverence and in charity."

TO

RALPH E. ALLEN, ESQUIRE,

OF HAMPTON MANOR, BATH,

COLONEL OF THE 2ND BATTALION EAST YORKSHIRE REGIMENT,

THIS LIFE

OF HIS DISTINGUISHED RELATIVE,

RALPH ALLEN, ESQUIRE, OF PRIOR PARK, BATH,

IS DEDICATED,

WITH THE MOST CORDIAL FEELINGS OF RESPECT

AND ESTEEM BY

THE AUTHOR.

CONTENTS.

Contents.

ILLUSTRATIONS.

PREFACE.

ERRATA.

In Preface, page xv, line 12 from top, *for* p. 179 *read* p. 178.
On page 11, first line at the top, *for* Belgæ *read* Belgic.

„ 12, seventeenth line from top, *for* to have lasted *read* to last.
„ 51, sixth line from bottom, *for* who has visited *read* who visited.
„ 57, third line from top, *for* younger *read* elder.
„ 67, foot note, second line, *for* rooms now *read* rooms which now. (?)
„ 217, seventeenth from top, *for* victims *read* sharpers.
„ 221, foot note, tenth line, *for* Proteus-like *read* Protean-like.   (?)

of Lyncombe and Widcombe—we have endeavoured to supply merely such information as the general reader would care to possess without much trouble or research; and limited as that information may be, it is not to be found succinctly stated in any one book with which we are acquainted.

The Biography of Allen may fairly claim the attention of the general reader. Starting life very young under every kind of disability, pecuniary and social, Allen honourably amassed an ample fortune, which he dispensed in princely

vi   *Contents.*

PREFACE.

E have thought, in pondering for some years over a Biography of Ralph Allen, more complete than any yet published, that such a biography would be imperfect unless it were preceded by a short historical sketch of the ancient manor of Lyncombe, to the latter annals of which Allen lent a unique interest. Concerning Lyncombe — known only by that name from the earliest Saxon down to the Norman period, but in later times subdivided into the parishes of Lyncombe and Widcombe—we have endeavoured to supply merely such information as the general reader would care to possess without much trouble or research ; and limited as that information may be, it is not to be found succinctly stated in any one book with which we are acquainted.

The Biography of Allen may fairly claim the attention of the general reader. Starting life very young under every kind of disability, pecuniary and social, Allen honourably amassed an ample fortune, which he dispensed in princely fashion, and attracted to his mansion at Prior Park some of the foremost "men of light and leading" during one of the most stirring epochs of English history; and the mere narrative of such a life, passed in such times, cannot be otherwise than interesting. Allen, however, has claims not only on our interest, but as a Postal Reformer he has claims on our gratitude ; for—if we estimate his work with a due consideration of his opportunities and of the age in which he lived—it is scarcely too much to say that he was perhaps the most distinguished servant ever employed in the Post Office. An enormous capacity for work, extraordinary powers of organization, an almost unrivalled mastery of details, a readiness to sink himself in his work, an unruffled temper, a serene patience, winsomeness in attracting the well-disposed, and tact in dealing with rogues in such a way as to disarm them and yet secure their allegiance at the same time ;—surely all these rare qualities were never so severely tested at the Post Office as they were in the case of Allen, who found the postal system in such a chaotic condition, faithfully reflecting the folly of the government and the knavery of many of the subordinate officials, that none but a genius of the most resolute and commanding type would have dared to grapple with it.

Our admiration is kindled, as we follow the poor Post Office boy, with no advantages but those of a clear brain and a resolute and energetic temperament, skilfully and honorably surmounting great difficulties on his road to personal success ; and our gratitude is excited, when we think of the conspicuous benefits which he conferred on the nation by his postal reforms ; but, after all, the greatest charm connected with Allen is the marvellous charm of his personal character, as established by a large and varied body of competent and independent witnesses. Pope has immortalised Allen as one who would

"Do good by stealth, and blush to find it fame".

Bishop Warburton wrote :—" *He* (Allen) *is,* I verily believe, *the greatest character in any age of the world.* . . . I have studied his character even maliciously, to find where the weakness lies, but have studied in vain." Fielding, in *Tom Jones,* speaks of Squire Allworthy (*i.e.,* Allen) as walking on his terrace one morning, when, " in the full blaze of his majesty, up rose the sun, than which only one object in this lower creation could be more glorious, and that Mr. Allworthy presented,—a human being replete with benevolence, meditating in what manner he might prove himself most acceptable to his Creator by doing most good to his creatures." Bishop Hurd, not a man likely to be carried away by an excess of generous emotion, on publishing a new edition of his *Moral and Political Dialogues,* prefixed to it a portrait of Allen, with the following words from Seneca : " *Si nobis animum boni viri liceret inspicere, o quam pulchram faciem, quam sanctam, quam ex magnifico placidoque fulgentem videremus ! Nemo illum amabilem qui non simul venerabilem diceret.*" How highly esteemed Allen was by the elder Pitt (Lord Chatham), the correspondence contained in this Biography will show ; it is sufficient here to quote this one sentence from Pitt's letter to Mrs. Allen on the occasion of her husband's death : " I fear not all the examples of his virtues will have power to raise up to the world his like again."

If the Biography of Allen can rouse the interest, the

gratitude, and the affection of the general reader, Allen s special claim on Bathonians should assuredly never be forgotten by us ; for it was from Bath that his light shone forth, first to the ends of the Kingdom, and afterwards to every part of the world where English History and English Literature are read ; and no one man ever so signally benefited and glorified our city.   He founded the Mineral-Water Hospital ; he gave a fresh and enduring impetus to the Bath stone trade ; he infused a purer spirit into the Bath Corporation, which he rescued from the corruption into which it had fallen during the generations and the century that preceded him ; he took the lead in all good works, and lavished his hospitality and his wealth on all those who, possessed of talent or of merit, were brought to his notice ; but not the least pleasing trait in his character was the helpful sympathy which, as our local annals abundantly prove, he was ever ready to extend to interesting or deserving persons whom he himself sought out and found "any way afflicted or distressed—in mind, body, or estate".   The marvel is how Allen found time to cultivate the graces and courtesies of private life amidst the exacting demands of business and public work.   The superintendence of the building of his mansion, the management of his estates at Hampton, Claverton, and Combe Down, the direction of a vast stone business, the anxieties and labour connected with the execution of the Government postal contracts, and a predominant share in municipal duties, did not exhaust his time or his energies ; he seemed to be always fresh, always calm, never in a hurry, and found ample leisure for the occupations and duties of a hospitable and benevolent private gentleman.

Allen's position as the foremost citizen of Bath, in his own or any age, was clearly recognised at the time ; and the wonder is that historical justice and proportion have been subsequently so far lost sight of and ignored that the popular mind associates the renaissance of Bath with Beau Nash. Yet the relative proportions of Allen and Nash were forcibly stated, at a time when both of them were living, by Burton in his *Iter Bathoniense.* Nash's everlasting white hat and his black morals were happily hit off by Burton, who saw in Nash nothing but a frivolous and an unprincipled rake ; while Allen is described in these glowing words : " *Tandem inveni virum ; instar mille unum . . . . virum inter Bathonienses suos facile principem, quem undequaque præsentem parietes ipsi loquuntur.*"

If Bath had depended for her popularity solely on the capricious favours of the merely fashionable and pleasure-seeking world, her questionable prestige might well have departed with Nash ; but Bath owes her continued importance to causes more enduring than fickle fashion—to the interest excited by her venerable antiquity, to the perennial efficacy of her springs, to the salubrity of her climate, to her geological conditions, to the beauty of her surroundings, to the general air of cultivated repose which pervades the place, and, in later times, to her convenient position on two great railway systems (Great Western and Midland). In such a city the two Woods, contemporaries and *protégés* of Allen, saw a suitable field for the execution of noble architectural designs ; educationalists recognised an appropriate scene for " the still air of delightful studies", which should raise Bath to the foremost place amongst the educational centres of the Kingdom ; and a large number of the cultured classes have found pleasant, convenient, and economical quarters for a permanent home ; and it is to these and other stable elements, not to changing fashion, that Bath must ever look for all-round benefits and for her continued prosperity and importance.

Seeing that Allen was so greatly esteemed, not only by his fellow-citizens, but by men of the highest rank and influence in the land, we may well be astonished that there is no record of royal honours offered to him, especially as he was a staunch Hanoverian ; but, of course, honours may have been offered to him, though there is no record of the fact, and Allen's refusal to accept them would not surprise us, nor should we expect to hear a word on the subject from his lips—his unostentatiousness and his dignified reserve being remarkable traits in his remarkable character. In illustration of this point, we would draw special attention to Allen's short letter (p. 203) in reply to Mr. Strahan.

It is pathetic and even melancholy to reflect that the days of such a man were darkened at their close ; but so it was, and the result came about in a way familiar to most readers. When George III acceded to the throne in 1760, Newcastle and Pitt were co-ordinate leaders of a remarkably strong Whig Ministry, which had achieved a rapid succession of brilliant victories abroad and suppressed faction at home ; but the new King, resolved to take the reins of government into his own hands, contrived by the agency of a reptile class of politicians—called "King's Men"—to oust first Pitt and then Newcastle, in the midst of the Seven Years' War, and to patch up, in 1763, what Pitt considered an inglorious peace. The peace, however, was acceptable to a large class of people, and numerous addresses of congratulation were sent to the

King, and amongst other places from Bath ; and in the Bath address, inspired by Allen, who was the leading spirit in the Corporation, the King was thanked "for an *adequate* peace". The word *adequate* turned out to be unfortunate, and there is no doubt that Allen, if he could have foreseen the consequences, would have avoided the word, though it faithfully represented his opinion. Pitt, who was at that time Member for Bath, and owed his seat there to Allen's influence, took offence at the term *adequate*, "so repugnant to my unalterable opinion, . . . and fully declared by me in Parliament", that he resolved to resign his seat at the next dissolution of Parliament ; and thus the two friends parted, with expressions of sincere esteem on both sides and regretting their honest differences of opinion. But Pitt, who still retained over the people that ascendency which he held at the time of the accession of George III (when Macaulay says that "in the House of Commons not a single one of the malcontents durst lift his eyes above the buckle of Pitt's shoes"), had given a serious rebuff to the Bath Corporation and, through the Corporation, to Allen, the leading member of it. Simultaneously with this, Allen's health, undermined by cancer, began to break down. Then came the old story ; the lion was sick, asses kicked him, and Allen became the subject of caricature (pp. 179-185), originating, it is believed, from Pitt's worshippers in London and circulated in Bath. It is only reasonable to suppose that Allen smarted under these caricatures, for

"Of all the griefs that harass the distressed,
Sure the most bitter is a scornful jest ;
Fate never wounds more deep the generous heart,
Than when a blockhead's insult points the dart" ;

but whatever Allen's feelings may have been, he never expressed them. Not only did no word of murmur or complaint escape his lips, but he confirmed by an additional codicil the codicil which he had appended to his will in 1760—the codicil of 1760 running as follows: "For the last instance of my friendship and grateful regard for the best of friends, as well as the most upright and ablest of Ministers that has adorned our country, I give to Right Honble William Pitt the sum of one thousand pounds", etc. In a month or two afterwards he was forced by ill-health to retire from the Corporation ; and happily his dark days were shortened, for before the close of the year following the untoward address he had breathed his last. The Great Commoner was not so fortunate ; he gradually lost his hold on the country, and completely so when he ceased to be the Great Commoner and became the Earl of Chatham in 1766, about which time his intellect (and, some think, his character) began to deteriorate, and he entered upon dark days, from which the cloud was rarely, if ever, wholly lifted, down to the time of his tragic death in 1778.

The caricatures to which we have referred are responsible for the idea entertained in some unreflecting quarters that Allen was dictatorial, and this idea has been hastily appropriated by superficial readers, who have not gone beyond the caricatures and studied Allen's character all round. Another idea, the exact contradictory of that just mentioned, is that Allen, while overflowing with the milk of human kindness, was deficient in the stronger elements of character ; and for this notion Fielding is largely answerable, but we must bear in mind that it would have been inconsistent with Fielding's general plan to portray anything beyond the softer and more amiable qualities of his model ; and, moreover, it is absurd to *wholly* identify a novelist's representation of character with his model, just as it would be absurd to *wholly* identify the domestic scenery amidst which Squire Allworthy moves with the scenery of Prior Park.

These apparently contradictory ideas are easily reconcilable. Allen could be firm and resolute on supreme occasions, when he maintained it was " the duty of every honest man, after he has made the strictest inquiry, to act pursuant to the light which the Supreme Being has been pleased to dispense to him" (p. 179) ; and Allen was also conspicuous for all the gentle and amiable attributes of humanity ; but those who study his character in its totality, and have eyes to see, find no difficulty in realising the conception of gentleness and strength harmoniously blended in a beautiful character, set off and adorned by " the white flower of a blameless life".

> " His life was gentle ; and the elements
> So mixed in him, that Nature might stand up
> And say to all the world : ' This was a man'."

To such a man the author is conscious of having done but scant justice, and it would have been very gratifying to him to have handed the results of his own labours and researches to more competent men, who might have been found willing to undertake the task ; but this opportunity has not presented itself, though the author still hopes that some one may yet arise, who, animated with the same love for the subject, but endowed with a larger measure of literary skill, will utilise all the available materials and throw them into a more artistic and pleasing form.   Meanwhile, the author tenders his sincere thanks to Colonel Allen for permission to consult the family archives, and to Mr. Austin King, Colonel Allen's courteous and accomplished solicitor, for facilitating the examination of these archives.

Gateway to Carriage Drive

INTRODUCTION.

THE ROMAN PERIOD.

IT may be well to give a brief summary of the origin of names appertaining to this very beautiful part of our city. One of the most remarkable characteristics of historic cities is the vitality of ancient names, and this fact is signally illustrated in the case of Bath, and more especially in Lyncombe and Widcombe. Four of the most remarkable objects of antiquity round or near our city are the *Wansdike*, *Via Badonica*,[1] *Via Julia*,[2] and the *Fosse*. The first of these is unquestionably the most ancient work, being possibly executed some three

[1] The *Via Badonica* in its construction was similar to the Fosse. Whilst the latter extended northward, the former extended from London, and formed a junction with the Fosse at Bathford. Upon this road, in fact, the London Road, *viâ* Devizes and Marlborough, of the last century, was made.

[2] The *Via Julia* was constructed by the Romans as a strategic road to enable them to get into Wales from Bath. They found the British station between them and the Severn—the almost impregnable station of Stoke—a stockaded defence on the scarp of the village now called *Northstoke*. The Romans got round it from Lansdown, from which they made a detour. They had penetrated to the Severn when they evacuated the country, but the road was used for centuries.

B

centuries before the arrival of the Romans. The aborigines, or earliest historic inhabitants of Britain, are supposed to have been Celts, once, no doubt, the dominant race in Europe, who migrated from Gaul several centuries previous to the Christian era. For a considerable time they seem to have continued in peaceable possession of their acquisitions, till a fresh body of adventurers from Gallia Belgica (thence called *Belgæ*), of Celtic origin, pushed across the Channel, and made a landing on the south-western parts of England. But the prior possessors of the coast were not easily to be driven from it ; the numerous earthworks and barrows in Cornwall, Devonshire, Somersetshire, Dorsetshire, Hampshire, and Wiltshire prove that the success of the invaders was very gradual, and that many a bloody battle was fought ere they gained a permanent settlement in this island. At length, fatigued and perhaps exhausted by this contest, the two tribes agreed to a compromise, by which a certain allotment of territory was to be made to the Belgæ, who should thereafter cease to disturb the possessions of the old inhabitants of the country. To mark the limits of this district, the immense and extended ditch and mound called *Wansdike* were constructed ; the term, which sufficiently explains its nature and design, being derived from the Celtic word *Gwahan*, or separation. This ditch is still in many places sixteen feet deep, the vallum being placed on the south side. This work (which left all the western counties in possession of the Belgæ) commences at Andover in Hampshire, and passes from thence nearly in a straight direction to Great Bedwin. From thence it crosses the forest of Savernake and the Downs of Marlborough. These downs remain in their ancient condition, and the Wansdike, therefore, is still seen in its pristine condition. It then visits Tan Hill, Sheppard-Shord, Heddington, passes through Spye Park, appears on the lawn at Lacock Abbey, and may be traced on Whitley Common, near

Monks' House. At Bathford we again meet with a bank, which tradition asserts to be the Wansdike. This may be pursued for a considerable distance, making an intermediate line between Hampton Manor House and Church ; but at the row of elms, below the canal, half a mile from Hampton, it

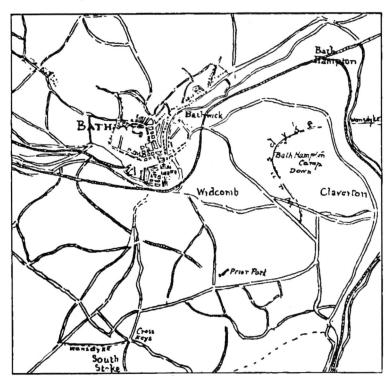

disappears. From this point till it enters Smallcomb Wood, on Bathwick Hill, its course seems to be through the bottom, a district which has been ploughed up and otherwise interfered with, so that the traces are less perceptible, the *dorsum* (or ridge) being almost obliterated. When, however, we come to the uncultivated steep of Smallcomb Wood, it becomes again sufficiently conspicuous not to be mistaken ;

crossing the Claverton road, it proceeds through the firs to the enclosure at Prior Park, and crosses the lawn above the house in a diagonal line and south-western direction.

On reaching the wall that separates the park from the road, it forms the basis of the fence for 200 yards. Issuing from the park at the upper lodge gate, and crossing the road to Bath, it follows the course of a halter-path or bridle-road, and becomes the right-hand bank of the same, appearing very lofty, and bearing on its summit several fine beech and oak trees. The nicest investigation cannot now detect it till we reach the ancient Warminster road, *viâ* Entry Hill and Combe Down, just at the point opposite the intersection of the South Stoke Lane, and that leading from Newton to Warminster. These two public ways it crosses, and then forms, for half a mile, the bold basis of a stone wall of separation between arable fields, which is reared so high, by availing itself of this ridge, as to be seen at a considerable distance. At Burnt-House Gate it crosses the Wells Road, and, pursuing a lane for a short distance, takes the brow of the hill which curves through the middle of an arable field. For a short distance its progress is again obscured, but we soon perceive the ridge once more, in the foundation of a hedge, which drops down a descent towards Englishcombe Wood,[1] having a coppice on the left hand. The next meadow discovers it in great perfection. Having crossed and ascended the western side of it, Wansdike penetrates into English-combe Wood, and follows the brow of the rock entirely through its shades. Thence it intersects a farmer's barton, a few yards to the south of the church ; and pushing on to the westward through an orchard, enters a meadow, where it appears in its original grandeur, exhibiting a mound twelve feet high, and a deep trench on the south side. A quarter of

[1] The most perfect and characteristic example of this interesting relic in this locality.

a mile to the westward of the church it makes a sudden bend to the southward, and is lost for some time, but presents itself again at Stanton Prior, Publow, Norton, and Long Ashton, and at length loses itself in the Severn sea near Portishead, after having pursued a course of nearly ninety miles in length.

We shall have occasion to speak of the Fosse Road when we refer to the excavation of the oolite in early times, and the part that that great Roman work played in Bath in relation to the Norman city and vast Abbey raised by de Villula.

Now, interesting as are these records, it must be observed that later history reveals the fact that the two sections of the Celts were assimilated, and ultimately became as one people, and during the Roman occupation were known as the *Belgæ*. After the departure of the Romans from Britain, moreover, it is clear that this people had made great advances in civilization and in the art of government. The departure of the Romans in the fifth century encouraged them to attempt the government of England and Wales; but with equal certainty it excited the Picts and Scots—*i.e.*, Caledonians of the Celtic race—to renew those attempts which the Romans had kept in check by the Cumberland Vallum, or Picts' Wall. With more or less success the Belgæ struggled against these formidable and rapacious foes. It was during this struggle that the Roman city of Bath gradually became a scene of desolation. The magnificent buildings which the Romans left behind them fell, partly by unavoidable neglect, partly by violence, into ruins. In the early part of this struggle the Belgæ invited the Saxons into Britain to help them. They came, drove back these Picts and Scots, and formed themselves into small States, leaving the Belgæ in possession of Bath, as well as other cities and territory.

In the year 557 it was that, after earlier futile attempts, the Saxons, under Ceaulin and Cuthwin, advanced to and en-

trenched themselves at Sodbury; and it is curious here to
note that they were assisted materially by one of the minor
roads made by the Romans connecting this portion of
Gloucestershire with Cirencester by way of Birdlip Hill.
They then advanced to meet the British, under their chiefs
Commail, Candidan, and Farinmail, whom they utterly
defeated; and Bath, with all dependent upon it, fell for the
first time under Saxon rule.

It is necessary, in order to understand Bath history, and
more especially as it concerns Lyncombe and Widcombe,
to state, if only in the briefest manner, the part played by
the Roman road called the *The Fosse*, signifying *Artificial
Way*. "For arts,[1] military and civil, that become a wise
government, the Romans beyond compare exceeded all
nations, but in their roads they have exceeded themselves.
. . . . . It is altogether astonishing to consider how they
begirt the whole globe, as it were, with new meridians and
great circles, all manner of ways.

> " Magnorum fuerat solers hæc cura Quiritum
> Constratas passim concelebrare vias."

It has been said that the Romans, " as well as use, studied
eternity in all their works"; and the truth of the saying is conspicuously illustrated by their wonderful works in the city of
Bath. Their prescience, not less than their constructive genius,
strikes us with wonder to this day. Bath manifestly was the
object of their special, perhaps their supreme care, and for
obvious reasons. There was an exhaustless supply of stone
and coal, and the great Fosse road they constructed was made
to intersect their city so that it should pass close to those coalfields with which the district abounds, as well as those vast
stone quarries, which were not only to meet all the wants of
early civilisation, but which, in a measure, are to this day
evidences of the scientific skill and the industry of the
Romans.

[1] *Itin. Cur.*, vol. i, p. 76.

THE SAXON PERIOD.

The British period after the departure of the Romans, we have already partly referred to. It was a period of violence and bloodshed, which did not cease with the early Saxon occupation. The efforts of Arthur and successive chieftains, whose valour and achievements, it may be, pass under his name, for a time kept the Saxon "hordes from the shores of the Baltic" in check, but only for a time. The first Saxon conquerors were not more civilised, but perhaps more cruel, than the British whom in the sixth century they overcame at Dyrham. We can trace to them no superior policy, no apparent desire to organize and develop the resources of the country, no wise and systematic toleration of the British, who were by this time materially weaned from their isolated habits and rude savage camp life by the influence of the Belgæ. In this the Saxons exhibited a marked contrast to the Romans, of whose power and organizing genius they had at that period ample evidence before them, but were unable to imitate. Warner, in the chapter on the "Saxon and Danish History of Bath", gives a picture, a hundred years after the Saxon conquest, of what he calls "the new religious rites, less elegant [than those of the Romans and more disgusting], poured into the temples of *Aquæ Solis;* and the fanes and altars of Minerva, Apollo, Jove, Hercules, and Diana beheld themselves polluted and deformed by the monstrous mixture of Celtic worship with their own classical ceremonials." The distinguished historian is here indulging in one of those fits of absurd exaggeration to which he was so prone, and of which he gives us another example in his description of the corrupt state of Christianity, almost before the sound of it had been heard in the Kingdom of Wessex. The first picture is simply a caricature, the Roman temples having for the most part, during the prolonged internecine contention, fallen into partial ruin, from which the Saxons rescued many of those altars and those wonderful examples of Roman art which we possess to this day.   In the second instance he indulges in the language of the modern fanatic in condemning the terms used by Osric[1] in 676,[2] in granting one hundred *manentes* to Bretana to found

[1] Osric was not originally a Wessex chief. He was King of the Huiccii, who occupied Worcestershire, Warwickshire, and part of Gloucestershire. He was an absolute and wise ruler.   The Saxons in this part of Wessex had, for 100 years after the battle of Dyrham, been subject to frequent attacks by the Belgæ, and had become weak and demoralised.   This period, indeed, was one of bitter humiliation to Bath ; and the accession of Osric to power here, with the consent of Kentwin, King of Wessex, was, in fact, the beginning of Saxon rule, Saxon laws, and Saxon civilization.

[2] The Very Rev. H. Donald M. Spence, D.D., Dean of Gloucester, the custodian, claims to have made the very important discovery that the actual remains of Osric, King of Northumbria, who was buried A.D. 729, lie beneath the beautiful shrine erected to his memory, which stands on the right hand of the high altar in the choir of Gloucester Cathedral. This shrine is the work of Abbot Malvern, Abbot of Gloucester in the days of Henry VIII, and it has been generally supposed to be merely a memorial—simply a cenotaph, or empty tomb.   This supposition probably arose from the distance back to which the interment dates—namely 1,162 years.   Britton speaks of the memorial as a " cenotaph, or empty tomb", and all local guide-books repeat what is now believed to be a mistake.   It was certainly a natural thing to doubt that the remains of one who had passed away in the eighth century were preserved, and that the dust of the bones of the founder of the Abbey still reposed beneath its sacred roof.   It seems incredible (as the Dean remarks in a short history of the discovery he has had printed for private circulation) that the hallowed dust of Osric could have escaped the ravages of war, time, and neglect, the forays of the Vikings and Norman pillage, the confiscations of Henry VIII, and the yet more dangerous guardianship of Cromwell's Ironsides.   Thus it was that successive historians spoke of the memorial as simply an empty tomb, and that the statement until now has never been questioned.

Dean Spence adopted the tradition of his predecessors in the Deanery

a nunnery, merely because Osric uses the pious language of that
and a later period, in that he performs the good deed for the
redemption of his soul, a formula of almost universal adoption

of Gloucester Cathedral, until quite recently. It is stated in Leland's
notes, which he made in the course of his official visit to Gloucester
Abbey, by the desire of Henry VIII, shortly after the dissolution in 1540,
that "Osric, founder of Gloucester Abbey, first laye in St. Petronell's
Chapell, thence removed into our Lady Chapell, and thence removed of
late dayes and layd under a fayre tombe of stone on the North side of the
High Aultar. At the foote of the tombe is this, written on a Norman
pillar, ' Osricus rex primus fundator hujus monasterii, 681.'" There is no
reason to suppose that Leland's "memory" was inaccurate, since it was
probable that he had heard it from an eye-witness of the translation of
the founder's remains from the Lady Chapel. It was reasoned, therefore,
that the memorial tomb marked the actual resting-place of the remains of
the great Northumbrian King and founder of the Abbey. Two panels
were taken out of the stone *loculus*, and a long leaden coffin was disclosed,
lying exactly beneath the King's effigy. The contents of the coffin disclosed the remains of a very ancient interment. Much of the cement
which had once fastened down the stone effigy of Osric had fallen into
the end of the coffin, broken by the weight of the superincumbent figure,
and a few small bones were discovered mingled with the cement. No
attempt was made to discover Royal insignia or fragments of vesture, and
the remains were left untouched. Dr. Spence claims that by this search
he has verified beyond all doubt the statement of Leland in 1540-41,
concerning the translation of the remains of the Royal founder of
Gloucester Cathedral, and that the beautiful tomb, known as Osric's
tomb, is no mere monument raised in pious memory of the King, but the
actual resting-place of the founder's remains.

The importance of this discovery lies in the fact that it is believed that,
in the tomb of Osric, Gloucester may claim the guardianship of the oldest
known remains of the Saxon kings. Fragments are known to exist in
other minsters. Winchester possesses some of the ashes of Kynegils,
King of the West Saxons, who died A.D. 643 ; and at Durham the skull of
King Oswald rests with the bones of St. Cuthbert. But beyond these it
is not known that the remains of any Saxon kings have been preserved.
The fact of the remains of King Osric being found in a leaden coffin is
thus of almost unique interest. The lead coffin probably replaces a more
ancient stone *loculus*.

then and centuries after in similar documents. This grant by Osric was one of many others of that period. As Mr. Grant Allen says—

"Before the conversion to Christianity we have not a single written document upon which to base our history ; from the moment of Augustine's landing we have the invaluable works of Bæda, besides a vast number of charters or royal grants of land to monasteries and private persons. These grants, written at first in Latin and afterwards in Anglo-Saxon, were preserved in the monasteries down to the date of the Dissolution, and then became the property of various collectors.

"Those who judge monastic institutions only by their later and worst days, are apt to forget the benefits which they conferred upon the people in the earlier stages of their system. The state of England during the first Christian period was one of chronic and bloody warfare. With such a state of affairs as this, it became a matter of deep importance that there should be one institution where the arts of peace might be carried on in safety ; where agriculture might be sure of its reward ; where literature and science might be studied, and where civilising influences might be safe from interruption or rapine. The monasteries gave an opportunity for such an ameliorating influence to spring up. They were spared even in war by the reverence of the people for the Church : and they became places where peaceful minds might retire for honest work, and learning, and thinking, away from the fierce turmoil of a still essentially barbaric and predatory community. At the same time, they encouraged the development of this very type of mind by turning the reproach of cowardice, which it would have carried with it in heathen times, into an honour and a mark of holiness. Every monastery became a centre of light and of struggling culture for the surrounding district. They were at once, to the early English recluse, universities and refuges, places of education, of retirement, and of peace, in the midst of a jarring and discordant world."

Now it must be mentioned here that in reference to the development of the various physical resources, from Osric to Eadgar, the Saxons did little. They found one road and they left one road—the Roman Fosse. The Romans had long before discovered those vast oolite beds whence they derived their supplies to construct those magnificent temples and other edifices which, in their fall, through neglect during the later Belg̸æ and the early Saxon rule, fell near and into those baths, the ruins of which a happy accident revealed in 1755.[1]

Then, it must be observed, not only did the Romans construct this celebrated *way*, the Fosse,[2] but they also constructed three other primary fundamental ways — *Icening Street*, *Watling Street*, and *Hermen Street ;* and this vast system traversed the kingdom from south-west to north-east. Besides these, there were many subordinate or subsidiary *ways* in Britain connecting various stations, besides the *Via Badonica*. [See note on page 1.]

The importance of the Fosse passing through the steep ascents at Lyncombe will be understood when it is shown that throughout the ages, from the earliest times of the Romans until the beginning of the last century, every stone used in building and every bit of coal consumed in the city and suburbs came from the Down quarries in Lyncombe, and from the coalfields in the country in a direct line beyond ; all being brought with comparative facility, by means of sledges, down the road which we now call Holloway.

That now despised road or way, dating from the Christian

---

[1] Those who desire to study the whole question of this discovery in 1755 will need no other authorities than Dr. Lucas and Dr. Spry, both of which are cited by the author in the work (*The Thermal Baths of Bath*) which he edited for H. W. Freeman, Esq., in 1888, pages 17 to 25, which citations are accompanied by the artist Hoare's beautiful plan.

It was in 1878 that the portion now open was uncovered. The masonry and *débris* which had fallen into this Roman work about the early part of the seventh century had in the next four centuries become so consolidated that, towards the close of the eleventh century, the first Norman bishop, John de Villula, built his palace immediately over it, the remains of which were still standing in the sixteenth century, and are described by Leland. After de Villula it was never occupied by Bishop or Prior. An ancient record, quoted by Bishop Hobhouse, states that it was let for 10s. per annum and fell into decay.

[2] The Celto-Saxon name is used to describe nearly all the Roman works, and the same remark applies to much of the Norman period to this day.

era, is, beyond all doubt, not only the most ancient one we possess, but is, moreover, the road identified with much of the ancient greatness of our city, and with the promotion and preservation of its prosperity for centuries. We forget all this when we enter that squalid suburb. If, half-way up the "Holloway", we turn to the left, we see the origin of the comparatively modern name; there are the denudations which indicate whence much of the oolite was hewn of which mediæval Bath was built. Ascending, still on the line of the Fosse, we pass the ancient "Repway"[1] until we come to the "steppe" (if it may be so called) opposite Westfield, and there on the left we see the exhausted quarry whence all the stone required for completing our revered Abbey was obtained.[2]

Proceeding, we come to those sites to the right and left, on Odd Down,[3] where the Romans, with their almost instinctive foresight, perceived not only stone, but stone possessing all the qualities they needed for structures which were to ~~have~~ lasted for all time, as the existing Roman baths attest. Their vast basilica and temples were for the most part built with the stone hewn with scientific skill from the quarries close to the site of the grand city they raised.

It has been said, with absolute truth, that the Saxons were

[1] Rope Way or Rope Walk. It signified also a public way or walk; and, in fact, was the field at the rear of Beechencliff, and opposite Elm Place.

[2] Much of the stone of de Villula's Cathedral was worked in from the walls of the ancient Roman buildings.

[3] *Odd Down.* Collinson, who was a careful antiquary, says the name is derived from Woden. The early Saxons appear to have regarded the Wansdyke with some superstition, and hence they called it *Vodenerdic.* The dyke passed close to this down, and therefore would be called Woden Down, of which Odin or Odd is the corruption. Wood gives a similar origin, but he adds two or three absurd suggestions.

The early Saxon kings were in the habit of tracing their descent to Woden, "father of victory, wisest of gods and men." Woden, in fact, was their "bogie" man, before they became enlightened by Christianity.

neither road-makers nor architects. We cannot, in any part of the beautiful and historic domain of Lyncombe, from the time of Osric to the death of Harold, find a trace of a road or a building attributable to them. Every local name that was known from the time of Osric, or before, until now, is Saxon, or Celto-Saxon; and yet we can only form a conjecture, founded on historic analogy, it is true, that the ancient Saxon chief's palace and wic, or village, stood on or near the site of the old Widcombe Church. It is more than probable that Osric, by whom the nunnery was founded, built a small church near it. But the only ecclesiastical edifice of which we have any account is that built by Offa in the eighth century on the site of the present Abbey, and which survived to be the scene of the most important event of the Saxon rule, the crowning of Eadgar. Much that preceded that event savoured of violence and bloodshed; but, so far as Bath is concerned, amidst all this there was a progressive advance in civilisation, and in the development of constitutional forms of legality and municipal order. With the final triumph of Christianity all the formative elements of Anglo-Saxon Britain are complete. We see it, even at this time, a rough conglomeration of loosely-aggregated principalities, composed of a fighting aristocracy and a body of unvalued serfs; while interspersed through its parts are the bishops, monks, and clergy, centres of nascent civilisation for the seething mass of noble barbarism. The country is divided into agricultural colonies, its only wealth being land. We want but one more conspicuous change to make it into the England of the Augustan Anglo-Saxon age—the reign of Eadgar—and that one change is the consolidation of the discordant kingdoms under a single loose overlordship. To understand this final step we must glance briefly at the dull record of political history. King Eadgar succeeded Eadwig in 958 as King of all three provinces, then finally uniting the whole of Teutonic England into one king-

dom. Eadgar was not crowned till years after being called
to the throne ; this has been to some a matter of surprise,
but it must be remembered that Eadgar and his great adviser
Dunstan had good reason for delay, and that was the complete
supremacy of Eadgar's power. The oft-repeated tradition,
that Dunstan delayed the ceremony to punish Eadgar for his
sins, is nonsense. Dunstan knew when to use pious terrors,
and when to exercise the wisdom of the statesman.

When that great ceremonial took place it was in the
Cathedral of Offa,[1] in the "ancient West Welsh Royal City of
Bath", by St. Dunstan, probably the first Englishman who
seriously deserves the name of statesman.   He was, says Mr.
Allen, born in the half-Celtic region of Somerset,[2] beside the
great Abbey of Glastonbury, and a good deal of the imaginative
Celtic temper ran probably with the blood in his veins.   But
he was above all the representative of the Roman civilisation
in the barbarised England of the tenth century.   He was a
painter, a musician, a reader and a scholar, in a world of fierce
warriors and ignorant nobles.

The Saxons were simple, and, even in their rudest state,
not without domestic virtues.   They were unaccustomed to
state and ceremony.   They were "skilful in the use of the
sword and the spade, of the oar and the sail".   They were
brave and warlike, and were, in their perpetual incursions
upon British soil, the dread of the Britons and almost a terror
to the Romans.   The remarkable quality about these Saxons,
however, was their innate sense of order and the power they
possessed of ruling themselves in their village communities,
and their inability to grasp those great principles in the

---

[1] The story of Offa's church having been destroyed by the Danes is a
fiction, resting upon much the same evidence as that which goes
to show that de Villula's cathedral at a later period was destroyed by
fire ; both stories are baseless.

[2] We, Bathonians, claim him as a native of Weston, close to our city.

growth and development of cities which so peculiarly characterised the Romans and the Normans.

It was, however, not only in architecture, but in all the arts demanding genius, taste, and execution, that the Saxons signally failed. Nor does it seem to have been the result of indifference ; on the contrary, it is clear that they aimed at excellence, for the coins that have been found of the seventh to the tenth centuries are distinguished for the excellence and purity of their metal and the utter meanness of their design and execution. It is singular that a people and a government such as the Saxon, roughly speaking, in whom the organizing and governing faculty seemed to be innate, should have lacked the faculty referred to.[1]

With all the disturbing elements, from the earliest Saxon times down to the Conquest, we trace that distinguishing characteristic, the recognition of legal principles ; and out of this instinct gradually were developed those municipal regulations which in time became the basis of our national laws and liberties. Our own city is, perhaps, the most notable illustration of the truth of this statement, and there would be special reasons for it. If Bath had occasionally been the focus of rebellion and violence, it was favoured by successive chiefs and kings. It was a royal city, with all the privileges and immunities which its rank conferred ; and these advantages grew and attained to that comparatively complete state of municipal government which the Normans found in force, and

---

[1] Of Saxon antiquities we are unable in Bath to boast of a single example. This is the more remarkable, seeing that Bath was, probably, more closely associated with Saxon rule than any other city. Since the publication, in 1807, of Ducarel's *Historiæ Anglicanæ*, only one perfect example of Saxon architecture has been discovered, viz., the church at Bradford-on-Avon, which is eminently characteristic of Saxon faults and, in a measure, of Saxon merits. The old church of Saxon architecture, St. Peter's, at Oxford, built by St. Grymbald in 886, is well known. (See Leland's *Collectanea*, vol. vi, and *Archæologia*.)

which, to their honour be it said, they fostered and encouraged, until it assumed that complete corporate form in the thirteenth century which lasted until the reign of Queen Elizabeth.

The Manor of Lyncombe was ecclesiastical property from the time of Osric in the seventh century down to the Conquest ; nor is it too much to say that it was in its compactness, fruitfulness, and beauty, and from its contiguity to the capital city, the gem of all the Church's possessions in Wessex. And again this supremacy was maintained, in spite of waste and mismanagement, from the time of John de Villula down to the Dissolution. But there was another advantage which the city derived from the domain of Lyncombe. The resources of this large range of fertile land were enormous. Cattle were fed on its plains and in its combes. The corn-fields lay to the south of what, after the Conquest and the Domesday Survey, was called the Wide Combe,[1] and on the south-east slope of Beechen Cliff, and the corn was made into flour in the two ancient mills deriving their water-power from that stream which still retains its Celtic name of Lyn. This stream, with its occasional pools, formerly wider and with greater volume than now, taking its rise in the hills to the west, flowed down the combe at the foot of those slopes which it watered and enriched. This was and is the Lyn proper ; but there is another stream, whose watershed is at the top of the *wide-combe*, and which originally flowed down the centre. This stream formed a dam at the bottom of the manor fields, and, having turned the mill wheel, passed through a culvert and joined its sister stream near the end of the combe, flowing on together towards the second mill,[2] turning its rude wheel, and then gently retiring into the Avon.

On the southern slopes, at the western end of Greenway

---

[1] This is a term first employed in *Domesday* to denote its character and its separation from Lyncombe, for local convenience.

[2] These mills are referred to in *Domesday*, each being gelded at 10s.

Lane, there were splendidly cultivated fig-groves and vine-yards, the latter producing wine in abundance, and of a quality something like that of a thin dry port ; while every species of vegetable was cultivated then (as now) on patches here and there throughout the various vills or farms, by the villeins, who, more highly favoured than that class in general under feudal law, held the land by the modified tenure of the law of socage. The ancient village was scattered about the sides of the combe, but besides this there were other houses in different parts of the manor, especially on the slope of Beechen Cliff ; and there is little doubt that on *Akerland*, on the eastern side of the cliff, the chief cultivators or villeins resided. From Odd Down a pleasing view may be seen of the vale of South Lyncombe, but to see it in all its varied and extended beauty the spectator must descend some distance, and enter the grounds near Westfield, whence it may be seen from the true picturesque point of view. There is no possibility of classifying valleys, but this landscape is perfect in its calm repose and picturesque beauty. " To be beautiful is enough," said Thackeray ; but to beauty and grace must be added its variety of scenery and remarkable richness of soil and productiveness. On the south it is bounded by the Barrow ridge.[1] An

---

[1] Near this ridge is the *mound* or *barrow*, which has been the subject of much controversy. Doubtless, this arose from Wood's absurd description of it, first published in 1749. He says : " This mound seems to me to have been King Bladud's sepulchre, for it stands within half-a-mile of a place called Hakim—a name expressive not only of a wise and learned philosopher, but the very title given to Zoroaster—and it is so situated as to make the angle of a triangle with Hakim and the Castle of Inglescomb." This theory, even supposing that Bladud was a real personage, is not only absurd, but is based, archæologically, upon an erroneous theory. "Barrow" is an Anglo-Saxon word, *beorh*, signifying a hill, and is liable to be confused with the names derived from " burgh", an earthwork. Some forty years ago the mound was examined, and found to be stone from base to summit.

C

adequate description of the rest of the scene would be difficult. Turning from the west to the east we are in Mid-Lyncombe, near the site of the Priors' Park, the most historic portion of the manor before us.

> "Straight mine eye hath caught new pleasures,
> Whilst the landskip round it measures."

This scene appears to have been the centre of interest in ancient as well as in modern times. Where now stands the venerable sixteenth-century church, there formerly, as early as the ninth century, stood the Saxon church; and on that same site was erected its Norman successor, which was superseded by the present. On the site of, or near, the Widcombe House stood the ancient thane's or chief's manor house, around which were grouped the dwellings of the freemen or enfranchised citizens.

From the time of Eadgar, through the Danish epoch and the restored Saxon rule, little occurred to affect the interests of the city or the development of Lyncombe. Fresh taxation was imposed by Edward the Confessor, but although the same terminology was employed as under the Domesday Survey to describe its import, yet it differed essentially, from the fact that in the Saxon system the admeasurment was by *rule of thumb*, whereas the Norman system was approximately accurate. *Hide, carucate*, and many other terms were all Anglo-Saxon, but they are all perpetuated in Domesday.

During the Saxon period in the City of Bath we really know little of the ecclesiastical government and policy. The entire manor of Lyncombe, as we have seen, was Church property, and all that concerned its management and Church government was under the direction of an ecclesiastical dignitary, subordinate to the ancient see of Sherborne. This see comprehended the whole of Wessex (Dorset, Somerset, Wilts,

Devon, and Cornwall) until 704. King Ina in that year divided the province into two portions — Winchester and Sherborne. It was in 1075 that Sherborne was removed to Salisbury. Again, in or about 905, the county of Somerset was taken out of Sherborne to form the diocese of Wells, and finally the see of Sherborne was wholly dismembered to form two sees, which ultimately were recorded under the see of Exeter, now again separated nearly upon the ancient lines in the see of Truro.

The see of Wells was created about 905, the first bishop being Athelm, between whom and Giso (1059) there were thirteen bishops. Giso was a native of Lorraine, and was chaplain to Edward the Confessor. He experienced much of the ill usage which honest prelates in those days received from such monarchs as Edward, having been banished the country. Singular as it may seem, Giso was recalled from banishment and reinstated in his see by the Conqueror, after which he continued to preside over his diocese until his death in 1087; and then began a new *régime.*

THE NORMAN PERIOD.

It is evident that so far as the Conquest affected Bath, its influence and general effect were by no means prejudicial. All the traditions and customs of the later Saxon times were respected. The local government was carried on upon the old lines without interference or arbitrary check of any kind ; indeed, it is evident that all that was capable of expansion and development in the Saxon municipal system was continued after the Conquest. Warner says :

"That the English [however] were rather surprised into submission than completely conquered, William soon discovered from the general dis-

C 2

contents which growled around him, and the many plots and insurrections which succeeded each other on every side. The attempts of enemies, foreign and domestic, kept him in continual anxiety, and at length induced him to adopt measures so severe against his English subjects as justify all the censures passed upon his conduct, and all the execrations with which they have loaded his memory. But amidst regulations the most unjustifiable, exactions the most unconscionable, and laws the most tyrannical, the Conqueror occasionally exhibited specimens of sagacity which mark him at least for a discerning politician, if not an amiable character."

This, perhaps, was the general estimate formed of William up to Warner's time. Mr. Freeman, however, gives us a very different picture of the Conqueror. He gives a vivid description of William's character, his genius and statesmanship :—

"Now that the Norman duke has become an English king, his career as an English statesman strictly begins, and a wonderful career it is. Its main principle was to respect formal legality wherever he could. All William's purposes were to be carried out, as far as possible, under cover of strict adherence to the law of the land of which he had become the lawful ruler. He had sworn at his crowning to keep the laws of the land, and to rule his kingdom as well as any king that had gone before him. And assuredly he meant to keep his oath. But a foreign king, at the head of a foreign army, and who had his foreign followers to reward, could keep that oath only in its letter, and not in its spirit. But it is wonderful how nearly he came to keep it in the letter. He contrived to do his most oppressive acts, to deprive Englishmen of their lands and offices, and to part them out among strangers, under cover of English law. He could do this. A smaller man would either have failed to carry out his purposes at all, or he could have carried them out only by reckless violence.

"When we examine the administration of William more in detail, we shall see that its effects in the long run were rather to preserve than to destroy our ancient institutions. He knew the strength of legal fictions ; by legal fictions he conquered and he ruled. But every legal fiction is outward homage to the principle of law, an outward protest against unlawful violence. That England underwent a Norman conquest did in the end only make her the more truly England. But that this could be was because that conquest was wrought by the Bastard of Falaise, and by none other."

Nothing, perhaps, in that early age marked more distinctly the instinctive wisdom and statesmanship of William than the great Domesday Survey. In its general results it not only led to a more accurate knowledge of property, but it formed an approximately correct basis, on which assessment for taxation, local and general, was to rest. It was a measure, moreover, which enabled him to ascertain the number and state of his own demesne lands, and, what was equally important, to obtain a clear knowledge of the estates held by the tenants *in capite, i.e.,* estates held in direct tenure from the Crown. Another result followed, namely, it enabled the king to obtain an exact knowledge of those estates which he had lavished upon his nobles, and thus to take care that they should be subject to equitable taxation. In a sense, this great measure was the first great step towards the settlement of real property, founded upon a definite law and a definite method of levying. The Saxon method was arbitrary and ill-defined. The tenures were more or less uncertain, and the holdings, according to Saxon customs, often insecure. The Domesday Commissioners appointed for every shire made their inquisitions upon the oath of juries empanelled on the occasion to ascertain the quantity of land in every county, *rape*,[1] *lathe*,[2] *hundred*,[3] *liberty*,[4] etc., together with the number of freemen, socmen, villeins, slaves, cattle, sheep, hogs, horses, which each estate contained ; to take an account of the cities, towns, vills, and hamlets ; the quantity of arable and pasture land, wood,

---

[1] *Rape*, a division of a hundred or shire ; a geographical expression.

[2] *Lathe*, a part or large division of a county.

[3] An indefinite expression, a territorial or administrative district, peculiar to Southern and Central England. In the North it is called a Wappentake. In earlier times it represented 100 hides, the hides differing in extent in various counties.

[4] A district exempt, as a community, from certain legal conditions and taxation of county government.

and meadow. There is no doubt, says Hearne, that the Norman Survey was one of the greatest strokes of policy ever accomplished.

"The Burgh of Bath we account to have been at the date of the Conquest the capital of Somerset. By 'capital' we mean the seat of the Summa Justicia, of the highest, though by no means the only, Crown Court which existed in the county.

"Bath, previous to its constitution as a burgh, which was towards the end of the tenth century, was but a member, however valuable, of an estate of Royal Demesne. . . .

"The Burgh of Bath, together with whatever pertained to it of royal estate, came to the hands of King Edward at his accession. Whether by way of dotation, or by subsequent gifts, the king seems to have bestowed the whole upon his wife, Edith. The estate, thus passing from the Crown, was then subject to hidation, and so became geldable.[1] On the other hand, it retained one great note mark of royalty. It continued to be a seat of high justice. Queen Edith herself exercised the function of a high justiciar. She paid the Tertius Denarius of the crown-pleas of Bath to her brother Harold, while Earl of Somerset. Queen Edith retained Bath, and her office as a high justiciar, after the Conquest. Surely it was in that capacity that on February 28th, 1072, she presided in the Church of Wilton over that memorable contract, whereby the Saxon Thane, Alsor, sold the Somerset manor of Combe to Giso, Bishop of Wells. This Combe was Monkton Combe, with Combe Down, the former consisting of 720, and the latter 173 parochial acres. Such a transaction could have had no validity save by warranty of the King or his *vicegerent*."

---

[1] That is, it became subject to the ordinary laws of taxation, based upon hidation or admeasurement, the hide differing in extent in different counties ; in Somerset it was about 249¾ acres. Originally, in its essence, it was a *tenement* or *occupation* of uncertain area calculated to bear a certain weight of taxation. When such property ceased to belong to the king, it became geldable, that is, to accurate measurement or hidation and taxation. At the death of Queen Edith the Burgh of Bath reverted to the Crown, and King William dishidated the Burgh. This process of dishidation involved no benefit to the tenant, the king in such a case simply remitting all taxes and royalties due to himself. There were other meanings of the word *hide* in connection with the lands ; but we confine ourselves strictly to its accepted meaning in relation to *Domesday*.

On the death of William, the Burgh reverted to Rufus, by whom it was sold to John de Villula of Tours, Giso's successor in the see of Wells. The sale purported to convey the Burgh and its local privileges and all its appurtenances as previously enjoyed by the King's father, but the justiciarship did not pass by the grant of William to the Bishop, but was entrusted to Edward of Salisbury, then Sheriff of Wiltshire, who was filling the said office at the date of Domesday. At the same date the Burgh and Manor of Batheaston was being farmed of the King by the burgesses as a body corporate, Edward of Salisbury now paying the Tertius Denarius of the Crown-pleas of Bath to the King, as Comes.[1]

It was in 1086 that John de Villula succeeded Giso as Bishop of Wells; and shortly afterwards Rufus sold the Burgh to the Bishop,[2] the sale purporting to convey the said borough, its local privileges and all its appurtenances, as previously enjoyed by the King's father. The estate thus acquired did not include the external territory, as is shown by the fact that the *Tertius Denarius*, the "third penny", brought only £11, whereas the Crown Pleas of that jurisdiction realised £33 per annum. The local territory within the borough comprised the Abbey-fee in Bath, *Bade Caput Abbatiæ*, consisting of twelve acres of meadow (the King's Mead), and a further area being in the old burgh within the walls, Lyncombe and Widcombe (*Lincuma*), Walcot and Bathwick. This last district was then

---

[1] In ancient Rome a companion of, or attendant on, a great person. The corporate body paid the tax to the Earl of Salisbury, the King's *Comes* or *representative.*

[2] It is curious to note the construction put by all the guide writers and many others upon this transaction. They seem to have thought it meant literally that William sold, and the Bishop bought, Bath bodily, and was able to rule and govern it as he pleased. It simply meant that de Villula acquired the King's legal rights in property subject to the laws then in force ; the justiciary being Edward of Salisbury as representative of the Crown.

called *Wicke* or *Wica ;* and the late Mr. Eyton, in his most valuable work on *Somerset Domesday Studies,* implies that the Wica was divided into three. He says : " Alured, a Saxon Thane (a term signifying a member of a rank above that of a freeman, but below that of a noble), appears in *Domesday* as *tenant-in-capite* of two hides in Wica, one of which he held in demesne. The name given to him in 1084 was from his estate in Wick (now Bathwick)." This is one of the few slips made by the accomplished author. There were two Wicks. Bathwick, distinct altogether from Lyncombe, was Wick or Wica proper ; the Wick held by Alured was on the western part of Lyncombe, known as Berewyke or Berwick[1] (prefix *Bere* or *Ber*, signifying water, from its contiguity to the small stream which runs just below it), the tithes of which were assigned to St. Mary de Stall in Bath. There is no trace of any other ancient village in Bathwick than the one which stood on the site of Bathwick Street. At the northern extremity of this village, near the bank of the river, stood the small Early Norman church, within a quaint little churchyard. This church had been patched up in every conceivable style of architecture until it would no longer hold together, and was pulled down in 1814.

The aggregate acreage sold to the Bishop was 3,348 statutory acres, to which must be added Woolley (Wilega or Heorleia) as an integral part of Wica, with an area of 366 acres, thus making an aggregate of 3,714.

---

[1] The modern corruption of the word is " Barracks".

THE

NORMAN AND PRE-REFORMATION PERIOD.

From the death of Giso in 1087, and the accession of John de Villula to Wells in 1088, the city of Bath seems to have undergone no change in relation to the Church. The Saxon church of Offa was still standing, and the rites of the Church were still carried on therein.

By whom or under what dignitaries the ecclesiastical affairs of Bath had been directed under Saxon rule there is little or nothing to show. It is certain that some sort of state and pomp was maintained, under a deputy prelate, or one subordinate to the Bishop. Formerly the heads of religious houses and certain other dignitaries were deemed prelates.[1]

> "A prioure that is a prelate of any church Cathedralle
> Above abbot or prioure with-in the diocise sitte he shalle."

The Abbot's dwelling before 1092 was called the *Manerium*, and belonged to the see. Of such houses, besides that in Bath, there were thirteen in the diocese.

It was, no doubt, in 1087, and before the death of William I, that John de Villula was appointed to the see of Wells, in succession to Giso. This fact effectually disposes of the statement that he practised medicine in the city of Bath, whatever he may have done in Tours, in which city he received Holy

---

[1] Professor Earle reminds us that there used to be in the garden of Weston Vicarage a coffin slab incised with the name of a priest who is entitled "Antistes", a name equivalent to prelate. Prior is an official in the monastic Orders next in dignity and rank to an abbot. Before the thirteenth century he was called *provost*, and prior seems to have meant any superior or senior. If in an abbey, and an assistant of the abbot, he is called a *claustral* prior; if in a priory, he is called a *conventual prior*. There were many other kinds of priors.

Orders. When de Villula was invested with the Bishopric of Wells, Bath would have been under his jurisdiction. Whatever the preferments and privileges may have been which he obtained from Rufus for the 500 marks could have made no difference in his ecclesiastical status. He seemed for some reason to have preferred Bath to Wells, and to have transferred the seat of his episcopal power and administration to the former city in 1091, four years from the time of his investiture at Wells.

This transfer of the see from Wells to Bath led to important and immediate changes in Bath, and in Lyncombe and Widcombe. De Villula was a man of the type of St. Dunstan, only with less of that great man's fiery religious zeal and temperament. He found the mean Saxon church still standing, and this he pulled down. The great prelate showed that if he and his countrymen could not make roads, he and they could conceive and carry out magnificent designs. De Villula's cathedral was one of the most stately in the land. The monastery at the south-west end, and the palace immediately in front over the Roman Bath, and the baths he constructed, one for the Bishop and one for the monks, all point to a completeness and a grandeur surpassing all others before and after. The level of the site, as the foundations show, was raised very much above that of the Saxon building. Even its ruins bore witness to that beauty and dignity and grand construction which had been allowed in successive ages, by shameful neglect, and in spite of episcopal remonstrance and censure, to fall into premature neglect and utter ruin.[1]

[1] The details of these particular facts are all given in Britton's History of the Abbey, edited by R. E. M. Peach, 1887. The bases of the pillars on the north side are preserved. Gratings are placed above them, and these, on being removed, admit of a personal descent. Taking the position of these pillars themselves, and their relative distances, the length and breadth of the ancient structure is shown to have been double the length of the Abbey.

The great work carried on by de Villula in this city was only a part of his achievements during the thirty-five years of his episcopate. He developed the episcopal domain of Lyncombe and Widcombe, which by the great Domesday survey had been brought more under equitable and judicial authority and management. Above the Wide Combe, which we now call Prior Park, the Bishop built the Grange and such offices as were necessary in the cultivation and development of all those higher tracts which extended eastward, southward, and westward. In the lower parts of the estate he also did all that was known in his day to foster the cultivation of the slopes, with their vineries, fig groves, and orchards, which the Saxons had promoted. But as early as Bishop Jocelyn in the thirteenth century, the prior and monks brought upon themselves episcopal censure for their neglect and mismanagement of all the resources placed under their control. At the Reformation the Grange and the group of minor buildings on the estate were little better than the dilapidated buildings on a sixth-rate farmstead. But this was not the worst, for the timber had suffered, so that all the umbrageous beauties of the hills and the combes had disappeared. We must recur however, to de Villula.

Professor Earle says, no doubt with much truth, that " a person who reads through the history of Bath does, in effect, read a history of England in small, because there is no important epoch that is unrepresented in the history of our immediate locality, and that from the very earliest times." Most people who have given any attention to the annals of Bath, recognise the force of the Professor's remarks. He likewise calls attention to some of the remains of Norman architecture, etc., to be seen in various churches near Bath, and makes especial reference to St. Michael's *intra muros*, which, he says, was near the present St. Michael's. This is a misconception. St. Michael's *intra muros* was near the site of the Cross Bath; and at the period when Mr. Lansdown made a sketch of it, partly real, partly ideal,[1] more of the structure was in existence than at present. The church in question enters partly into this history at a later period. Besides this early Norman church, dedicated to St. Michael, there was another beyond the walls, which stood on the site of the old bowling-green[2] in Green Street. This was succeeded by the curious little sixteenth-century structure which stood on the spot occupied by the present church, and was surrounded by a quaint churchyard.

There was another Norman church, to which we shall briefly refer, St. Mary Magdalen. This church was not only Norman in its character, but in its historical associations, especially in connection with the Hosate or Hussey family. The first of the Hosate family was Walter, a knight who came over with the Conqueror. He had various possessions near and around Bath. His son, likewise Walter, was contemporary with de Villula ; and whilst the great prelate was raising his vast cathedral, Walter was erecting that little Norman church near the Fosse in Holloway, in Lyncombe. It was saved from destruction by Prior Cantlow in 1495. Hosate designed the church for the Lepers' Hospital, of which at that time there were two others in the city in connection with the mineral springs. The Hussey family were long associated with Bath and the neighbourhood, their seat having been at Shockerwick.[3]

[1] More than sixty years ago.

[2] When this old bowling-green was built over in the last century many human graves and bones were discovered, not merely indicative of an ancient churchyard, but of an ancient church.

[3] Shockerwick derives its name from Adam de Socherwicke, who lived as early as the reign of Henry II. He held of the Bishop of Bath as part of a knight's fee. Under the feudal system this tenure signified a *perequiste* or ownership of a certain amount of land, and bound the owner to definite military service and other obligations—

In 1322 there is a curious decree of Bishop John de Drokensford with regard to the vicarial endowment of St. Mary in Bath [with Widcombe Chapel], hitherto undefined and so leading to strife between the Priory, the Appropriator, and the Vicar, J. de Didmarton. The Vicar was to have manse, etc., tithe of wool and hay in Widcombe, Lyncombe, and Berwick, with milk and small tithes, obituary services, legacies, and all customary dues, and to find a resident Chaplain at Widcombe. Prior to have great tithes of the villeinage and of other parishes in Lyncombe, of lands of John de Weston, and the Brethren of St. Mary Magdalen ; to bear all "onera". One copy to be kept in Priory, one by Bishop's registrar.

"For that dangerous fight
The great Armenian King made noble Bevis *Knight.*"

After passing from the Socherwicke family the manor, with Batheaston, Bathford, and much besides, came into the possession of the Hosate (now softened into Hussey) family, whose principal seat was called Husei and then Hussey Court, standing on or very near the present mansion. The Husseys, during the reign of Edward III, sold the manor to Sir Walter de Creyk, whose family continued to occupy the old mansion until the manor, with Batheaston and Bathford, in the reign of Richard II, passed to the family of William Brien. Sir Guy, his son, left two daughters, Philippa and Elizabeth. From Philippa, the elder, the manors passed to her husband, John Devereux ; from him to the Scroops ; thence to Boteler, Earl of Wiltshire, through his wife Avicia, whose heir was Humphrey Stafford. In the reign of Edward V the manors were held by Edmond Blunt, then by Simon, who lived at the aforesaid Hussey Court. In the reign of Philip and Mary the manors were held by Thomas Earl of Northumberland. Hussey Court then suffered from neglect, until in 1667 Shockerwick was sold, with Batheaston, to James Lancashire ; and from that time until about eighty years after, when Shockerwick passed into the possession of the Wiltshire family, not much can be recorded of it.

The Court had become a ruin, scarcely one stone standing upon another, and the Park little better than open fields. Then, with the Wiltshires, came the great transformation, the revival of all that was picturesque and beautiful in the charming domain.

Another reference should be made here. In the first map of Bath extant, 1568 or 1572, by Smith of the Heralds' Office, by whom a general survey of the large towns and cities of the kingdom was made, he represents, on the south bank of the Avon, close to the entrance to the bridge, a small *Early English Church*, which has been a puzzle to antiquaries. Mr. Emanuel Green inclines to the opinion that it was not intended to represent an ecclesiastical edifice at all. It must, however, be remembered that the early maps were very realistic; and, moreover, there exist tangible grounds for believing that an ecclesiastical edifice did stand near that spot. Mr. Austin King thinks it is the Church of St. Mary *extra muros*, or that, inasmuch as it is not mentioned by Leland, it may have been a second Oratory. We do not think so, but incline to the belief that it was a small church or chapel-of-ease to St. Mary Magdalen.

One of the interesting aspects of early local history is the growth or evolution of early names, early local laws, and early customs. Now when we speak of Lyncombe we are too apt to think the term itself is as old as, and no older than, the Conquest, whereas the name is very ancient, and, in fact, older than Bath itself. It is as old as the Saxon rule in Bath. The name of Bath has changed with every dynastic change of government, and this was in a sense a necessity. Names, however, of ordinary and general detail used by the Saxons were preserved in the local nomenclature for centuries after the Norman Conquest. The value and importance of this fact in relation to local historical investigation, as well as in itself, cannot be overrated, and it constitutes an especial interest in this ancient part of our city.

But what is so remarkable to note in our own history is the gradual process of legal evolution—to observe how, amidst internecine contentions and occasional violence, the municipal or self-government system, as opposed to the centralizing or bureaucratic, was gradually taking root. In this respect we may claim even more than Professor Earle, inasmuch as these municipal rules were administered in a popular form as early as the tenth century,[1] and after the Conquest the system grew and assumed more popular and definite proportions.

We, moreover, from time to time get clear and interesting aspects of legal procedure. We had in the twelfth century achieved the " Reign of Law"—*i.e.*, the recognition of those principles of human government in their application to property and conduct ; those general rules of external human

[1] From the Conquest until the thirteenth century, the chief officer was called the *Prepositor*, or bailiff, and the place of meeting the *burg-mote* or *moot-court*. [The word is A. S. *mōtian*, cite to a meeting ; *mōt gemōt*, a meeting.] The earliest mayor referred to by Warner is John Savage, in 1412, but the name is much more ancient, as will be seen by the following document, which is a copy translation by the late Mr. H. Riley of a Deed belonging to the Bath Corporation :—

" Know present and to come, that I Walter, Son of Serle, in my lawful power have given to Juliana, daughter of William Springod one seld to the south of the Stalls of Bath which I bought of Robert Prither for 4 marks and a half mark of Silver ; to hold and to have to himself and to whomsoever he shall wish to give or assign it ; rendering for it yearly to the Lords of the fee at the Feast of St. Michael 7 pence, and at Heck day 5 pence for Land gable (Land tax) for all service exaction and demand. And that this my gift may have the strength of perpetual security, this present charter I have corroborated with the impression of my seal. These being witnesses, Caskil de Westone, John Duport, at that time Mayor of Bath, Andrew the clerk, Geoffry Wissi, Hugh de Aystone, Thomas Sweyn, Walter Cabbell and many others."

[It will be seen by this document that surnames at this date were beginning to be used.]

(" Date about A.D. 1230. It contains perhaps the very earliest mention of a Mayor of Bath. The device of the Seal has much of the appearance of an ancient gem.")—*H. R.'s note.*

The first Mayor of London was in 1208. " This yere began the names of Mayers and Sherefs" (*Arnold's Chronicle*). Bath, therefore, was not far behind the capital.

action which are enforced by a sovereign political authority ;
rules of human conduct presented by established usage or
custom.   Henry II had bruised the heel of feudalism, and in
our small way we were soon to see and feel some of its effects
in Somersetshire and our city of Bath, of which some examples
may be cited, chiefly relating to Lyncombe and Widcombe.
Mr. Emanuel Green, who has done so much for Bath history,
has recently edited for the Somerset Record Society a volume,
Pedes Finium, commonly called "Feet of Fines", from 1196
to 1307, a work of unusual interest.   Roughly rendered, it
may be said to mean an account of fines paid to the King for
licences to alienate lands, for freedom from knight's service,
for pardons, wardships, and ordinary justice.   Nor is this all,
for it also shows the manner in which surnames were first
acquired.   Several cases are quoted, all of which are highly
interesting ; but one instance will suffice to illustrate the
manner in which law and justice were administered, and how
in its administration it tended to fix names[1] on individuals, to
perpetuate and explain ancient nomenclature in localities.

Feet of Fines.   Somerset.   44 Henry III.

At Westminster in the quinzaine of Easter ; between William de
Berewyk, querent ; and Thomas, Prior of Bath, deforciant ; for common
of pasture which William claimed to have in the lands of the Prior in
Lincumb and in the wood of Horscumb by fine made at Exeter between
David de Berewyk father of William, whose heir he is, querent ; and the
aforesaid Prior, deforciant ; for the said common of pasture : and whereof
William complained that by the said fine he ought to have common for
all his cattle in Lincumb in all the hill of Lincumb and in all the fields of
the Prior[2] in the said vill of Lincumb, and in a meadow called Sydenham

---

[1] With reference to the history of surnames, those acquired by reason of
legal decisions, or by ownership of distinctive estates, were of a much
earlier date than those of the dwellers in cities and towns, who, early in
the fourteenth century, were called after their professions and their various
callings.

[2] The Prior here referred to was Prior Thomas, who was a litigious

after the hay is lifted and the corn carried : the Prior contrary to the said fine deforced him of the common of pasture. The Prior acknowledged that William in future should have pasture throughout all the manor of Lincumb, and the wood and pasture of Horscumb,[1] for ten oxen with the oxen of the Prior, and likewise pasture in the said places for beasts at grass (*otiosa*), with the Prior's beasts at grass, according to the free tenement which William held in Berewyk the day this concord was made ; except the enclosures and closes underwritten, namely, Dolemede, the vineyard, garden, grove next the court, park, Akerlond, Mellecroft, and Bicchenclyve, in which William shall have no common. If it happen that the Prior remove his oxen or beasts at grass from any cause, William by this fine, may keep his oxen or beasts at grass to feed in the said pasture without hindrance from the Prior. Further, the Prior gave and granted to William a messuage in Berewyk and four acres and a half of meadow in the manor of Lincumb, namely, an acre on the hill near the quarry (quarry opposite Westfield), an acre under Repwey (or rope-walk), towards the Fosse, two acres in the tilled ground called Clyves, half an acre of meadow in Charlemede near the Brodecroft (Broad Field, above the park), and the messuage under the garden of the said William,

---

ecclesiastic, between whom and the civil powers and the citizens frequent misunderstandings occurred. In this contest with William and David de Berewyk, the Prior doubtless wanted to wrest from them the "pasture" referred to, to add to the Prior's Park, which was immediately adjoining. At the same time, Prior Robert was a man of considerable energy, which in the main was well directed. Edward I assigned Bath, with its barton and appurtenances, to his consort Eleanor in dower for her life. The assignment was speedily retracted, and the rights were granted by Bishop Burnell to the churches of Bath and Wells, "except the berton of Bath which the prior and convent hold of us in fee-farm." This act of justice was no doubt due to the sagacity of Robert and his successor, Walter de Aona (Avon), who was the receiver of the monastery. Prior Thomas died in 1261, and was succeeded by Walter. Thomas de Winton was Prior in 1301, and was succeeded by Robert de Cloppecote in 1303. In 1321 Bishop John de Drokensford addressed to him the following remonstrance :—" Has heard of scandalous waste of revenues, and consequent stinting of monks' diet, etc., exhorts him by most sacred motives to be a careful steward and a kindlier ruler in word and deed."

[1] Most of the local names quoted in this reported judgment we have dentified. They are all pre-Norman.

D

which messuage Master John Teyke once held ; to hold to William
of the Prior, doing therefor the regal services to the said tenements
belonging : and the Prior warranted against all men. Further the
Prior quit claimed all the right he had to demand or to have common of pasture in the meadows of William in Lincumb and Berewyk,
namely, in la Brodecroft, Wychegenemed (the Wyke Mead), and Cher-
mesmed (Cherrymead, now Perrymead), so that William may enclose,
ditch, or hedge, and cultivate and take profit from, the said meadows at
his will, without hindrance from the Prior. For this William remitted all
the damages which he was said to have suffered by reason of the Prior
not having held to the aforesaid fine, to the day this concord was made ;
and be it known that the fine first made between the said David and the
Prior for the said common of pasture, by this fine is annulled."

Somerset Fines.   41 *Henry III*, A.D. 1256-7.

At Exon in the octave of St. Martin ; between William de Berewyk,
querent ; and Robert de Atterbere, impedient ; for fifteen acres of land,
excepting one rod, in Berewyk and Lincumb.   Plea of warranty of deed
was summoned.   Robert acknowledged the right of William as being by
his gift, to hold of him, rendering yearly one clove gillyflower at Easter,
and doing to the chief lord of the fee all services belonging ; and Robert
warranted against all men : for this William gave one sore sparrowhawk.

At Exon in the morrow of All Souls ; between William de Berewik,
claimant ; and Adam, Master of the Hospital of St. John of Bath, tenent;
for a messuage in the suburb of Bath.   William acknowledged the right
of the Master and Brethren, to hold of him, rendering per annum five
shillings, half at Easter and half at Michaelmas, and doing to the chief
lord of the fee all services belonging ; and William warranted against all
men ; for this the Master gave William one sore sparrowhawk.

These ancient references cast a very vivid light upon ancient
legal and local nomenclature, many of the names referred to
in the document being retained until this day ; for instance,
the wood and pasture of *Horscumb*, now called *Horsecombe*
Bottom, at Midford ; the meadow called *Sydenham*, situate
near the Midland Railway Station ; the *Dolemeads*, now a
familiar locality in Widcombe parish, near the river, was no
doubt in times even previous to the reign of Henry III the
scene of charitable doles, made from time immemorial by the

various religious orders. Here the ancient vineyard and garden grove next the court are again referred to. The reference, moreover, to Bicchenclyve establishes beyond all controversy the origin and meaning of the name. Wood affected a far-fetched and learned derivation. He, for instance, without any apparent authority, calls it *Blakeleigh*, and as an alternative meaning, the Cliff near the Beech Avenue, and the latter only as a modern invention of his own time.

The name is a very natural one. The south bank of the Avon, even as late as 1700, was a shelving beach, which was embanked in the early part of the century, when the Avon was "canalized" and Claverton Street built. *Beechenclyve* is manifestly a form of Beachenclyve, or Cliff near the Beach. The term *clyve* is used by many of the old authors—

> "And romying on the *clyve* by the sea."
> CHAUCER, *Good Women.*

> "Here es a knyght in theis *klevys*, enclosside with hilles."
> *Morte Arthure.*

Another form of the word is *clough* or *cleugh*, applying more especially to a cleft or rift.

> "Into a grisly *clough*
> This and that maiden yod."

In our edition of Britton's *History of the Bath Abbey* we have endeavoured to trace the history of the Priors in relation to the property and their dealings with the Cathedral. It was in the time of Prior Cloppecote that the Lyncombe and Widcombe estate began to be neglected, the Grange and granaries to fall into disrepair. Episcopal remonstrance was useless; and this strange anomaly occurred: the Prior obtained permission to establish two fairs annually, the one in Lyncombe[1] and the other on their manor of Barton; both having been

---

[1] This fair was held for many years at the foot of Holloway, and until recently, *i.e.*, from the sixteenth to the early part of the present century. That of Barton came to an end at a much earlier date.

a source of great profit to the Prior. The monks complained of oppressions, so that the bishop, Drokensford, interfered on their behalf; and it was at this period, about 1324, that, partly by the neglect of some of his predecessors, but especially of Cloppecote himself, de Villula's cathedral fell so much into dilapidation, that a general collection was made throughout the diocese towards its repair.

It is clear from historical evidence that Bishop Jocelyn of Wells, in the thirteenth century, was the last Bishop who systematically exercised a vigorous and personal supervision over the Bath prior, monastery, and the domain ; and further, from the end of that century the fact appears to be certain that although men like Cantlow, Bird, and Holway[1] (or Gybbs) were men of holy lives and good intentions, the state of things was such as to defy their best efforts to improve them ; so that when the great crisis came a general wreck ensued. The monks were not only too numerous, but nothing could be said for them ; they were drones, and ate up the honey—more honey than the estate could produce. Bath was not in a position to make a successful stand at the Reformation. Some of the Church estates had been well managed—for instance, Montacute, Bruton, and Waltham—hence, so far as the pensions, gratuities, and compensations were concerned, better terms were awarded than to the Bath community. The functions of the three Somersetshire Royal Commissioners, of whom Layton acted for Bath, were to report to Cromwell on the state of the woods and lands, and on the internal administration of the finances generally. Layton, although a lawyer, must have been, even for those days, very illiterate. This man,

[1] The pension to Holway is set forth as follows : "ffurst to William Holewey, prior, for his yerely pencon in mone, xxx*l.*"

"More is appoynted to hym for his dwelling howse, one tenement sett and lying in stalles strete wiin the Southgate of bathe, wherein one 'effrey Stayner lately dwellyd, being of the yerely rente of xx*s.*"

in writing to Cromwell, gives a horrible account of the monks, and, it would seem, of the utter helplessness of the Prior :

"Hit may please yor goodness to vnderstande that we haue visit^e bathe wheras we fownde the priour(Holloway)a ryght vertuose man and I suppos no better of his cot (cloth) a man simple and not of the gretesteste wite, his monkes worse than I haue any fownde yet both in . . . . and adulterie, sum one of them haueying X women sum VIIIth and the rest so fewer. the howse well repared but foure hundredth poundes in dett."

This was not edifying, and the estate at "Wydcomb" might well be impoverished, its grange, its granaries, and its cattle-sheds dilapidated, and its woods cut down, and a *"dett* of foure hundredth poundes"! One is reminded of Chaucer's quaint lines :

"A monk, when he is reccheles,[1]
Is likned to a fissch that is waterles,
This to seyn,[2] a monk out of his cloystre."

Kennet says that the poverty of the surrounding clergy was so great that most of them in Henry VIII's time took to farming, and were very much alarmed when the statute, 21 Hen. VIII, seemed to prevent them from leasing land of the convents any longer. But one finds it difficult to believe this. Kennet was a man with a case to prove, and, as far as Somerset is concerned, there seems evidence to the contrary from the Survey, where the values of the livings are often enumerated. Further, we have the evidence of the *Valor* which shows that the vicar had enough for a single man to live on. Not a large income, but more than Kennet would have us believe, or else, in the stagnation period of rent which followed, and the small improvements in agriculture, the vicar could never have paid his first-fruits and tenths at all, more particularly as he was deprived by statute of part of a small augmentation often accruing. All the historians of the time considered the parson to have been fairly well off. In the

---

[1] Reckless.   [2] Say

Survey we find a vicar keeping two curates. From the *Valor*, a vicar would appear to get some six pounds a year, but he often got more than that, and sometimes, as appears from the survey, he had his food or wood as well. Fish laments the wealth, rather than the poverty, of the clerics. In the diocese of Bath and Wells there were 125 rectories appropriated before the Dissolution. Most of these were in the hands of the convents, an example of which may be seen in the Taunton accounts, the Austin canons there having the rectory of Dulverton. But others besides convents were in possession of impropriated rectories before the Reformation. It was a very favourite method of paying a man a salary, to make him a non-resident rector of a country living. He put in a vicar, and drew the difference between the whole tithe, and whatever the vicar had to live on, generally the small tithe. The chancellor of the diocese, the prebendaries, the archdeacon, and others received money in this way, and sometimes laymen. Also, when the visitations were in progress, and during the troubled years between the various stages of the suppression, the convents, in order to bribe or please certain of their friends, made grants of rectories to laymen, but the practice was not at all common, and was considered illegal. But when the monastic property changed hands a very different state of affairs presented itself.

The laity who held land in manors, formerly the property of a convent, very naturally objected to pay large sums of money (amounting in our values almost always to several hundred pounds) to other than religious persons; and it appears that they did not pay until admonished so to do by the Act 32 Hen. VIII on the subject. One computation assigns 3,335 as the number of rectories which passed into lay hands.[1]

[1] Archbold, *Religious Houses in Somersetshire.*

THE REFORMATION PERIOD.

The statute referred to portended the great measure which was to come. If we refer to the Reformation here, it is because in its relation to Lyncombe, and its bearing upon the destinies of the Abbey, it furnishes us with a chapter in our ecclesiastical annals of which we have no reason to be proud. If the monks had erred, and if Henry VIII could not, with the consent of the Pope, follow their evil example with that celerity which he desired, it was a bad reason for depriving Bath of all her endowments ; the " carcase" of the Abbey being left to be carted away like an old barn. If it was saved, it was saved partly by Colles,[1] by whom it was purchased, together with the larger portion of Church property in Lyncombe, Widcombe, and other parts of the city. The enumeration of the various items of the property, if not edifying, is curious.

It will be observed that within this " ambit" there was much scope for evasion and nepotism, not to say great roguery. The opportunity was not neglected ; but what added to the turpitude of the transaction was the fact that it was done ostensibly to preserve some endowment for the Abbey—in a word, to make a provision to maintain and perpetuate the Church and public worship in the oldest and most important city in the county.

The original document, after the preamble, goes on as follows :—

"And also all that site Sept circuit ambit and precinct of the late Monastry or Priory of Bathe in our said county of Somerset, and all and singular houses, edifices, Gardens, Orchards, Kitchen Gardens, Barns, Dovecotes, Pools, Vivacies, Waters, Fisheries and Fishings, Land and

---

[1] See *Bath, Old and New*, by R. E. M. Peach.

Soil within the same site being sept circuit ambit or Precinct of the said late Monastry or Priory. And also one Close or Meadow called the Ham and two Closes or Meadows called Amebrye Meades, with all and singular their appurt's lying and being near the Site aforesaid and in the Parish of St. James in our said County of Somerset, to the said late Priory or Monastry of Bathe lately belonging and appertaining. And also all and singular Messuages, Lands, Tenements, Meadows, Feedings, Pastures and other our hereditaments whatsoever known by the name or names of Beechingclyft, Brodecrofts, Brodemede, Wrogsmede, Horselease, Belle-mede, and Priours Park, with all and singular their appurt's lying and being within the Manors or Parishes of Lyncomb, Widcombe, Holloway, and Walcot, or any of them, in our said County of Somerset, and to the said late Monastry or Priory of Bath lately belonging and appertaining, and also all that our Messuage or capital Mansion of Combe, situate, lying and being within the Parish of Combe in our said County of Somerset, and all and singular houses and edifices, structures, Gardens, Orchards, Kitchen Gardens, Dovecotes, Pools, Vivacies, Lands and Soil within the site and Precinct of the same Capital Mansion being to the said late Monastry or Priory of Bathe late belonging and appertaining."

Previous to and at the time of the Dissolution, the Wid-combe manor and estate included "Lyncombe, Widcombe, and Holway", and are so described in the schedule, a copy of which was published by the Society of Antiquaries, *Valor Ecclesiasticus*, Henry VIII, page 175. After the Dissolution, the Commissioners, for reasons to be stated hereafter, sepa-rated the Prior's Park from the other portion of the eccle-siastical manor. It was (with other large estates) sold to Humphrey Colles, from whom it passed to Matthew Colthurst ; and after a lapse of time it was acquired by purchase by Fulke Morley, from whom, in the early part of the last century it descended to the Duke of Kingston, whose representatives, as is well known, sold it to Ralph Allen.

Then we come to what is commonly called Widcombe Manor, which, it is enough to say, included the manor house and surrounding estate ; in other words, that portion of the ecclesiastical domain separated from the Prior's Park. Now, then, comes the reason for that separation. The Commissioners, two of whom were local gentlemen, were not authorised to assign funds for the completion of the half-finished Abbey, nor to make any sort of provision for the continuity of any kind of public worship in the church. It is needless to enter upon the history of the danger which followed to the very existence of the Abbey, as every intelligent person knows it only too well. But, perhaps, the incident that followed is very interesting, as illustrating some of those evils to which reference has been made, and against which no provision whatever, at any rate in portions of Somerset, Bath more especially, had been made.

The Commissioners, prompted by laudable zeal, were anxious to preserve a portion of the ecclesiastical revenues for the future sustentation of the church and public worship. To this end they proposed to grant a portion of the Widcombe estate in trust to the Mayor, Richard Chapman, and the Corporation, for the use of the churches in Bath. The Mayor, with a refined distinction in honesty, suggested that the transaction might be too open to be safe, and that a covert grant of the property (he taking the lion's share) should be made to him and the Corporation, the better to achieve the objects of the Commissioners in securing an endowment for the churches in perpetuity. This Richard Chapman was in reality from that moment the owner of the Widcombe estate. But here follows another quiet piece of rascality, equal to, though perhaps differing in its nature from, modern accomplishments of that character. The chief actor in the later refined combination of sacrilege and vulgar iniquity was also a Chapman, as well as Mayor—John Chapman. Shortly after R. Chapman's deed of plunder—that is, about 1557—the Vicar of St. Mary de Stalls[1]

---

[1] There is an excellent account of the Norman church by Mr. Austin King, in vol. vi, *Field Club Proceedings*, p. 283. It should be known that some forty years ago a part of the crypt of the church was discovered.

died, and from that time until 1584 no successor was appointed and there were no systematic public ministrations in the city.

In that year the said Mayor, John Chapman (who succeeded to his father's property and virtues), and the Corporation, by whom the patronage had been secured, appointed the Rev. Sir R. Meredith to the Rectory of the Abbey and Vicarage of Stalls (which retained certain properties in the precincts of the Abbey and churchyard). With this unprincipled cleric the Mayor and members of the Corporation entered into an unholy compact. Sir Richard was to grant leases of sites for building around the Abbey and on the said precincts, which by that time had acquired a value. It was at this time that every foot of available ground was built upon up to the very walls of the Abbey, on the site of the old Stalls Church, the church-yard thereof, and any nook and cranny these vampires could appropriate, nearly all those buildings remaining until they were pulled down between 1819 and 1832.[1]

Between the period of the Dissolution and the advent of Ralph Allen to Prior Park, Lyncombe and Widcombe experienced unfavourable vicissitudes. The land was let to the butchers, dairymen, and jobbers, all of whom naturally got as much out of it as they could. The slopes, and the valleys, and the combes were denuded of as much of their beauty and loveliness as seemed needful to those whose business was profit. Enclosures were destroyed, the coppices cut down, the approaches badly kept, except near and about the Manor House.

When Allen, therefore, about 1730, purchased Prior Park and its contiguous surroundings, he began with a clear course and no favour, and he was soon to prove to the city that he understood his position and appreciated his opportunities.

---

[1] Of the Chapmans we shall have more to say in connection with the Bennets and Widcombe House.

LIFE AND TIMES OF RALPH ALLEN.

LIFE AND TIMES OF RALPH ALLEN.

ESIDES the difficulties inherent in the postal system itself, at the beginning of the eighteenth century, the roads and means of locomotion presented tremendous complications, in dealing with which Allen had neither Government help nor much experience to guide him. He was left to his own unaided resources in devising practical means to ensure regularity of transmitting the mails by the shortest, the most practicable, the safest, and cheapest routes. Up to Allen's day the Post-Office was one of the worst managed and most abused departments under the Government control. Two Post-masters-General appear to have been prompt and efficient in nothing except receiving each a large salary, paid quarterly. With some exceptions, few attempts (as we learn from Mr. Herbert Joyce's able and valuable work, and others, on the Post-Office) were ever made to work out with the genius, energy, and determination afterwards displayed by Allen, a postal system adequate to the growing needs and the resources of the nation.[1] Nor was this the only consideration.

[1] Even now it needs the penetration and wisdom of a Postmaster-General to say why printed matter may go at the cheap rate, whilst type-written matter cannot. The matter may be identical, but only the intelligence of a P. M. G. can see why the poor type-writer is to pay a penny for an open letter and the printer a halfpenny.

The acceleration of postal arrangements, and the adaptation of means to that end, especially involved the question of roads. It will be well to give a slight description of the Roman roads, all of which were, as far as possible, roughly adapted to the growing needs of commerce and the public service. These roads had become little better than rough tracks, wholly unfit for any kind of vehicle to traverse in winter, and very difficult for horses on which were laid very heavy loads. The *Fosse* and *Icening Street* traversed the kingdom from south-west to north-east, parallel to one another; *Watling Street* crossed them quite the contrary way, with an equal obliquity; and the *Hermen Street* passed directly north and south. We need not describe these roads more minutely,[1] but it may be well to state that the roadways, with the exception of being here and there cobbled, were not "made"[2]—*made* being a technical word, signifying the distinction between a road which has undergone the scientific process of being metalled by broken stone, etc., and a mere path or track from one point to another, which really the ancient roads had become.[3]

The Fosse begins at Seaton, thence passes to Ilchester, Bath, Cirencester, through Warwickshire to Cleybrook in Leicester-shire, thence to Lincoln, and ends at Saltfleet on the sea-coast. The *Via Badonica* was from London to Batheaston, where it formed a junction with the Bath line, and is almost on the identical lines of the London road by Devizes, while,

[1] The two books by which these roads are most clearly depicted are Ogilby's *Kingdom of England* and John Owen's *Britannia Depicta*.

[2] The Roman roads were originally paved with flints, Roman bricks, and large flagstones ; but few examples were left when these roads were incorporated with the "made" roads in the last century.

[3] The laugh excited by the clumsy epigram on Marshal Wade's Scotch roads was without point or wit :—

"Had you seen these roads before they were made,
You'd have lift' up your hands and bless'd Marshal Wade."

as above mentioned, the Fosse and Icening Street traversed the kingdom from south-west to north-east, parallel to one another, the Watling Street crossed them quite the contrary way with an equal obliquity, and Hermen Street passed directly north and south.

The early part of the eighteenth century may be regarded, especially in relation to Bath, as the beginning of that great transition which was soon to effect a new epoch in the national habits. New energies were brought into action, and the vast inherent resources of the nation were about to be developed. In Bath this fact was to be illustrated in very many ways. Not a few of the old walled cities had been for some time emancipated from their fetters —their walls—which had not merely become anachronisms in themselves, but were impediments to progress in every sense of the word. Many towns and cities there were that still loved and clung to the old order of things, apparently for no other reason than because they were venerable. Bath, however, clung to its old city and its old walls for reasons different from these. In the previous century the uselessness of the city walls as a defence had been proved more than once, and no pretence whatever could be or was urged by the authorities for maintaining a *cordon* of walls around it to protect any interest, curious enough, except their own. The marvel to us in these days is how a city, badly ventilated, ill-drained, lying, too, at that period on the lowest levels, with no means of expelling foul air by the admission of fresh, could, as it certainly did, maintain its reputation as the healthiest city in the kingdom.

Bath was, at this period, under a very paternal corporation; and these city fathers had, by this time, become masters of the city. The city fathers, as we know, drew the parental ties a little too close ; their power was, locally, very great, indeed, almost absolute within the walls ; they elected one another, and the ties of brotherhood or fatherhood were deeply laid in the foundations of self-interest. The time had come, however, when, if the breath of heaven were not permitted to blow into and purify their city, public policy, public opinion, and public necessity, had become too strong for them, and their walls were soon to fall down like the walls of Jericho before the trumpets of the priests and the shouts of the people.

The removal of the walls[1] opened up the streets and let in the fresh air; public dust-heaps were no longer allowed to accumulate around the walls; the various other abominations were rigidly removed from certain localities, which were then converted into beautiful sites, on which now stand some of the most dignified and beautiful groups of buildings in the world. The resistance to change and progress is to be looked for in one of those exceptional features which were at that time peculiar to Bath.

The corporate body, from the time of Queen Elizabeth down to the beginning, and some time after, of the last century, had consisted chiefly of the professional men of the city—lawyers, doctors, apothecaries, and a few moneyed nondescripts, to whom the gains of corruption and peculation were always sweet. These men began, as we have often shown, by robbing the Church, the charities, and the public institutions, and they ended by robbing the citizens generally.

The peculiarity of Bath consisted in this. From the middle of the sixteenth to the close of the seventeenth century, and a little later, not only was the whole municipal power in the hands

---

[1] It by no means follows that we can approve the barbarous methods employed. The gates and walls were simply knocked down and carted away, no systematic effort having been made to protect and preserve the interesting historical and traditional figures which ornamented the north and south gates etc.

of this class of men, but individually they possessed all the best houses,[1] some of which (notwithstanding Lord Macaulay and Wood[2]) were fine, stately old mansions, affording ample accommodation for their own private wants, and capacious state rooms for wealthy cripples and delicate valetudinarians. These privileges manifestly constituted profitable monopolies, which they knew must vanish in the face of open competition and healthier abodes. It is an axiom that no reform is so effectual as that which proceeds from within, and in this case it proved so. The man who had the courage to risk the displeasure of his colleagues was George Trim, who, after gaining his point, was the man by whom the first street was built outside the walls, which bore, and still bears, his name.[3]

At a little later period [1720[4]] began the great work of the first Wood, by whose genius, enterprise, and energy arose, within a period of thirty years, a city (even before the noble continuation of the work by his son) without an equal, or at that time a rival, in the kingdom.

The corporate body of Bath, as has been shown, from the time of Queen Elizabeth to the close of the seventeenth century, if not a scrupulous body, possessed perhaps what

---

[1] See Gilmore's map.

[2] The 12*s*.-a-week lodgings, of which Wood speaks, and to which Lord Macaulay refers, as the average character of Bath lodgings, were such as the needy fortune-hunter or the low gambler was glad to get in the minor houses in the minor streets.

[3] It contains some fine houses, but has long been superseded by the later and nobler streets of Wood, Chambers, Baldwin, Harcourt Masters, and others. The house in which General Wolfe was living, with his father, when he was summoned to take charge of the Quebec expedition, was a beautiful mansion ; but as one passes it now, with its war emblems over the door, there placed in honour of the gallant soldier after his death, it is difficult to suppress a sigh.

[4] He became a resident in 1727.

E

they deemed to be the utilitarian virtue of economy, especially when the exercise of that virtue failed to touch their own pockets. There were two Norman churches within the city, built immediately after the Conquest—St. Michael's and St. Mary's. The former occupied a site close to Westgate Street, at the termination of St. Michael's Place; the latter was placed just within the North Gate. St. Michael's was used as a church until 1590, and St. Mary's until 1553, the last rector having been presented in 1541. Both churches fell into disrepair, but such portions as could be utilised were pressed into the public service. St. Mary's Tower was used as the city prison, whilst the nave was appropriated to the use of King Edward's Grammar School, so that very opposite ideas were " shooting" under the enlightened auspices of the Bath corporation. St. Michael's fell into decay, the tower having been removed late in the seventeenth century, and only the nave and an aisle remained; and it would be difficult to say to what uses this comparative ruin had not been put. Early in the eighteenth century, however, on the appointment of Quash as Postmaster, what was left of the place was used as the local post-office.[1]   The condition of the English Post-

---

[1] Since 1730 the building has been used, first, for many years, as a tavern, then as a printing-office, then as a warehouse, then as the office of *The Bath Herald*, and since that period again as a warehouse under various forms. On one of the old windows (all of which have now been removed) various lines were written, and on one, curiously enough, the autograph of Cowper :—

> "Bath for distinction may cope with old Rome,
>   But sulphur and fire are reserved for both's doom."

> "If thy good-spoken tongue thy bosom shows,
>   Then let the secrets of my heart repose."

> "Oh, ye gods, what have I done?
>   Spent all my money and had no fun."

> *Farewell to Bath*, April 22, 1730.

Office at this period seems to have been most unsatisfactory in every respect ; in fact, it seems not to have grown with the growth and public wants of the country, and the Postmasters-General never seem to have risen to a due sense of the importance of their department. Public roads[1] there were none, and the local offices were allowed to drift into sad disorder. No post-office out of London could have been

---

" Heavy and strong is the delightful chain
  By which Clarisda does my heart retain."
" No tongue my pleasure or my pain can tell,
  'Tis heaven to have you, but without you, hell."
" If to her shame some trivial errors fall,
  Look on her face and you 'll forget them all."
" I will love for ever,
  But ne'er shall have her."

[1] In spite of some precautions, roads were often neglected, so that those who were not obliged to go on foot travelled almost entirely on horseback, women almost always riding astride like men. It was only at the end of the fourteenth century that a few ladies rode sideways. Kings and queens and exceedingly great people occasionally used lumbering but gorgeously ornamented carriages ; but this was to enable them to appear in splendour, as this way of travelling must, at least in fine weather, have been far less agreeable than the ordinary ride. The only other wheeled vehicles in existence were the peasants' carts on two wheels, roughly made in the form of a square box, either of boards or of a lighter framework. It was one of the grievances of the peasants that, when the king moved from one manor to another, his purveyors seized their carts to carry his property, and that, though the purveyors were bound by frequently-repeated statutes to pay for their hire, these statutes were often broken, and the carts sent back without payment for their use.— *Rawson Gardiner.*

Every great personage who has visited Bath before 1720 rode on horseback, except Queen Anne, who travelled in a chariot, and nearly came to grief. Queen Elizabeth had an enormous retinue of horsemen and horsewomen in making her journey westward. Nearly all the eminent personages who visited our city as late as 1710, and even later, rode on horseback. See Hon. Miss Fiennes's account of her westward journey.

E 2

much worse managed than that of Bath. Quash either could
not deal, or did not care to make the attempt of dealing,
with the disorders, which were of every sort and kind. But,
as Mr. Herbert Joyce says, "there was one who realised
not less fully than the Postmasters-General themselves the
difficulties by which they were beset. He knew well, even
better than they, how letters were being kept out of the
post and transmitted clandestinely, and how, even on letters
which fell into the post, the postage was being intercepted.
But while the Postmasters-General regarded the evil as in-
curable, he thought that it might, at all events, be mitigated.
This was Ralph Allen"; and he was soon to show, not only
that he possessed the capacity to conduct the local Bath
post-office, but the foresight and the ability to devise and
carry out a system which was of incalculable importance
nationally, both in its immediate and future results.

The Rev. R. Graves of Claverton, author of the *Spiritual
Quixote*,[1] writing about the year 1800, says : " An ingenious
young gentleman, who has lately made a tour of the west,
showed me a drawing of the house where Mr. Allen was born,
which is still shown to strangers, not merely as an object of
curiosity, but by many of those who had partaken of his
bounty and are still living, with a kind of religious veneration.
The house," he continues, "seems to have been the residence
of a gentleman's family, and though now converted into a
farmhouse, by no means warrants Mr. Pope's epithet of
low-born Allen."[2]

From an entry in the Registry of St. Blazey there is, under
the year 1686, an imperfect entry, the legible parts of which
are : " Will. All . . . . and Grace was mar . . . . 24th August."
And then, in 1687, a John Allen and Mary Elliott were married.

---

[1] For many years Rector of Claverton, occupying the old manor house
[now destroyed] above the beautiful terraces.

[2] A subject on which more will be said as we proceed.

Neither of these couples, however, were the parents of Ralph. This would be tolerably clear from the fact that, as Ralph was the first-born of the family, and his birth took place in 1693 or 1694, his parents must have been married after the dates given. But we find in a deed, dated 1724, that the name of Ralph Allen's father was Philip, and that he was the owner of the property he occupied at St. Blazey, upon which he was raising a mortgage from his son, Ralph, of £206.

Many entries of births, marriages, and deaths of the Allen family occur in the Registry of St. Blazey even as late as the year 1810, but these may be passed over as foreign to the present design, even if these Allens were of the same family, which is doubtful. Of Ralph Allen himself the baptismal register does not appear, and it seems probable that Ralph was born before his parents came to St. Blazey. The name of Allen is now no longer known in the parish.

Mr. Allen's father seems, from the brief records that have come down to us, to have borne a high character for honesty and straightforwardness. Mr. Polwhele gives the following anecdote of him :—

" In a severely-contested election for the county (Cornwall), in which the candidates were Edgcumbe, Boscawen, Granville (of Stowe), and Trevanion, Mr. Boscawen called upon Mr. Allen and asked him for a pint of his beer, requesting Mr. Allen to drink with him. Mr. Allen, being naturally obliging, had no hesitation in complying with the request of the stranger. Mr. Boscawen (who was *incog.*) took occasion to inquire the news of the neighbourhood and day, and the election being then most prominent, the subject was immediately introduced. After conversing in a mere cursory manner, Mr. Boscawen began to inquire into the general opinion of the private characters of the candidates, which Mr. Allen as freely gave him. Mr. Boscawen then inquired who this Boscawen was, and what Allen thought of him ? Allen observed, ' He

is much respected, I believe, in his neighbourhood ; but in his
public capacity we all suspect him to be unsound.' The conversation having proceeded thus far, several of Mr. Boscawen's
attendants came up and addressed him in his proper form.
Mr. Allen felt abashed, and apologised for the freedom which
he had ignorantly taken. 'Give me your hand, my honest
friend,' cried the gentleman ; 'you have given me no offence ;
here is your money for the beer. I hope soon to undeceive
the county, and prove that Boscawen is not unsound.'" This
anecdote is given for what it is worth. We confess we should
have thought more of Allen if he had displayed a little more
independence by sticking to and defending his opinions. The
"dropping-down-deadness", on learning the dignity and importance of his visitors, detracts from the sturdy independence
which the freedom of his criticism implied.

The first mention of Ralph Allen is his having been
placed under the care of his grandmother (whether paternal
or maternal does not appear), who kept the post-office at St.
Columb.

"He there discovered", says Mr. Graves, "a turn for
business, a cleverness in arithmetic, and a steadiness of
application, which seemed to indicate his future eminence.
The Inspector of the post-office having come into Cornwall,
and among other towns having visited St. Columb, was highly
pleased with the uncommon neatness and regularity of young
Allen's figures and accounts, and expressed a wish to see the
boy in a situation where ingenuity and industry might have a
wider scope and more encouragement. Not long afterwards
Allen's friends consented to his leaving Cornwall, and he
appears to have come to Bath." Graves further said : "In
what I am going to relate in these few anecdotes I do not
pretend to great accuracy as to time and other circumstances;
but they are what were generally known and circulated fifty
years ago (about 1750), when I first came to reside in the

vicinity of Bath,[1] as facts of which few people in the neighbourhood could be ignorant." Graves then goes on to say :
" In the year 1715, Mr. Allen was one of the clerks in the
post-office in this city. In this situation, having got intelligence of a waggon-load of arms coming up from the West
for the use of the disaffected in this part of England (who
were supposed to have projected an insurrection in order to
co-operate with that in Scotland and in the North of England),
he communicated this to General Wade, who was then
quartered at Bath with troops ; and who finding him a
sensible, prudent young man, got him advanced after the
death of Mr. Quash, who was then Postmaster, to that
station, and afterwards married him to Miss Earl, his natural
daughter."

We give this story for what it is worth. The incident was
said to have happened in the year when Graves was born,
and was not related by him until eighty-four years after.
At that time Graves, after a long, interesting, and exemplary career, was enfeebled by age and infirmities. Mr.
Herbert Joyce, C.B., briefly refers to the supposed incident,
which, if it rested upon any trustworthy evidence—evidence
surely would have been found in the archives of the Post
Office, and quoted. We doubt the truth of the story altogether. In the first place, Marshal Wade never was quartered
with troops in Bath ; in the second place, no rising in the
West was at any time imminent ; and in 1715 a waggon
was a vehicle unknown, and if it had been, there was not
a road at that period on which it could have travelled
at the rate of a mile a day ; and lastly, from whence could
arms have been procured in the West to have supplied the
disaffected ? It is a romance ; and we need not go far for

[1] As Rector of Claverton, about a year before Allen acquired that
estate.

other and more legitimate reasons for the rapid advancement of Ralph Allen in the postal service.

Tradition says that Ralph Allen was born in 1693 or 1694, at St. Blazey. His father was Philip Allen,[1] the landlord of a roadside inn in that parish known as "The Duke William", now converted into private dwelling-houses. This was one of the old-fashioned inns of those days which were models of comfort and respectability ; and Philip Allen was one of the typical landlords of the roadside posting-houses of that day. He was, from a few glimpses we get of his character, a clear-headed, well-educated man, who wrote a good hand, and who, if we may judge from his two sons, Ralph and Philip, and his several daughters, took infinite pains

[1] "It is no uncommon popular fallacy in estimating the dispositions and characters of self-made wealthy philanthropists, to regard them as a simple, easy-going class of men who repose in easy chairs, spread a napkin over their knees, into which Providence pours His bounteous gifts, without an effort on their part, or the exercise of brains, or forethought of any kind whatsoever. Such creatures—the recipients of such bounty—there may have been, and such easy-come, easy-go beings may have dispensed freely that which cost them nothing, and of the value of which they never had a just conception ; but such people are not philanthropists, they are pauper-makers. Of such was not Ralph Allen. He was a true philanthropist. The wealth he acquired was through a keen and observant sagacity ; there were no means consistent with honour and strict integrity, no vigilance compatible with upright dealing he did not exercise in the pursuit of the fortune he accumulated. Hence he knew its real value. He gave not of that which cost him nothing ; but he gave with an open hand, a willing heart, and a noble spirit, when the object was worthy and the occasion opportune. His perception of what was good was quickened and enlarged by a never-ceasing desire to increase human happiness, and in his employment of labour he exhibited the keenest solicitude for his men in their workshops and their dwellings. He sought to improve their moral and material welfare, and so far recognized the obligations he felt towards those through whom he amassed no little of his fortune. If he obtained wealth he conferred happiness."—*Author's Preface to another little work.*

to train them practically, wisely, and well. In after life Allen received his sisters at Hampton and Prior Park, and corresponded with them kindly and affectionately. Of his ~~younger~~ *elder* brother, Philip, frequent mention will be made in these pages. Ralph Allen as a lad was unusually grave, thoughtful, and intelligent, but without the least conceit or moroseness.

When Allen came to Bath in 1715, it is clear that he had given, and was soon to give, further evidence of those peculiar qualities—personal and official—which were to inspire confidence and respect. His personal appearance at this period was impressive rather than striking. About the middle height, with well-knit frame, head well set upon his shoulders, with very fine features—large mouth, and nose well-formed, clear large dark eyes, well-chiselled but rather too small a chin. But with this comely person he never, even in his *salad* days, seems to have had the least vanity. He was always plainly dressed in the style of the period, and his manner and address were set off by an inbred courtesy and a grave self-possession. " Hail, ye sweet courtesies of life, for sweet do ye make the road of it." At this time he laboured as few men laboured, but his duties and responsibilities increased, and none can tell how in those days he accomplished the official duties he had to perform whilst simultaneously carrying on the vast self-imposed duties in relation to the social and philanthropical work of the city.

The earliest glimpse we got of him in his official career is from the pen of Mr. Herbert Joyce, C.B., in his most interesting and able *History of the Post Office.* He says, speaking of Allen at an early age : " Allen's experience in postal matters was probably unrivalled. He had, it might almost be said, been cradled and nursed in the post-office. He had, at eleven years of age, been placed under the care of his grandmother, who, on the post-road being diverted from South to Mid-Cornwall, was appointed Post-mistress of

St. Columb. Here the regularity and neatness with which he kept the accounts gained for him the approval of the District Surveyor when on a tour of inspection ; and shortly afterwards, probably through the surveyor's influence, he obtained a situation in the post-office at Bath. When Quash, the old Postmaster, died, Allen was appointed in Quash's room."

In 1719, Allen[1] offered to take in farm the bye and cross-post letters, giving as rent half as much again as these letters had ever produced. It was a bold offer, and, coming as it did from a young man only twenty-six years of age, and presumably without capital, not one to be accepted precipitately. Allen proceeded to London and had frequent interviews with the Postmaster-General. The earnestness of his convictions, and the modest assurance with which he expressed them, invited confidence, and on April 12th, 1720, a contract was signed, the conditions of which were to come into operation on the Midsummer Day following.

" Much as we desire to avoid the employment of technical terms, it is necessary here to explain that letters, exclusive of those passing through the penny post, were technically divided into four classes—London letters, country letters, bye or way letters, and cross-post letters. For purposes of illustration we will take Bath, the city in which Allen resided. A letter between Bath and London would be a London letter, and a letter from one part of the country to another which in course of

[1] After Quash's death, Allen continued to conduct the postal business in the old church nave until about 1727, and even a little later. This old church at that period was closely surrounded by houses and dwellings of the most objectionable character, and the neighbourhood infested by the "post-office hangers-on", who were the terror of the honest, and the "pals" of the dishonest officials within. The Cross Bath, near it, was at this time in a "tumble-down" condition. At a later period the Royal Baths were erected by Wood II, but at this time they were not much better than a *wash-house.*

transit passed through London would be a country letter. A bye or way letter would be a letter passing between any two towns on the Bath Road and stopping short of London—as, for instance, between Bath and Hungerford, between Hungerford and Newbury, between Newbury and Reading, and so on ; while a cross-post letter would be a letter crossing from the Bath Road to some other—as, for instance, a letter between Bath and Oxford. It was only with the last two classes of letters that Allen had to do. The London and country letters were outside the sphere of his operations.

"On the bye and cross-post letters the postage for the year 1719 had amounted to £4,000. Allen was to give £6,000 a year ; and in consideration of this rent he was for a period of seven years to receive the whole of the revenue which these letters should produce. Some letters, indeed, were excepted, namely, Scotch letters, Irish letters, packet letters, and 'all Parliament men's letters during the privilege of Parliament', and such letters as usually 'goe free', that is, letters for the High Officers of State, or, as we should now say, letters on His Majesty's service. No post under Allen's control, whether a new or an old one, was to go less than three times a week ; and the mails were to be carried at a speed of not less than five miles an hour. He was also to keep in readiness a 'sufficient number of good and able horses with convenient furniture' not only for the mails, but for expresses and for the use of travellers. One condition of the contract may seem a little hard. Allen's own officers were to be appointed and their salaries to be fixed by the Postmasters-General, and to these officers he was to give no instructions which had not been first submitted for the inspection of the Postmasters-General. Allen, by his sterling qualities, had won the confidence of his fellow-townsmen at Bath, and there can be little doubt that they now gave him a practical proof of the estimation in which he was held."

This period was, no doubt, the turning point of Allen's career. From the last sentence quoted from Mr. Joyce, that gentleman evidently thinks Allen received pecuniary help from the citizens. "It is difficult", he says, "to understand how else he can have raised the funds necessary for the purposes of his undertaking. In the very first quarter, between the 24th June and the 29th September 1720, he expended in what may be called his plant as much as £1,500, and made himself responsible for salaries to the amount of £3,000 a year." The citizens of Bath, at that time, were not at all likely to have helped Allen; they, with a very few exceptions, "cared for none of these things".[1] It was about 1718 that Allen's marriage with Marshal Wade's natural daughter, Miss Earl, took place; that beautiful lady receiving from her father a large fortune. Marshal Wade was, even at that period, not only very rich, but he was also a very prudent, generous, and far-seeing man. No one in those early days was likely to understand and appreciate the sterling qualities of Allen better than Wade, between whom a lifelong friendship subsisted; nor to have been more impressed with the vigilance, sagacity, and foresight of Allen. The Marshal could not have failed to observe the disorder which prevailed in the old Bath Post Office, and the disgusting scenes that took place within and around it. After the arrival of every mail a large proportion of the letters arriving were handed over to the hangers-on for delivery, and on every letter an extra penny, and sometimes twopence, was charged by these men to the receiver.

The serious minor difficulty, with which Allen in his early official days had to contend, doubtless was the disorganised

---

[1] Seeing by the official evidence before him what manner of man Allen was, and what he had achieved in connection with the post-office, Mr. Joyce might well have formed such an opinion, but it was without foundation.

state of the staff which he found in the Bath Post Office. Quash had been for years entirely at the mercy of the clerks and the sorters, who were in league with the outside irregulars. When Allen entered upon his duties in Bath it is difficult to conceive a state of things more discouraging or more difficult to deal with ; and the locality of the office at the bottom of that narrow, dirty, and loathsome street (as it then was),[1] whilst it aggravated the special irksomeness of postal organization, increased the difficulties of applying an efficient remedy. Another source of perplexity to a Bath Postmaster was the perpetual fluctuation of the population. In 1715, and from that time almost until the death of Allen, the houses were not numbered ; and this, as may be imagined, facilitated the operations of the outside " hangers-on". There was some check afforded in that a large number of the distinguished visitors to Bath took up their abode at some of the "lodgings" distinguished by the names of the owners upon the houses[2] ; these owners were the big men of the city, and realised very large incomes by this means. For instance, a careful correspondent, writing from Bath, would write thus : " From Mr. More's Lodgings in the Churchyard", or, " From the Royal Lodgings by the Abbey Church", and so on. This method usually ensured a reply to such address. This, no doubt, was a special feature in the social life of Bath ; and therefore it would to a great extent be less liable to the confusion to which London and other large cities were subject from the absence of specific addresses.

Of course, the first duty imposed upon Allen as Postmaster was to deal with the disorders of the local office. In this he

[1] The old one (Bath Street) was pulled down early in this century, when the present street was erected.

[2] These houses, with the names of the owners, the leading men of the city, were illustrated in Gilmore's Map, recently republished by the Bath booksellers, with a History, by Mr. R. E. M. Peach.

showed on a smaller scale what in course of years he was to
display on a larger. He knew that if he dismissed a rogue he
would get a bigger one in his stead. The process he adopted
was to make the rogues see that in the long run honesty
would pay them best. It is needless to say that this process
demanded the exercise of all the patience, beneficence, and
firmness even of Allen. This great moral duty was rendered
the more difficult by reason of its having to be carried on in
the locality of which mention has been made, with all the
hindrances and impediments of which the "outsiders", over
whom he had no control, were capable. If an irregularity, or
a theft, or any sort of violation of post-office rules was com-
mitted, the culprit was "carpeted", and Allen, with a calm,
kind smile would chide the wrongdoer in his own impressive
manner, and at the same time would show him that no false
pretence or evasion could deceive that calm and clear-headed
employer. No man who was susceptible of moral impressions
could resist appeals thus made to his sense of right, and fail
to conform to the principle of duty. Allen knew if the appeal
failed the case was hopeless. Be this as it may, the staff
of local clerks and other *employés* in Bath was transformed
from a nest of rogues into a respectable body of men.

There were great difficulties at that period in obtaining a
suitable post-office ; and notwithstanding the unfitness of the
Bath Street office and the serious objections to the locality,
the business, with all its vast accession from the cross-post
system, was conducted there until 1728 ; and then, entirely
through the enterprise and public spirit of Allen, a new era in
all that concerned the policy and post-office business, not
merely in Bath but throughout Great Britain, was to be
instituted.

It was about 1722[1] that Allen lost his first wife, and it was

[1] We are here bound to admit that we have been unable to trace

in that same year Allen was elected a member of the Bath Corporation. It has been the fashion on the part of local writers to attribute to Allen, as a member of that body, the exercise of an undue share of power ; that, in truth, he was dictator of the assembly. We shall have more to say on this head when we come to deal with the later period of his life. All that need be said here is, that whatever influence he exercised upon the policy and proceedings of the corporate body was done without any effort or ostensible desire of his own. It is probable that no important measures affecting the interests of the city were passed or contemplated without the bulk of his colleagues consulting him and deferring to his judgment. As a matter of fact he was not a regular attendant at the council meetings, and never given to much talking. During his mayoralty in 1742 he was frequently absent from the council. No one was less of a busybody than Allen, and we repeat here, what we have already said in *Historic Houses*, that there was a calm, dignified reserve about Allen which he seldom or never broke through. Nor was this incompatible with that courtesy and kindness which during his whole life he never forgot. At this period, 1722, Allen would have been twenty-nine years of age.

From the beginning of the eighteenth century there was a great improvement in the tone and character of the corporate body. Public opinion to some extent had something to do with this ; but doubtless that improvement was chiefly attributable to the class of men who were chosen on that body. Certain it is that direct corruption and misapplication of public property may be said to have ceased. Still there was a little quiet nepotism. The good things going were not

the date of this lady's marriage with Allen, or the place or date of her death ; and further, we cannot find in any of the local registers when and where his marriage with Elizabeth Holder of Hampton took place.

allowed to go out of the municipal circle ; there were always professional uncles, sons, nephews, and friends amongst whom to distribute the good things of which these fatherly citizens were the patrons.   The Corporation was deeply imbued with Hanoverian principles, and it is clear that this was due to the influence of Wade and Allen.   Although Allen always exercised the most prudent control over his opinions, and expressed them with wise moderation, we think there is little doubt that on public questions he felt stronger on politics, so far as the subject affected the dynasty, than on any other ; and we have as little doubt that he was partly induced by this motive to enter the council, in order to serve the interests of Marshal Wade, who for some years had been wooing the Corporation —the then elective body of the city.   Nor is this surprising, seeing the close relations which existed between the two men.

It was in 1726 that the Marshal began his Highland roads, five hundred soldiers being employed in the work at sixpence a day extra pay, and it was well advanced in 1729. He treated his men, whom he called his *highwaymen*, liberally and humanely, and the qualities which made him so popular in Bath, shown in a different manner, made him the idol of his men.

For a long time Wade had spent a portion of each year in Bath, and by his general manners, affability, and generosity had become very popular in the city.   In 1722, William Bush being Mayor, there was a general election, and Trotman, who in conjunction with, first William Blathwayt of Dyrham, and then with John Codrington of Dodington, represented the city from 1702, retired, and Wade was elected, with Codrington as his colleague.   At the following election, in 1727, Robert Gay[1] was Wade's fellow-member ; in 1734, Codrington again, with Wade, was chosen.   In 1741, Philip Bennet of Widcombe

---

[1] R. Gay was a considerable landowner in Bath, near Queen Square and Gay Street ; hence the name of the latter.

House, whose sister, Jane Bennet, was the wife of Philip Allen, became the colleague of Wade in the next Parliament, when both retired.

During the whole of this period, *i.e.*, from 1722 to 1747, Wade maintained the closest friendship with Allen, and the most cordial relations with the Corporation and the citizens at large. His popularity was maintained during the fifty years he was connected with the city. His urbanity and friendly manner, his love of Bath, and his activity, made him a familiar figure ; and his unbounded hospitality tended very much to endear him to, and to keep him in touch with, all classes. No appeal was ever made to him in vain, and he often gave, in the spirit of Allen, to deserving cases ; and his liberality to public institutions in the city was very great. The Abbey Church experienced his bounty ; St. Michael's Church[1] received a large contribution towards its erection. At his own cost he made a passage through that odious pile of buildings which disfigured the north front of the Abbey, to enable the public to get from the churchyard to the Grove, and at the same time to cleanse the odious den from its detestable impurities.[2] The whole block was removed[3] in 1823-34.

[1] The church before the present.

[2] To remove these buildings, the sites of which were originally granted, or rather dishonestly appropriated, by the Corporation after the Reformation to members of its own body, cost the city £10,000. Just before these houses were erected the Abbey itself was imperilled, the question of selling the "carcase" thereof having been seriously discussed.

[3] These buildings really surrounded the Abbey, but those on the north side blocked up the avenue from the west to the east, *i.e.*, at this time, into the "Orange Grove", so that the only public way thither and back was through the north aisle of the Abbey. The clergyman officiating sometimes seemed to be offering thanks for "all the blessings of this life", in the shape of mutton-chops and beefsteaks (and such-like creature comforts) on the butcher-boys' trays, which were being carried through to the classic pipings of those refined youths. Not infrequently these

F

An old epigram runs thus:—

"The citizens of Bath, with vast delight,
To hide their noble church from vulgar sight,
Surround its venerable sides with shops,
And decorate its sides with chimney tops."

One curious fancy seized the Marshal, and that was to have the portraits of the members of the council, as well as his own in uniform, painted to adorn the council (of the former) chamber. A few of these portraits were good, and are still to be seen. The larger portion are consigned to the lumber-room of the Guildhall. The Marshal's is to be seen on the landing as you approach the banqueting room, and he was a dignified, soldier-like-looking man; another was of Allen, by Hoare [see frontispiece].

About 1730, the Earl of Cork and Burlington designed two houses in Bath, one for himself in the Orange Grove, and the other for Wade in the Abbey churchyard. The latter, with others, formed on the north front one side of Cheap Street; and when this street (long since the Marshal's death) was widened, it was necessary to get the extra space from this side of the houses, which were very handsome structures. The Marshal's mansion on the south (now used as the Depository of the Tract Society) retains some of its architectural beauty. The Earl also designed the Marshal's house in Cork Street, London. Marshal Wade was a gambler, and Walpole tells a good story of him. Wade, being at a low gaming-house, and having a very fine snuff-box, he suddenly missed it. One man only in the company refused to be searched, unless the Marshal would go into another room with him. There the man told him that he was born a gentleman, was reduced,

youths were followed by their favourite dogs, and then ensued a "woful battle" in the nave with the turnspits, an army of which, " in the intervals of business", took shelter there.

and lived by what little bets he could pick up there, and by fragments which the waiters occasionally gave him. " At this moment I have half a fowl in my pocket, I was afraid of being exposed. There it is ; now, sir, you may search me." Wade was so much affected that he gave the man a hundred pounds, and afterwards found the snuff-box in his own inner pocket.

When Wade was in Bath he sometimes could not resist Wiltshire's Rooms, but he was a more constant frequenter of Lord and Lady Hawley's.[1] There was little to choose between these gambling-shops and between those by whom they were respectively kept—"the trail of the serpent was over them all."

Now, essentially different as were Ralph Allen and the Marshal in almost every respect, there were points of contact between them which led to the most cordial and sympathetic relations. Decided as were the Marshal's political opinions and obligations, he was free from all rancour and bitterness ; and if his methods of dispensing his generosity were eccentric and oftentimes imprudent, he was actuated by warm, kind, and generous impulses. These qualities would have endeared him to a man like Allen, and made him gentle to the failings of his friend and relative.

The Marshal died on the 14th March 1747, in his eightieth year, and his memory is still cherished in the city of Bath. It was in the year of Marshal Wade's first election, 1722, that his daughter, Allen's wife, died ; and it is, we are constrained to admit, a source of mortification to us that we are unable to discover where or when. We think it probable that on his marriage Allen and his wife resided in one of the adjacent

---

[1] Lady Hawley was Miss Hayes, the successor of Harrison as the lessee of the rooms, now, with some alterations, the Literary Institution. These rooms were opposite Wiltshire's Rooms (*vide* Nash), and the two establishments were known as the Lower Rooms.

ALLEN'S HOUSE.

villages, and that after her death her body was buried in London, at the wish of her father.

The seven years, 1720 to 1727, must have been the most trying period in Mr. Allen's official experience. The inherent difficulties involved in carrying out his contract, which under the most favourable conditions would have taxed his resources to the utmost, were aggravated by the general disorder which prevailed throughout the post-office generally. Mr. Joyce shows that many of the postmasters received no salaries, and others very little, and therefore the Government were delibe-rately encouraging such officials to help themselves. It was not surprising, therefore, that these men robbed Allen wherever they could ; but seeing also that if his plans and policy were successful, as they bade fair to be, their nefarious habits must come to an end, they withheld all co-operation, and obstructed him by every means in their power.

There is no doubt that Allen, apart from his contract and his personal interest in its success, was an earnest postal reformer. He foresaw that, compatible with the then state of the public service, the state of the roads, and the limited means of transmission, the cheaper the rate of postages the greater would be the revenue to the nation. The result of his first contract, which was dissolved by the demise of the Crown a fortnight before its legal expiry, was to open the eyes of the nation. The upper and middle classes began to under-stand something of the inherent vitality of that branch of the public service which had been so flagrantly neglected and abused, and which was opening up to them and the country at large new ideas and enlarged views of the capacity of the nation.

It was in the year 1727, and after the contract with the General Post Office was renewed, that the old quarters in Bath Street were to be given up, and Allen's private residence so enlarged as to afford accommodation for the conduct of the cross-posts branch of the business, the local postal business being carried on in a house at the south-west entrance of Lilliput Alley.[1] The basement and first stories were used for the local postal business, whilst the upper portion was the residence of Philip Allen, who, though not officially connected with the post-office, was in this, as in all other operations, his brother Ralph's worthy coadjutor.

The house now represented was Allen's private residence, to be enlarged by Killigrew. The centre was originally surmounted by a low, plain attic story above the first floor. This story was removed, and the present double story, uniform with the original work, substituted. The right wing was enlarged for Allen's private use. The left wing was the office for the clerks and secretaries employed exclusively in the cross-posts business, and formed the north side of Lilliput Alley. The house, or rather group of buildings, is, no doubt, somewhat idealized, although its general effect was very picturesque. From the centre a sloping terraced walk led down to Harrison's Walks, opposite, and the house commanded a view of the bare Hampton Down, on the brow of which, some few years later, in order to break the monotony, Richard Jones erected what is now called *Sham Castle.*

The group of buildings was associated with the post-office and Ralph Allen until his death in 1764, and there the postal business, we believe, was conducted by his nephew, Philip Allen, until his death in 1785 ; then the place was

---

[1] This house was just within the city walls, a portion of which may still be seen in the area. It is now a part of the North Parade, and is used as a printing-office. Forty years ago the original panelling of the peculiar square-shaped front was to be seen, having on one of the centres the usual kind of slit, and the words *Post Office* painted above it. This locality of *Lilliput* was the residence of the famous Sally Lunn, the immortal inventor or originator of the tea-cake called after her name.

neglected. At the beginning of this century the right
wing was pulled down to make way for the new street
(York Street), the sloping path was levelled up, houses
and offices were built in front of the centre and left wing,
which now are hemmed in on every side, and are approached
only by a narrow passage. The sight of what remains of the
buildings is not pleasant. The ornate centre is still whole,
but dirty within and without, whilst the other portion is still
worse.

It was, so far as we can ascertain by various comparisons

Sham Castle

and allusions, about 1727 that Allen's second marriage, with
Elizabeth Holder, of Hampton Manor House, took place.
This lady was the daughter of Richard Holder, and sister of
Charles Holder, who at this time was the nominal owner. It
is evident from the numerous deeds relating to mortgages,
etc., that the Holders were in much pecuniary trouble, and
that Allen, in respect of considerations not explained, had
acquired the right of exercising the privileges of ownership for
many years before he purchased the property in 1742. There
is no doubt that Allen's generosity was called into full play

both here and at Claverton, which was also in the possession of a Holder, where also Allen possessed certain recognised rights long before he became the owner of the estate about 1752. In Hampton, it is probable that Allen took upon himself the full responsibility of meeting all claims in respect of mortgages, for we find that in 1735 such mortgages were consolidated, and a sum of £15,000 advanced by Elizabeth Baker, the deed of conveyance to Allen being dated 1742. Charles Holder continued to live in the village, chiefly upon the bounty of Allen, dying one year before him, in 1763, aged eighty-nine.

Bathampton is one of the most picturesque and interesting villages near our city. The Domesday manor and the modern parish[1] are in exact coincidence. The Domesday measures were as follows, namely, 720 acres of ploughed land, 100 acres of woodland, 28 acres of meadow, 60 acres of pasture, and 24 acres of waste, and we have the modern parish of 932 acres.

The manor was a part of the possessions of the Church of Bath, and has been held by many of the local historic families. In the reign of Henry III, Bishop Button obtained a charter of free warren here, as well as Claverton, of the Church lands.[2] In the reign of Edward IV the manor was held by the family

---

[1] The Liberty of Hampton cum Claverton constituted the Hundred of *Bada.*

[2] In a small garden in the village is a very curious ecclesiastical relic of the fourteenth century. It is the remains of a monkish cell, which would have been in connection with and attached to the monastery of Bath. The arch of the doorway is almost perfect. On the buttress of the wall, which skirted the road in the village, was a *hip knob.* This was in imminent danger of being injured by boys throwing stones at it. About eight years ago this finial, to ensure its safety, was removed from this building and placed on the gable of the chancel of the church. The drooping form is somewhat remarkable, typifying, by the inclination of the foliage, the drooping head of the Crucifixion.

of Blunt under Bishop Barlow, who, in 1548, exchanged the manor of Bathampton with the King for other lands late the property of the Prior of Bath ; but it did not long continue in the Crown, for, 7 Edward VI, both the manor and the hundred or liberty, appear to be the property of William Crowch, Gent., in whose name and family the same continued to 36 Elizabeth, when Walter Crowch had a licence for alienating his possessions here to Thomas Popham.[1]   From this family the manor passed to the Hungerfords, and from them to the Bassets.   Sir William Basset was lord thereof in 1688, of whose heirs and executors it was purchased in 1701, under a decree of Chancery, by Richard Holder.

Mr. Joyce has given us information to which local historians have never before had access.   As in his private affairs, so in his official relations, Allen was prudent, cautious, and reserved. He always seemed impressed with the importance of keeping the counsels of the Government as well as his own.   In the exercise of his private beneficence he seems to have guarded himself against the slightest charge of ostentation.   When he gave openly, it was as an example to others ; when *he did good by stealth*, he did so as few others ever did ; and an illustration will be cited which in this respect is a summary of the practice of his life.   It is not meant to imply that Allen was cold and wanting in sympathy in his intercourse with the various classes of Bath society ; on the contrary, he was never out of touch with either—frank, cordial, cheerful, kind. One of his best beloved friends was Leake, the publisher and

---

[1] After the Dissolution the vicarage and advowson were granted to the Dean and Chapter of Bristol (consolidated with that of Bathford about 1770, and again separated in 1835).   The great tithes, however, with other property, were conveyed to Robert Fisher, a citizen of Bath.   The chancel of the church was also assigned to him.   Beneath the chancel is a vault in which Fisher and others of the family are buried, and on the walls are several memorials of the family.   The family have sold all rights to the Allen family.

bookseller.   In that well-known citizen's cheerful, vaulted-
roofed reading-room[1] on the " Walks", close to Lilliput Alley,
Allen daily read what there then was to read in the way of
newspapers and the literature of his day.

We do not know the result of Allen's first contract, so far
as profits and loss concerned him.   In itself, however, it was
not simply a success, but promised the full realization of
Allen's most sanguine expectations.   Nationally, it meant
more than this.   Allen's system was not merely extending
throughout the length and breadth of the land, but his work
was far better done than that of the Government.   Great
officials had been vapouring, formulating, and indulging in
dignified proclamations, but all to little or no purpose.   The
department was infamously managed, the rogues unchecked,
and the public service neglected.   Great "statesmen" knew
how to set the egg on its end when they had been taught the
way ; and when Allen had elaborated a series of efficient
checks, proved them, and carried them out, the *statesmen* saw,
apparently for the first time, that organization was not the
exclusive gift of Allen.   We must do these " statesmen" the
justice to admit that, whilst they thought it well to show
their peculiar wisdom in pompously making now and then a
few needless, but harmless, conditions, they treated him con-
siderately, not to say generously, and wisely picked up and
appropriated the best of his ideas and his methods, and then,
with transcendent condescension, imparted to him their
superior wisdom on the manner in which he should conduct
postal affairs.[2]

[1] At a later day, in the same room, Sheridan was said to have written
The Rivals, of which the locality forms the scene.   The room is still to
be seen almost unchanged, and is a worthy solicitor's office.   The buildings have been shorn of their fair proportions in front to obtain a wider
public road.

[2] From the time of Allen to the present, Postmasters-General have

Gradually Allen extended his labours, devising an effective code of regulations and checks, and bringing the whole system into perfect subjection. Mr. Joyce bears testimony, not merely to Allen's diligence, but to his local knowledge, and to the further fact that in all "post-office matters affecting the provinces" the initiative came from Bath. As an example of Allen's methods in all that concerned the obstructions, the roguery, and deceptions practised by the old officials in their attempts to arrest progress and reform, Mr. Joyce says :

"Allen was better qualified, probably, than any other man living for the task he had set himself to perform. Of a temper which nothing could ruffle . . . and possessed of an amount of local knowledge which even at the present day is perhaps unrivalled, he enjoyed a combination of advantages which might have been sought elsewhere in vain. His patience, indeed, was inexhaustible. No subterfuge, not even a transparent attempt at imposition, would call forth more than a passing rebuke : ''Tis faulty,' ''tis blameable'; and then, perhaps, would peep out a gleam of merriment at the clumsiness of the contrivance."

It may be inferred that with the second contract the full success of Allen's enterprise was assured. What the income derived at that or any subsequent period was, has never been known, and never will be. So long as he fulfilled his obligations to the country and to the Government, he considered in

always been a curious study. The universal acceptation of certain fundamental principles is nothing to them. The process of conviction has always to be worked out in their minds, and if it be possible (as it always is) for a new Postmaster-General to interpose a vexatious and irksome regulation, it becomes a most pleasing duty at the beginning of his reign and at occasional intervals thus to display his idiosyncrasy. If a new privilege is to be introduced for the public good, the Postmaster-General invariably deems it his religious duty, for the good of humanity, to mix up with the benefits a due proportion of blister ointment. There was once a philanthropist who occasionally gave doles of bread and meat, and he indulged always in the peculiar luxury of saving a little in the shape of short weight !

this, as in the vast stone trade which he opened up on his own estates, that it was his own business, and that he was accountable to *One* only for the righteous use of that which was righteously gained. The income from the national sources, and from his estates and quarries, averaged large sums; no doubt more than has ever been conjectured.

It may have been two or three years after his second marriage, with Elizabeth Holder, *i.e.*, 1730, that Allen took up his residence at Hampton Manor House. The mansion at that time consisted of the centre, without western and eastern annexes, which are quite modern. The doorway and the rest of the front have been much altered. Over the doorway or hall was a small belfry, and the country adjacent was rough and unenclosed. The low-lying lands near and around the house were cultivated as kitchen gardens, from which Bath derived a considerable supply; the whole scene was monotonous and deficient in the picturesque. Allen was a man of taste, and to remedy this defect he built a hawhaw, and laid out the lawn; removed the belfry, and made the centre what it now is. To the east and to the west may be seen extending, each way, an avenue which he planted, of great beauty. Allen also made roads to the Down and about the estate. It was also about this time that he began to develop the stone works on Hampton Down, which, as we shall show, he carried on with the same energy and the same humanity as he did shortly after on Combe Down, above Prior Park. The machinery used in this earlier work for bringing down the dressed stone from the quarries to the banks of the Avon differed from that referred to later as to Combe Down. Nearly all the beds of oolite on the former were hewn in the open, dressed with much care, and laid by for seasoning. A series of short trams were laid on to a centre, where was constructed a large drum worked by some kind of machinery, but we cannot quite tell what. A tramline or way was constructed, extending from the drum along the Down, then descending the slope to the edge of a rather steep gorge. The stone was here unladen and conveyed to Allen's stoneyard and basin, but what was the precise mode of conveyance is not clear.

In 1810, or a little earlier, the old quarries were again worked by the Directors of the Kennett and Avon Canal for the construction of the locks, but the quality of the stone left was very inferior. The old tram-road was used to the edge of the gorge, and then passed over a bridge and down

The Dry Arch.

an inclined embankment to the canal bank. Since the Warminster Road was made, which passes under the bridge, it is called " The Dry Arch".

There were two things to be done by Allen when he acquired Prior Park, namely, to get into and out of the estate on the north-east and north-west sides of it. He made a private carriage-road down the former, and the stone tramway down the other [see illustration]. The document quoted is characteristic. Only two strips were wanted of the adjoining property, of which Bennet was the owner. The tram itself was not to emerge beyond the Prior Park boundary.

" THIS INDENTURE made the twentieth day of March in the fourth year of the Reign of our Sovereign Lord George the Second by the Grace of God of Great Britain France and Ireland King defender of the faith &c. Anno D'm' One thousand seven hundred and thirty Between Philip Bennet of Lyncomb and Witcomb in the county of Somerset Esq. and Jane his wife both dec'd which said Jane was the sole daughter and heir of Scarborough Chapman late of Lyncomb and Witcomb aforesaid Gentleman also dec'd of the one part and Ralph Allen of the City of Bath in the said County of Somerset Esq. and Elizabeth his wife of the other part   Whereas the said Ralph Allen hath lately made and cut a certain Waggon-way or road for the carriage of stone from the quarries of him the said Ralph Allen in and through a certain piece or panel of ground called the Mill Ground late belonging to the said Scarborough Chapman (which among other lands) by the last will and testament of the said Scarborough Chapman stands charged with the payment of a debt of Two Thousand Pounds or more due by Mortgage on the Joynture Estate made to the said Jane the Daughter which according to agreement ought to have been paid of long since the greatest part thereof having been raised out of his said daughter's estate which was settled to that Interest   And the said piece of Ground called the Mill Ground is by the said Will inter alia devised to Trustees of whom or of whose Undertenant or lessee the said Ralph Allen hath rented the same to protect the said Joinature Estate from the same debt and from any other dormant incumbrance as by the said will may more fully appear   And whereas a bill is shortly intended to be brought by the said Philip Bennet in the High Court of Chancery (amongst other things) for the due execution and performance of the said Will and for such releise as he the said Philip Bennet shall seek and pray therein   Now this indenture witnesseth that the said Philip Bennet for and in Consideration of the Grant and Covenant of the said Ralph Allen hereinafter mentioned and expressed and of five shillings of lawful money of Great Britain by the said Ralph Allen to the said Philip Bennet in hand paid at or before the sealing and delivery hereof and for diverse other good causes and considerations him the said Philip Bennet thereunto moving Hath granted released ratified and confirmed unto the said Ralph Allen All that the aforesaid waggon-way or road so by him made and cut in and through the said ground called the Mill-Ground together with the ground and soyle of the said road to have hold and enjoy the same to him the said Ralph Allen and his heirs and assigns for ever   And the said Philip Bennett doth hereby for himself and his heirs and assignes Covenant promise and agree to and with the said Ralph Allen his Heirs and Assignes that he the said Philip Bennet shall will as soon as conveniently may be make and execute a cause and procure to be made and executed a good and sufficient conveyance and assurance in the law unto him the said Ralph Allen and his heirs of the aforesaid waggon-way or road so by him made and cut in and through the said ground called the Mill-Ground and of the Ground and soyle of the said Road for and in consideration of the summe of Thirteen pounds nine shillings and sixpence of good and lawfull money of Great Britain to be paid to the said Philip Bennet his heirs and asignes by the said Ralph Allen his heirs or assignes at the time of making and executing of such conveyance or assurance But in case the said Philip Bennet should not recover the said ground by the said intended bill in Chancery so as to make or procure such conveyance or assurance to be made thereof unto the said Ralph Allen and his heirs aforesaid And in case the said Ralph Allen his heirs or assignes shall at any time hereafter be Evicted Ejected dispossessed or deprived of the Use Benefitt and enjoyment of the said waggon-way or road so made and cut in and through the said ground called the Mill-Ground by any person or persons claiming or to claim the same under the said Scarborough Chapman That then the said Philip Bennet his heirs or assignes make and execute or cause and procure to be made and executed a good and sufficient conveyance and assurance in the law to him the said Ralph Allen and his heirs of all that part and so much of the said Philip Bennet's Orchard lying in Lyncomb and Whitcomb aforesaid at the lower end of his Garden there belonging to his New Mansion as contains forty-four leeygs in length and one leeyg in breadth to be measured from the highway leading from Witcomb Church to hanging land on the south side to the bounds or hedge at the lower end of the Orchard there belonging to Mary Wiltshire Widow or her son William Wiltshire for and in consideration of the said summe of Thirteen pounds nine shillings and sixpence of like lawfull money of Great Britain to be paid by the said Ralph Allen his heir or assignes unto the said Philip Bennet his heirs or assignes at the time of making or executing such last-mentioned conveyance and assurance And this indenture further witnesseth that the said Ralph Allen and Elizabeth his wife for and in consideration of the grant and covenant of the said Philip Bennet before mentioned and expressed and of five shillings of lawfull money of Great Britain to the said Ralph Allen and Elizabeth his wife by the said Philip Bennet in hand also paid before the sealing and delivery hereof the receipt whereof is hereby acknowledged and for diverse other good causes and considerations then the said Ralph Allen and Elizabeth his wife thereunto especially moving Have and each of them hath given and granted and by these presents Do and each of them doth give and grant unto the said Philip Bennet his heirs and assignes the full and free use liberty and priviledge from time to time and at all times hereafter with his and her family friends & servants with His and their horses coaches chariots chairs chaises to ride pass and repass in upon and through his the said Ralph Allen's new made waggon-way or road so far as the same extends from the gate called Dolemead Gate to the way or road newly made by the said Philip Bennet from the waggon-way or road of him the said Ralph Allen up to the mansion-house of him the said . . . Philip Bennet at Whitcomb aforesaid and to his estate and lands there provided the same be not made use of by him the said Philip Bennet his heirs and assignes or any of his friends or servants in any wise with any carts cars drags waggons or any other heavy carriages To Have hold use exercise and enjoy the said waggon-way or road of him the said Ralph Allen hereby granted in the manner before mentioned and expressed unto him the said Philip Bennet and his heirs And the said Ralph Allen for himself and for the said Elizabeth his wife and for their and for either of their heires or assignes doth covenant promise and agree to with the said Philip Bennet his heirs and assignes by these presents That he the said Ralph Allen and Elizabeth his wife and their heirs shall and will from time to time and at all times hereafter at the reasonable request costs and charges of the said Philip Bennet make do and execute or cause and procure to be made done and executed any further or other lawfull and reasonable act device convey-ance or assurance in the law for the better moveyure and absolute granting assuring and confirming the full and free use liberty and priviledge of his the said Ralph Allen's said waggon-way in the manner herebefore mentioned and intended to be hereby given and granted unto him the said Philip Bennet and his heires as the said Philip Bennet his heirs and assignes or his or their councell learned in the Law shall be reasonably advised or devised and required so as the person or persons required to make the same be not compelled for the doing thereof to have further than his or her or their respective place or places of abode In Witness whereof the said parties have hereunto interchangeably sett their hands the day and year first above written.

" PHILIP BENNET.

" Sealed and delivered (being first duly stampt in the presence of Ann Bennet)—John Noble.

"A true copy of the original deed examined therewith by us this twenty-eighth day of May One Thousand eight hundred and fourteen.

"William Merrick Gent.

Endorsed : --   " William Merrick Junr."

"20 *Mar.* 1730. Agreem't between Mr. Bennet and Mr. Allen about the waggon-way.—*Attested Copy.*

"The original deed is now in the hands of Mr. Dan'l Clutterbuck, the parish of Witcomb House, and to be produced by him to Mr. John Thomas [the purchaser of the estate] for inspection when desired.—28 *March* 1816."

COMBE DOWN.

The Combe Down tram-road was constructed in 1731, and consisted of two narrow lines, of which distinct traces remain. The frame and machinery were fixed upon the Down. The lines were so adjusted that the down laden tram drew up the empty one ; starting, stopping, and speed being regulated by it. The small square waggons were very strong, and were mounted on small wheels, running on a low platform.

In cases of contract the blocks of stone were sometimes dressed upon the down, having been long seasoned by exposure in the rough ; in ordinary cases the blocks were brought down in the rough. When the trams reached the level at the bottom of the hill, the waggons, after emerging from the road proper, were unloaded on to an ingenious sledge (invented by Richard Jones), and the stone was conveyed either to the boats at the basin or deposited on the quays.

The method of excavating the stone on the Combe Down was different from that pursued on Hampton Down. For the greater part a boring was made, the operations being carried on as in a coal mine, though nearer the top, which mostly was supported by cross-beams in the workings ;[1] and this arrangement, whilst preserving the surface for pasture, at the same

[1] The circular openings, protected by low walls, are still to be seen on various parts of Combe Down.

time concealed the unsightly exhausted open pits, except in a few localities about the village.

As a proof of Allen's kind consideration for his fellow-citizens, it may be well to refer to some special features in the tram-road. It was constructed some years, apparently, before he contemplated building the great mansion in the park, and was evidently intended not only for the tramways, but for ordinary public business vehicles running between the city and the Down. The road entered at the bottom of the hill, and went almost in a straight line from north to south, up to the Down, right through the estate. The west side of the road was embanked with protecting masonry ; whilst on the eastward, parallel with the tram lines, a low wall was built, from which the land sloped towards the valley, a footpath being made for the public use. A stranger now looking at the four lodges in this road is puzzled by their peculiar arrangement, but the matter becomes perfectly clear when it is seen that they were built to suit the road, long after the latter was constructed.

The opening up of these sources of industry, especially at such a juncture, was of incalculable advantage to Bath. Wood was carrying out his great building projects in the city and all around, so that in addition to the vast market for the stone created in London, the home consumption was very large ; hence a demand for skilled industry was developed in and around the city, which more or less continues to this day.[1]

Now, it will be seen, began that part of Allen's career which, no doubt, was the most trying period of his life. The post-office difficulties, though practically overcome, still involved responsibility and anxiety, whilst the organization of these new fields of labour and enterprise added largely to his

---

[1] Extensive new quarries have from time to time been discovered ; and recently excellent stone has been found over the Box Tunnel, at Bathford, and elsewhere, and worked with enterprising energy.

daily toil and mental task. True, in all his vast and complicated duties he was largely assisted by his brother Philip; but there was no part of the details appertaining either to his official or private business, from the supervision of his labourers' cottages and their social and moral welfare to the most important official correspondence with the Government, which does not more or less bear the impress of his own careful hand; and yet he was always calm, cheerful, and hospitable. It has been already shown that, as an employer of labour on his estate, he had effected improvements in the interests of the labourer, and especially of the quarry-men; but in addition to this his solicitude for his large staff of clerks and superintendents was quietly shown in all his dealings with them. In return he was served by men who loved him. From 1731 until his death, his clerk-of-the-works, one Richard Jones,[1] served him with rare ability and indefatigable zeal. This man was wholly untrained and almost uneducated, but displayed an amount of natural aptitude and knowledge in relation to building, architecture, and engineering, which amounted almost to genius; and he was one only of a large number of equally devoted servants.

BATHAMPTON AND BATHEASTON.

From about 1731 until 1733 Allen was engaged in improving his Bathampton estate, especially the Manor House.[2] It was a small, old-fashioned house, which had been much neglected, standing on the south bank of the Avon. Near it were the "old mill and the sparkling weir". The river was crossed by a ferry to Batheaston, through which ran, and still runs, the old Roman fosse road. By this road and the ford Bathampton

[1] After Allen's death Jones was elected by the Corporation one of the City Surveyors of Works, a post he filled with satisfaction to the City.

[2] The estate being mortgaged by his wife's father, Allen purchased he equity of redemption.

BATHAMPTON MANOR

could alone be approached, except on foot. Vehicles and horses were conveyed across on a ferry-bridge, and this continued long into the present century. It was at the Manor House from 1732, or about, that Allen received many of his distinguished visitors.

The church of Bathampton is dedicated to St. Nicholas, and now consists of a low square battlemented west tower, open at its lowest stage ; eastward, the church comprises nave, north and south aisles, south porch, chancel ; organ chamber on the north, and vestry on the south, sides of the chancel.

The original church had the tower, nave, and chancel only, the roof of the latter being higher than the nave. To meet the expansion of the village, the church has been from time to time altered and enlarged, as occasion required.

At the present east end of the south aisle, before its recent westward elongation, was a square attached mortuary chapel, under which sleep many of the dead members of the Allen family, its walls bearing their respective tablets.

The tower was erected in the Perpendicular era ; and, with the exception of the nave roof, hardly any part of the older church remains.

The cross on the chancel gable is of unique design ; formerly it was the hip knob or finial of a fourteenth-century building (see tail-piece, p. 96).

The remains of stone effigies of a cross-legged knight and lady are carefully preserved in the window-sills, internally, of the south aisle.

Opposite Hampton Manor, sloping down to the road, were the pretty grounds in which stood the far-famed villa of Lady Millar at Batheaston, and the

"Urn, an antique, as I think I've been told,
Stood in Tully's fam'd Tusculan villa of old,
And, a thousand years after and more, was here brought,
And long may it stand in this favourite spot."

The villa, with additions, still survives in all its pristine beauty. In the grounds are the pavilions, but the urn, crammed under a canopy too small for it, adorns the Bath Park.

Batheaston abounds with an interest all its own. Near and around it are some beautiful old houses, with St. Catherine's Valley, exquisitely wooded, on the summit of the south side of which stands the romantic and interesting mansion of St. Catherine's Court, with its Elizabethan garden, both the work of the famous wit, Sir John Harington of Kelston.

In a memorandum, Allen says he has on *The Waste*[1] at Batheaston twenty houses, of which he gives the names of the tenants, with a note at foot, in his own writing :—

" Memorandum, that the late Widow Bushell's husband (Mayor 1718) kept count for Sir W. Bassett[2] at Hampton, and 'tis probable Mrs. Ann Collibee (whose husband was Mayor 1719), now Dalamore, may have some of the Court Rolls which will explain the *Waste*, &c., at Bath Easton."

ALLEN'S GENERAL CHARACTERISTICS.

We should like to add a few sentences expressive of our conception of Allen in certain other aspects than that of a philanthropist. He was a high-minded Christian, gentleman ; and, in a sense, that summary may seem to leave little more to be said.

There was, however, another side to Allen's character besides that presented in his domestic relations, and in his bearing as a citizen and a public benefactor, on which many writers have descanted. A man may be, as Allen was, sympathetic, generous, and clear-sighted, and yet lack certain qualities which Allen possessed, but with which he is not usually credited. We might almost think that he was sub-

---

[1] The tradition as to the term seems to be lost, but the locality, we opine, was at the east end of the village on the left. We believe Allen made overtures, which were not accepted, to become Lord of the Manor of Batheaston.　　　　[2] Of Claverton Manor.

missive to the point of weakness ; that his " humility" was an infirmity rather than a virtue to be admired ; that, indeed, he was lacking in manly dignity, and that independence of spirit which is the natural result of it. Emerson says : " It is the mark of nobleness to volunteer the lowest service, the greatest spirit only attaining to humility." As Bishop Hurd said of him, " He comes up to the notion of my favourites in Queen Elizabeth's reign : good-sense in connection with the plainest manners—*simplex et nuda veritas.*" This was precisely the *humility* which adorned Allen's life and character—not the humility which, like that of Uriah Heap, was always proclaiming itself. There was in Allen a quiet reserve, a calm subdued dignity and courtesy, and the self-possession which indicates the well-bred gentleman. Then there was another quality possessed by Allen which has been almost entirely overlooked, we mean his instinctive aptitude for business, and his keen sagacity in the pursuit of it. It is a mistake to suppose that Allen opened his mouth and the good things fell into it. He had many a hard fight with the Government of the day, and his correspondence at each successive development of his great national work reveals the conscious power and self-reliance of the man.

We shall endeavour to show, moreover, that in Allen's local enterprises he was not simply the easy-going philanthropist of the come-easy, go-easy type. He was a man of large conceptions, full of resources ; and being rewarded by commensurate fruition, so he dispensed his hospitality and his bounty with an unsparing hand. The story[1] that Allen's

---

[1] The story, in short, is this : When Allen described the character of the mansion he proposed to build in Prior Park, Wood, in astonishment, asked him if he had counted the cost thereof. Allen, by way of answer, showed him a series of boxes filled with gold. To those who know anything either of Wood or Allen the story needs neither explanation nor denial.

notions as to the mansion he proposed to erect at Prior Park utterly confounded his friend and architect, John Wood, may be partly true. The error underlying this statement, however, is typical of many others relating to Allen : it imputes to him a kind of recklessness, whereas Allen was especially circumspect and vigilant in all his schemes and expenditure. In this particular instance, so far from Wood being "confounded", he first had to prepare the plans from Allen's instructions ; and having done so, and submitted them for his approval, Wood proceeded to carry them out.

Wood was a man who knew his own mind, and he had elaborated his designs not merely to secure unity of architectural grandeur, but also certain features which should realise several unique characteristics, especially in the roof and portico[1] (see illustration). Here, again, Allen's conduct illustrated the quality to which we have referred. When it came to the point of carrying out certain features in the roof of the stables, Allen resolved upon a modification of them ; Wood remonstrated, but to no purpose. Allen had his own way ; the relations between the two men became strained, and, on the completion of the first portion of the work, Wood's direct connection with Allen ceased. The eastern wing, the Palladian bridge, planting, etc., were entrusted to other hands, a year or so before Wood's death.

WARBURTON'S INTRODUCTION TO ALLEN.

The following extract, written in 1856, from the Rev. Francis Kilvert's Essay on Allen, whilst describing the incident which led to the introduction of Warburton to Prior Park, will also, to some extent, show the footing on which Pope stood in 1736 :—

"Mr. Allen lived in so noble and hospitable a manner, that no one distinguished by rank, learning, or eminence in any profession or public

---

[1] When built (and we believe still), the largest in England.

employment came to Bath, but was either invited to or introduced at Prior Park. Mr. Pope was almost a constant inmate in the family during the Bath season, for many years. This intimacy commenced previous to the year 1736,[1] and originated in the high opinion of Pope, formed by Mr. Allen on reading his first volume of letters, which led him to offer to print a second volume at his own expense. To these circumstances attestation is borne by Pope's letter to Allen (*Works*, vol. vi, p. 320, edit. 1770). During one of his visits, Mr. Pope, being one day at dinner, had a letter delivered to him by the servant, on which, having inspected it, he shook his head ; and on Mr. Allen asking what was the matter, he answered that a Lincolnshire clergyman, to whom he had very great obligation, was coming to make him a visit at Twickenham. 'If that be all', said Mr. Allen, 'invite him to come hither. Let him come to Chippenham in the stage-coach, and we will send our carriage to meet him and bring him to Prior Park.' The Lincolnshire clergyman was Warburton, then the simple Incumbent of Brand Broughton, in that county. In a letter to Warburton, dated from Prior Park, Nov. 12th, 1741, Pope says :—' My third motive of now troubling you is my own proper interest and pleasure. I am here in more leisure than I can possibly enjoy, even in my own house, *vacare literis*. It is at this place that your exhortations may be most effectual to make me resume the studies I had almost laid aside by perpetual avocations and dissipations. If it were practicable for you to pass a month or six weeks from home, it is here I could wish to be with you ; and if you would attend to the continuation of your own noble work, or unbend to the idle amusement of commenting upon a Poet who has no other merit than that of aiming, by his moral strokes, to merit some regard from such men as advance truth and virtue in a more effectual way ; in either case this place and this house would be an inviolable asylum to you from all you would desire to avoid in so public a scene as Bath. The worthy man who is the master of it invites you in the strongest terms, and is one who would treat you with love and veneration, rather than with what the world calls civility and regard. He is sincerer and plainer than almost any man now in this world, *antiquis moribus*. If the waters of the Bath may be serviceable to your complaints (as I believe, from what you have told me of them), no opportunity can ever be better. It is just the best season. We are told the Bishop of Salisbury (Dr. Sherlock) is expected here daily, who, I know, is your friend ; at least, though a Bishop, is too much a man of learning to be your enemy. You see I omit nothing to add to the

---

[1] In Bath 1734, afterwards continued at Hampton Manor until 1740.

weight in the balance, in which, however, I will not think *myself* light, since I have known your partiality.   You will want no servant here. Your room will be next to mine, and one man will serve us.   Here is a library, and a gallery 90 feet long to walk in, and a coach whenever you would take the air with me.   Mr. Allen tells me you might, on horseback, be here in three days.   It is less than 100 miles from Newark, the road through Leicester, Stowe-in-the-Wolds, Gloucester, and Cirencester, by Lord Bathurst's.   I could engage to carry you to London from hence, and I would accommodate my time and journey to your conveniency.'   Again, Nov. 22nd :—' Yours is very full and very kind : it is a friendly and a very satisfactory answer, and all I can desire.   Do but instantly fulfil it. Only I hope this will find you before you set out.   For I think, on all considerations, your best way will be to take London in your way.   You will owe me a real obligation by being made acquainted with the master of this house, and by sharing with me what I think one of the chief satisfactions of my life—his friendship.'   Of this invitation Warburton did not fail to avail himself.   On the 3rd March 1742, we find him writing, as follows, to Dr. Doddridge :—' In Nov. Mr. Pope sent me so pressing an invitation to come to him at Mr. Allen's, near Bath, seconded by so kind an invitation of that good man, that I could not decline a long, tedious winter journey by London.   I stayed at Widcombe in the most agreeable retired society with two excellent persons, so very dear to me, till after the Christmas holidays.'   This was the 'tide in the affairs' of that remarkable man, which he 'took at its flood', and which 'led him on to fortune'.   So successfully did he cultivate this advantageous introduction that, in 1746, Mr. Allen gave him in marriage his favourite niece, Miss Gertrude Tucker.   In 1757, through Mr. Allen's influence with Mr. Pitt, he was appointed to the Deanery of Bristol ; and in 1760, through the same interest, became Bishop of Gloucester."

It might be added that Allen repaired the Deanery at considerable cost, and subsequently the Palace at Gloucester.

"Low-born" and "Humble".

It was in 1735 that the famous couplet was written—

"Let low-born Allen with an awkward shame
    Do good by stealth and blush to find it fame,"

and in 1738 that the epithet *low-born* was changed to *humble;* and the incidents that followed illustrate the independence and dignity of Allen's character.

Pope's alleged aim in changing "low-born" to "humble" was to divert attention from the lowly *origin* to the modest and unpretentious *character* of Allen ; but the change of epithet makes no difference, as Pope must have foreseen. The general reader, not knowing the literary history of Pope's famous couplet, interprets *humble* with reference to birth ; and connoisseurs who do know the history and recollect the original reading, *low-born*, are not likely to interpret the word *humble* in the non-natural sense which Pope (a master of subterfuge) alleged to be his meaning, but will rather exclaim :

> " Who dares think one thing, and another tell,
> My heart detests him as the gates of hell."
> (Pope's *Iliad*, Book I, x.)

Let us reverse the case, and suppose that Allen, *ex hypothesi* a master of language, had first of all stamped Pope in literature as a *disreputable* person, and then changed the epithet *disreputable* to *low*, declaring at the same time that he meant *low* to have reference to Pope's stature ; would Pope's displeasure at the original epithet have been appeased by the second one, it being clear, under the circumstances, that neither the general reader nor the connoisseurs would be diverted by Allen's non-natural definition of the word *low ?*

There is no record, however, that Allen felt hurt or remonstrated[1] about the allusion to his humble parentage, which a man of his native nobility could well afford to treat with lofty disdain ; in fact, the only reputation injured by the allusion is Pope's.

It is said that Warburton remonstrated with Pope before

---

[1] The story has been told so often, like the story about Queen Elizabeth's visit to Harington, and some of the Sherston fables, that it has got into the warp and woof of our local Histories and Guides Warner, Tunstall, and others give it as an indisputable fact, without any investigation of their own.

he changed the epithet from *low-born* to *humble*. No such remonstrance can be traced, either in express terms or implied. Nor is it likely, seeing that Warburton did not know Allen until three years after the later version was written.

The history of this famous couplet is altogether independent of the quarrel between Pope and Allen, of which much was told us by Mr. Dilke in his *Papers of a Critic;* and Mr. Elwin and Mr. Courthope made quite clear what remained to be told. We believe both Allen and Warburton quite understood and appreciated Pope's *motive* in writing the couplet. They could not impute to him an offensive intention, because both versions appeared some years before the fatal quarrel took place. We will endeavour, as simply as possible, to relate this curious and interesting literary episode as affecting our local Mæcenas.

The couplet first appeared in the Epilogue to the *Satires,* which was published in " the folio" edition in 1735. In 1738, three years before Allen and Warburton had met, Pope writes to Allen :—

" Pray tell me if you have any objection to my putting your name into a poem of mine (incidentally, not at all going out of the way for it), provided I say something of you" (which, by the way, he had already said three years before, using *low-born* instead of *humble*) "which most people will take ill, for example, that you are no man of high birth or quality ? *You must be perfectly free with me on this, as on any, nay, on every other occasion.*"

In the November following he writes again to Allen :—

" I am going to insert in the body of my Works my two last poems in quarto. I always profit myself of the opinion of the public to correct myself on such occasions ; and sometimes the merits of particular men, whose names I have made free with, for example, either good or bad, determine me to alterations. I have found a virtue in you more than I certainly knew before, till I had made experiments of it, I mean humility. I must, therefore, in justice to my own conscience of it, bear testimony to it, and change the epithet I first gave you of *low-born* to *humble*. I shall take care to do you the justice to tell everybody this change was not made at yours, or at any friend's request for you, but my own knowledge you merited it."

This letter appeared in Warburton's edition of Pope's Works (9 vols.), 1751, seven years after Pope's death, without animadversion or comment. It is more than probable that Allen and Warburton perceived the bad taste by which such a letter was dictated. The tone of patronising condescension could not have escaped the observation of either of them, but they quite understood the little great man.[1] It is not likely that Allen, with his proud reserve, even if either of the epithets had given him pain, would have condescended to complain, or that he at a later date would have sanctioned any remonstrance on the part of Warburton. Besides, the letter of Pope surely would have elicited an expression of disapprobation if such feeling had existed.

We do not presume to deal with Pope, except so far as it may affect his relations with Allen ; and it affords some ground for amusement to find a man like Warner, if he did not invent it, accepting such a story as he relates, without any sort of reserve or qualification, as to the cause of the breach between Allen and Pope :—

"Amidst this constellation of geniuses, Pope shone the distinguished star ; he had become intimate with Allen from the personal advances of the latter, in consequence of an esteem he had conceived for him on reading the surreptitious edition of his letters in 1734. But the *friendship* of a wit is not to be depended upon. Pope, who visited *much* at Prior Park, and found the house so comfortable as to be desirous of being there *more*, requested Mr. Allen to grant him the mansion at Bathampton, in order that he might bring Martha Blount thither (with whom Pope's connection was somewhat equivocal) during the time of his own residence at Prior Park. This request Allen (whose delicacy was extreme) flatly refused, which so exasperated the little wasp, that he

---

[1] Pope was himself the son of a linendraper in the Strand.

quitted his house in disgust, and never afterwards expressed himself in terms of common civility with respect to his old host and former friend."

There is not one word of truth in this statement. All traditions affecting Pope and Allen associate the former with Prior Park. We have shown in an earlier chapter that Prior Park was not ready for occupation until Nov. 1741, and, therefore, Pope could have visited Allen there only twice. This alone would suffice to refute the foregoing silly statement; the ground of quarrel not being between Allen and Pope at all, nor is there any reason whatever for the imputation of immoral motives. The truth is that both Martha Blount and Mrs. Allen were women of high temper. Little is known of the merits of this dispute; but it appears that Martha Blount being towards the end of 1743 on a visit with Pope, at Prior Park, a difference arose between her and Mrs. Allen, of which the poet was in some way the cause, and they at once left Prior Park and proceeded to Lord Bathurst's at Cirencester.

Another explanation of the mystery was that Martha Blount, after her quarrel with Mrs. Allen, insisted that Pope should cancel his obligations to Allen, and refund the sums he had received from him. Pope yielded to her demand, and after bequeathing his books to Allen[1] and Warburton conjointly, he went on to say: " In case Ralph Allen, Esq., should survive me, I order my executors to pay him the sum of £150, being to the best of my calculation the amount of what I have received from him, partly for my own, and partly for charitable uses. If he refuses to take this himself, I desire him to employ it in any way I am persuaded he will not dislike, to the benefit of the Bath Hospital."

Allen allowed the money to go to the hospital, remarking

---

[1] Lord Orrery, writing from Marston, July 14th, 1744, to Mallet, a friend and (in Bath) a neighbour of Allen's, on the North Parade, says : " It is reported that Mr. Allen is extremely enraged at his share of money, not of books, or *rather at the manner in which it is given.*"

that " Pope was always a bad accountant, and that if to £150 he had put a cypher more, he had come nearer to the truth." Warburton received all the printed books and copyrights of the poet's own works.[1] At Warburton's death he bequeathed his library to Bishop Hurd.

Allen was hurt that his generous friendship should, coupled by a misrepresentation, be flung back to him with disdain ; and the indignation he expressed was natural. The public joined their censure, and Johnson says that Pope "brought some reproach upon his own memory by the petulant and contemptuous mention of Allen, and the affected repayment of his benefactions."   Allen, in a sense, cared not for the money or for the books, any more than he cared for being called *low-born* and *humble.* He knew his own motives, and if he expressed any sense of disappointment it was because he had less to bestow upon the hospital he loved so well. The moiety of the books he surrendered to Warburton, not because he was indifferent to books and literature, but simply because he did not wish to divide so precious a collection.

Overtures for a reconciliation were made by Allen,[2] and in reply to his letter, Pope (March 6th, 1744) writes : " I thank you very kindly for yours. I am sure we shall meet with the same hearts we ever met . . . I must see you here (Twickenham) or nowhere. Accordingly, Allen went to Twickenham, and there the reconciliation took place.

It was between the time of the quarrel and Allen's visit to

[1] Many of the calumnies touching Pope and Martha Blount, arising out of the quarrel at Prior Park, were promulgated immediately after Pope's death. Warburton had a perfect knowledge of the facts, and, as a gentleman and a bishop, ought to have given the true version on the opportunity afforded him in the edition he issued of Pope's works in 1751. He not only did not do this, but he suppressed many documents which, in justice to Martha Blount, he ought to have published.

[2] A fact in itself sufficient to refute the silly calumny of Warner and others.

Twickenham, on the 17th March, that Pope altered his will, inserting the offensive clause ; and, whether urged by Miss Blount, or by his own petulant and vindictive temper, to insert the offensive clause, he might, and probably would have altered it before he died, but his last illness came upon him too suddenly. It is at any rate reasonable to suppose that, after his letter, he would have done so. Martha Blount very earnestly declared that when Pope told her his intentions with regard to the mention of Allen, she in vain tried to dissuade him from it ; and there is no reason to doubt her word.

Hip Knob. (See page 85.)

PRIOR PARK.

[Three events were to happen in 1742 : namely, the election of Allen to the Mayoralty ; the opening of the General Mineral Water Hospital ; and the completion of a portion of Prior Park.]

Carriage Entrance, within
second Lodge Gate.

T may be well to introduce the subject by quoting Thicknesse's[1] bitter but amusing description :—

"A noble seat, which *sees all* Bath, and which was built, probably, for all Bath to see. The Founder of this House and Family was Ralph Allen ; of low Birth, but no mean Intellects. It is said, the Postmaster of *Exeter*, being caught in a Storm upon a dreary Heath, in *Cornwall*, took shelter in a poor Man's Hut, the property of ALLEN'S Father, and being kindly received by the humble Host, and seeing some Marks of Genius in this Boy, proposed taking him under his Care and Protection ; a Proposal very acceptable to all Parties. He was accordingly taught to read and write, and then employed in the Post-Office, to receive and deliver Letters ; during his Residence there, Mr. ——,[2] the Postmaster, had formed a Scheme in

---

[1] *Prose Guide*, 1788. Thicknesse was not a favourite of Allen's, and this explains the *animus* displayed by the former towards the latter on every occasion. The statement above quoted may, in the main, be regarded as an invention.

[2] The Postmaster's name, as we have shown, was Quash, of which the writer seemed in ignorance.

H

which young ALLEN'S Pen and Head were employed, of establishing a Cross-Post all over *England;* but Mr. —— was unable to carry it into Execution. Mr. ALLEN, however, possessed of some Materials for so great an Undertaking, and a much better Head, leaving his Master soon after, carried this great National Convenience into Execution ; and while he was supposed to be gaining a Princely Fortune by digging Stones from the Bowels of the Earth, he actually picked it off the Surface,[1] by traversing the whole Kingdom with Post-Horses. He was said to bear his great Prosperity with Humility, and to conduct all Business with the utmost Probity. That he affected a Simplicity of Manners and Dress, we can testify ; but we can by no Means allow that he was not a Man deeply charged with Pride, and without address enough to conceal it. His plain *Quaker*-coloured Suit of Cloaths, and Shirt Sleaves with only a Chitterlin up the Slit, might, and did deceive the vulgar Eye ; but he could not bear to let POPE (who was often his Visitor) call him what was true (*low-born* ALLEN), but made him substitute in its Place, that which was false[2] (*humble* ALLEN). He was not, however, mean, for we once ate a most magnificent Dinner at his Table, served to thirty Persons, off *Dresden* China, and he seemed to take infinite Pains to shew his Munificence in every Respect. He left behind him, however, a Nephew and Namesake, whom we lately followed to the Grave, amidst the unaffected Tears and Sorrows of all, but those who might profit by his untimely Death. For he was one of the noblest works of God !"[3]

For centuries the quarries, of what is technically called *Bath stone* or *oolite*, had been more or less worked, and the stone wrought for facing noble buildings, as well as being largely used for small ornamentations in courtyards, gardens,

---

[1] The insinuation meant to be conveyed by the writer is, that Allen needed a plausible pretext to cover his excessive gains by his postal contracts. If the reader has perused the notice of the Hampton and Combe Downs machinery, their nature, and extent of the works, the personal labour and anxiety which they both involved to Allen ; if, again, it be considered that the postal contracts were carried on eleven years previous to Allen entering upon those estates, the ill-nature which prompted Thicknesse's malignant suggestion will be only too obvious.

[2] A statement we show to be untrue.

[3] This was Philip Allen's younger son, Ralph, who died unmarried August 30th, 1777, aged 40.

etc. These smaller articles found their way to all parts of the kingdom, the stone being soft and easily worked into the most ingenious forms and patterns, while, after exposure, it proved as durable as the hardest stone known, and consequently admitted of little competition ; whilst the larger blocks were principally used only in the district.

One of the most enterprising of the ornamental stonecutters, early in the last century, was Thomas Greenway ; and for forty or fifty years the art continued to develop and flourish in the hands of many others, some of whom had been taught their business by Greenway. The house now known as the " Garrick's Head" was built by Greenway,[1] ostensibly to display the elaborate Bath-stone ornamentation. This is the house in which Beau Nash lived before he removed into the "next door", the house in which he died, and in which Mrs. Delany and the then Miss Berry afterwards respectively resided.[2]

The stone business in Allen's hands increased so rapidly that, about six years after he became possessed of the quarries at Hampton Down, he acquired the entire estate of Prior Park and Combe Down, with a single exception, as will be seen, with all the quarries and royalties ; and the first thing he did was to construct two tramways, one connecting the works on Combe Down with the basin and the river in the Dolemeads, and the other, which we have described, in connection with Hampton Down. At this time modern Bath was springing up ; Queen Square[3] was already built, the Parades were in progress,[4] and all these were built of Bath stone ; but still Allen had to contend with the prejudices, the professional

---

[1] Whom we have already noticed. " Greenway Lane" is so called after this ingenious person.

[2] The house is still standing in Gascoyne Place, next to the theatre. The entrance doorway is exceedingly fine, but is obscured by the atrium of the theatre.

[3] Begun December 10, 1728.   [4] Finished in 1735.

H 2

opposition of architects, and every species of difficulty by which interested persons could and did impede the sale and use of Bath stone for important buildings remote from Bath.[1] He seemed to have exercised all his faculties in the development of the stone trade; he built cottages for the workmen to be near their work; he erected sheds to protect them while dressing the stone; and in thus saving time he saved the cost of production, and also very greatly increased the "out-put"; he established the principle of piece-work, and he did also what seems to have been unusual in those days, he paid his men weekly, and treated them humanely.

The exception, to which reference has been made at the beginning of the last paragraph, was the quarry of Milo Smith,[2] one of the promoters of the navigation of the Avon. He, it appears, opposed Allen on his own ground. But there was another opposition from the master-masons, who were determined, if possible, to get the control of the business into their own hands. Allen dealt equitably with Milo Smith, whose quarry he purchased, and soon convinced the masons that he was too just to act oppressively towards them. Allen also proved to them that, in the matter of the domestic trade, he was their best friend. The London architects, as early as 1728, set their faces against the Bath stone. They were interested in other quarries, and refused to look at the product of those at Bath. They compared it to Cheshire cheese, not only in its colour and texture, but in its liability to breed maggots, which would soon devour it. They said it would not bear any weight, and was wholly unfit for London work.

At a meeting held in the presence of the Governors of Greenwich Hospital, Mr. Colin Campbell, their architect, being

---

[1] Block stone in the rough at this period was delivered at the Avon side for 7s. 6d. per ton, and, as Wood asserts, "stone fit for the walls of a palace for the greatest prince in Europe."

[2] Mayor of Bath in 1732.

present, Wood, with a Bath stonemason, attended to submit specimens of the Bath stone, and to compare it with other stone, all of which was laid upon the table. Campbell by mistake took up the wrong stone, and pointing to the defects, which he alleged were peculiar to the Bath stone, opened the eyes of the Governors to the unprincipled opposition to its use, the direct consequence of which was that they effected a reduction of thirty per cent. on the Portland stone for the work then to be added to the hospital. One of Mr. Allen's purposes was thus attained. He had exposed the selfish objects of those who opposed the use of the Bath stone, and opened the eyes of many whose minds had been prejudiced against it. Many men would have been discouraged by the great difficulties by which his efforts to bring Bath stone into the London market were met ; but, having so far succeeded, he continued for some time to persevere, though he did not attain complete success. In this spirit, as we show, he resolved to exhibit the Bath stone in a mansion "near his works to much greater advantage, and in much greater variety of uses than it had ever appeared in any other structure".

When Prior Park was built the fame of Bath stone spread everywhere, and contracts were sought for public and private buildings—in some cases *en bloc*, in others in detail ; and these contracts were entered into under the personal super-vision of Wood. This arrangement with Wood lasted for five years ; and although it terminated amicably, and a clerk of the works,[1] together with a staff of competent persons, was appointed to conduct Allen's business, Wood evidently thought himself inadequately paid for his services.

At the time Ralph Allen purchased the Priory Estate it was of comparatively little value, as has been shown. The

---

[1] Richard Jones, to whom Allen bequeathed one year's salary. In The '45 Rebellion, Allen at his own cost raised a company of volunteers, of which Jones took the command.

situation was noble, and the configuration admirably adapted
for a grand mansion.   In the "olden time", before the Dissolution, it would seem that the Priory lands were laid out
tastefully, and with some degree of grandeur ; but even as
early as Leland's visit to Bath, during Prior Holeway's time,
the "waulles" were neglected and the "dere" sold, and there
were other symptoms of neglect and decay.   The presage of
coming troubles seems to have cast a gloom over the capitular
executive, who, though anxious to build a new cathedral or
abbey, had allowed their estates to fall into decay, apparently
because exhausting demands had been made upon their
financial resources for the building of the present Bath Abbey.[1]
It may fairly be questioned whether it was a righteous act

---

[1] The Cathedral of John de Villula, especially the eastern portion of it,
even as early as 1400, was in a hopeless state of dilapidation ; but at the
close of the century little more than the bare walls were standing.   The
first effort made to build the Abbey was begun by Prior Cantlow in 1491,
by the clearing of the site, the preparation of the stone, etc.; and at that
period this was a work of time, patience, and cost.   In 1496 Bishop Oliver
King was translated from Exeter to Bath and Wells, and immediately
began that great work in his diocese which has made his name so
venerated.   He had no power to command with regard to the building
operations, but he had the power to exhort, to help, to infuse courage
and zeal into those by whom the great work was to be accomplished;
and this he did from the time of his accession to the time of his
death in 1503.   Cantlow died in 1499, and at that time much progress had
been made.   The Bishop, in proceeding to appoint a successor to Cantlow, whilst holding Birde in high estimation for his general qualities and
his personal piety, hesitated in his choice because he distrusted Birde as
to his qualifications in directing and carrying on the great work of building the sacred edifice.   It is a notable fact that, whether Birde was aware
or not aware of the good Bishop's distrust, he devoted his whole life, zeal,
and energies, to the work of his office and the raising of the sacred pile;
and this care, seeing what was to follow from neglect and indifference,
saved the building from destruction.   By this we mean that the work he
left completed was so done as to survive even the neglect to which it was
exposed during the Reformation as well as at a later period,

on Henry's part to reduce the Church to beggary ; to allow
this Prior, by whom the Bath Monastery was surrendered, to
starve on "£30 a yere" in a "dwellyng at 20*s.* per annum",
whilst nearly the whole of the Church lands were bestowed on
his illegitimate daughter, who married the first Harington of
Kelston.[1] Holeway's last days were spent in Sowter Street,
within the South Gate,[2] and the fair work of his and his
predecessors' hands (the Abbey) was sold with remorseless
disregard as to its sacred character, and without the smallest
provision being made for the clergy of Bath and all within
its jurisdiction. The Royal Reformer thought the Bathonians
had no souls ; and it is pretty clear that the members of the
Corporation had very small ones, if it be true, as there is little
reason to doubt, that the Commissioners offered them the
"carcass" of the Abbey, which they declined, on the ostensible
ground of their distrust of the Royal Commissioners, but
really because they shirked both expense and responsibility.
After the Reformation, many of the benefices that had been
confiscated at the time of the Dissolution were repurchased
and restored by the lord and the squire. The Priory lands at
the time of the Dissolution originally comprised the Widcomb[3] of Camalodunum,[4] the Lyncomb,[5] the Smallcomb,
Bathwick, and certain properties within the precincts of the
walls or liberties of the city.

It was in the year 1728 that the incident connected with
the Greenwich Hospital Governors occurred as to the relative qualities of Bath and Portland stone, which no doubt
decided Allen to build a large mansion with Bath stone, though

[1] The father of Sir John Harington, by his second marriage.
[2] Removed bodily when the walls and gates were pulled down about
1755.
[3] The wide combe, or valley, extending from the road bounding Widcombe House to the head of the Dunum, or hill, as the word signifies.
[4] This, so called by Wood, must not be confounded with *the* Camalodunum of Colchester.   [5] Lyncombe signifying the watery valley.

it was not until some years afterwards that he carried his resolution into effect. When the ground was broken and prepared for the foundation is not clear from any authority to which we have access; but from the nature of the soil, and some natural difficulties that had to be overcome, it is probable that the site was not ready until 1737. Some idea may be formed of the nature of the preparatory work from the fact that for the foundation, or stereobata, of the central mansion alone,[1] 800 tons of freestone, in large blocks, were required, so that for the whole work it may be assumed that the foundation walls required in the aggregate not less than 30,000 tons of stone. The conception of the general plan by Wood was on a larger scale, and the building itself more ornate than that which was finally determined upon and carried out. Nor was this the only important modification of the design. In the first dream of this big house—in the exuberance of his fancy to " exhibit the Bath stone in a seat he had determined to build for himself near his works"—Allen had pictured a mansion in which the " Orders of Architecture were to shine forth in all their glory". But ultimately this ideal yielded to a style less elaborate in principle and detail. Writing some seven years after the completion of the house, Wood says (vol. i, p. 96, 2nd edit.): " The Seat consists of a Mansion House in the center, two Pavilions, and two Wings of Offices

---

[1] We do not know, but we suppose the site was chosen by Wood, inasmuch as he is silent on the subject. It appears to us, as it has appeared to others better qualified to judge, to be too low down, occupying, in fact, the watershed of the East Lyn, one consequence of which was seen in the difficulty of getting good foundations and a safe outlet for the water. For, besides the enormous cost, provision had to be made by the construction of immensely strong permanent culverts under the foundations for its escape. If a higher site had been chosen all these evils would have been obviated, and the position would have admitted of an open south front, which is now "cribbed, cabined, and confined" under the excavated bank.

West.

East.

PRIOR PARK AND TRAMWAY.

(From a Print of the Period.)

All these are united by low buildings; and while the chief
Part of the whole Line fronts the Body of the City, the rest
faces the summitt of *Mar's Hill.*"[1] It is probable that the
adoption of the less magnificent and costly design was due to
Allen's own desire, because Wood says, in reference to the
grander design, " the warmth of this resolution at last abating,
an humble simplicity took its place".

STABLES AND PAVILION.

In pursuance of the modified design, the west wing was
begun, but again some deviation from the design was made
before its completion.   This wing consisted of a principal
and half-storey, extending 172 ft. 8 in. in front by 34 ft.
4 in. in depth on the plinth course of stone.   In the centre
there was the hay-house, 20 ft. high, with a pigeon-house
over it of the same altitude, four six-horse stables, three
coach-houses, with a harness-room behind them at one end,
a barn at the other end, and proper granaries in so much
of the half-storey as was to be over the stables, coach-
houses, and harness-rooms.   The stables and hay-houses were
arched or vaulted over with stone, which was so intended
from the first by the architect, who borrowed the idea from
the stables of Mr. Hanbury of Pontypool.   The rest of the
floorings and roof of the whole were intended to have been of
timber, covered with Cornish slate.   But in the execution of
the building Allen resolved to make use of nothing but stone
for a covering for this wing of offices.   This substitution of
stone for timber disarranged the architect's plan, and the
changing of the material for the roof not only interfered with
the altitude of some of the offices, but also greatly interfered

---

[1] Applied to that part of *Mons Badonica*, or Mount Beacon, which
we now distinguish as Lansdown. Wood says the name is so called
from *Lan*, signifying temple, and *Dunum*, a hill. A mere fanciful theory.
Lansdown simply signifies *Lan*, Celtic for *land*, and *Down*, a hill.

with the essential characteristics of the building itself. Of the external walls, only that which fronts the south was faced with wrought freestone ; and this was to have exhibited the Doric order in its plainest dress, but so high as to include a principal and a half-storey above it, separated by a fascia or band. A tetra-style frontispiece in the middle of the whole line, before such an advanced part of the building, was to have contained two of the staircases, one on each end of the hay-house, and at the same time appear as a proper basement of the pigeon-house, which was to have crowned the edifice with magnificence and beauty; for the basement extends 50 ft., and a square of that size in the middle of the building was to have been covered with a pyramidal roof, divided into two parts, and to have discovered the body of the crowning ornament. It will be seen, therefore, in what respect the change affected the edifice. The joists intended for the timber roof had such a projection given them in the design as would have afforded protection in wet weather to persons walking from one part of this wing of offices to the other. When, however, the ends of the joists came to be represented in stone, they were contracted to small corbels, of little use and less beauty, when considered as part of the crowning ornament to columns of the Doric order.

The stables were divided into six recessed stalls on every side, arched, and lined with dressed stone. Allen treated his horses like gentlemen. They were richly caparisoned, and he always had four to his coach,[1] in which his guests drove out with much state. Wood was not quite satisfied, however, with the stables ; he wanted a little more magnitude, and would have preferred a recess at each stall to contain a bin for each horse. This wing was finished about 1736 or 1737.[2]

---

[1] Allen seldom used a carriage, unless he went beyond Bath.

[2] It may be well to state that the domain, as well as the mansion, during the occupancy of Mr. Thomas, from 1817 to 1827, suffered very

After the completion of the west wing, the pavilion was to serve as an arch for coaches to drive under, and as a poultry and pigeon-house. This structure was built and finished with wrought freestone. The lower part of it was composed of four hollow legs, each 9 ft. square by 13½ ft. in length, every front containing an aperture of 16 ft. in breadth, all arched over. The body of the building was crowned at the altitude of 22½ ft. with a cornice, surmounted by a plain attic, 6 ft. in height, supporting a pyramidal design, terminating in an octagonal pedestal turret, 10 ft. in diameter, covered with a dome, the whole being finished with an ornament, consisting of a base, ball, baluster, and vane, making the extreme height 59 ft., or 39 ft. above the vaulted arch for coaches. The cells for pigeons were made of wrought freestone. The poultry were similarly provided for in the low building by which the west wing was united with the pavilion. It consisted of three rooms, facing southward, with three apertures to every room, arched over.

CENTRAL MANSION.

Some deviation from the general plan was rendered necessary by the addition of a closet, which destroyed the continuity of the original basement lines of the central mansion, from the necessity it involved of placing the pavilion lower than was intended. Another consequence was that the line having thus been broken, the architect felt no scruple in laying the foundation of the main central structure higher than was originally intended ; and the bottom of the plinth was,

much from parsimonious neglect. In 1829, Bishop Baines, of honoured memory, purchased the estate, and repaired, as far as possible, the mischief done ; and we believe it was he who built the stately flight of steps on the north side of the central mansion. Of this part of the history Monsignor Shepherd has written an interesting account.

THE MANSION, PRIOR PARK.

therefore, 15 in. higher than that of the west wing.[1]   The
building thus elevated stood upon the plinth course of
stone, 147 ft. in length by 80 ft. in breadth, inclusive of the
projections in front and rear, and consisted of basement,
principal and chamber stories, with garrets taken out of the
altitude of some of the rooms of the latter.

The mansion was constructed of solid blocks of very large
dimensions, in equal courses both within and without, with
a course of brick between; so that the walls were equally
strong on both sides, and were able to bear the superincumbent masonry without being liable to "buckle" under the
weight.   The rooms in the basement storey were 12 ft. high,
but a narrow passage, running through the middle of the
house from end to end, was lower by 1 foot.   The chimneys
in the several rooms were dressed with architraves, some of
which were crowned with their proper friezes and cornices,
all in freestone; and with the same material the door-cases
next the passage were made, architraves being worked upon
the external faces as the proper dress for the apertures.
This passage being divided into five equal parts, regularly
finished with freestone ornaments, became the beauty of
the inside of the basement story, the rooms of which received their light from square windows in the north front,
but those on the south from oblong windows.   It should
be added that not only were the walls of the entire house
outside and inside built of Bath stone of the best quality,
carefully wrought in the sheds, every stone for its place, but
the floors of the basement rooms were laid with the hard,
calcined, shelly ragstone, which is the first bed or stratum, or
as Wood further says, "the roof of the subterraneous quarries",
the next stratum being the "picking bed", which is not so
hard and durable.   On this basement storey were a servants'
hall, a housekeeper's room, a butler's pantry, and a room for

[1] The general illustration distinctly shows this.

the footmen, a small-beer cellar, a strong-beer cellar, wine vault, laundry, bakehouse, kitchen, scullery, larder, and pantry There were also a dairy and milk-room, with scullery, and an apartment set aside for W.C.'s should "any such conveniences be wanted within the body of the house". The several rooms were arched, or vaulted over by stone, and the stairs also made of stone, so that the defects peculiar to plaster were effectually avoided in this almost uniquely-constructed house.

On the first floor the hall extended from the front to the rear of the house, and to the eastward of the hall there were a parlour, study, store-rooms, chapel, and back staircase ; to the westward a dining-room, drawing-room, bedchamber, dressing-room, and principal staircase ; and to the northward a portico or grand pavilion. The altitude of this pavilion, as well as that of the chapel, was determined by the base of the roof ; but all the other rooms were covered over at 16 ft. of height, the whole of the architectural ornamentations being of Bath stone, though these were afterwards removed from the parlour and dining-room, which, to the disgust of Wood, were then lined with oak, the irate architect denouncing it as a "depredation". Some compensation, however, was vouchsafed to him by his being permitted to finish the whole of the upper stories, passages, and gallery (20 ft. high), as well as the chapel, with dressed stone. The chapel was of the Ionic order, sustaining the Corinthian. The parlour was finished in the Ionic order, and the dining-room, hall, principal staircase, and gallery were completed in the Corinthian order.

The portico, already mentioned, on the north front was a hexastyle ; and it seems that, although divested of some of its beauty for the convenience of the garret windows, it was designed by Wood to excel in grandeur that which had been just executed at Wanstead by his old rival, Colin Campbell. The portico consisted of Ionic columns supporting a Corinthian

Walter Kessler. Palladian Bridge.

entablature. The columns were 3 ft. 1½ in. in diameter, which exceeds the Wanstead column by 1½ in. ; the inter-columnation being what is called a *systylos* or systyle—*i.e.,* the space between the columns equalling two diameters of the shaft at the bottom, whilst the distance between each of the plinths on which the column or shaft rests is equivalent to its own diameter. The entablature was carried all round the house, with the exception of the west end, where it was sacrificed to the exigencies of the windows. Each front was crowned by a handsome balustrade.

The east wing was designed by Richard Jones, and the object was chiefly to provide bedroom accommodation. It contains a hall and a picture-gallery ; and this wing is connected with the centre by an open corridor. In the midst of the grove was a fine lawn, sloping down from the house ; near the summit of this lawn rose a plentiful spring, gushing out of a rock covered with firs, and forming a constant cascade of about thirty feet, not carried down a regular flight of steps, but tumbling in a natural fall over the broken and mossy stones till it came to the bottom of the rock, then running off in a pebbly channel, that, with many lesser falls, winded along till it fell into a lake at the foot of a hill, about a quarter of a mile or less below the house on the south side (facing north-west).

The lake was (and still is) in the midst of a grove, and the cascade gushed out of a rock ; but we have shown that the site of the mansion was the watershed of the south-east branch of the Lyn ; and after issuing from the rock, the water passed through the culverts constructed under the foundations, then formed the cascade, passed into the small lake in the grove, then entered an open channel, and passed into the pretty lake at the bottom of the park. Richard Jones designed the exquisite Palladian bridge by which it is spanned, and of which Allen, in 1751, laid the foundation stone. There is a

I

full-length portrait of Garrick, painted by Gainsborough, one of that master's greatest works, done at Prior Park. We wish we could give a more circumstantial account of the local associations which connect it with Prior Park. The figure of Garrick is very characteristic, and the attitude seems intended to represent *Genius* ; the right arm is carelessly thrown round the base of a bust of Shakespeare resting upon a plinth, whilst in the distance, to the left, the Palladian bridge is the conspicuous object.

Besides the east wing, Jones erected near it a small, but very pretty cottage for the gardener. After Allen's death this cottage was called *The Priory*, and has recently been enlarged and transformed into a lovely residence.

Within a few yards westward of the upper lodge gate is the entrance to what once was a very pretty and well-kept private walk, traditionally known as *Pope's Walk*. This walk runs parallel with the carriage road, and leads down to a picturesque old arch, which forms a roadway over a narrow chasm, and was manifestly intended in former times for, and used as, a path for the use of the shepherds to cross with their flocks. This walk was not laid out until ten years after Pope's death. On each side is a quickset hedge, and at intervals there are lovely peeps of the distant scenery to right and left.

THE ROYAL MINERAL-WATER HOSPITAL.

In Bath the institution of and for which the city has most reason to be proud and thankful is the "General Hospital", as it was originally called. It had its origin in, perhaps, one of the greatest evils that ever affected the city, an evil arising out of a crude Act of Parliament passed in 1597, giving a right to the free use of the baths of Bath to the diseased and impotent poor of England. Each parish was authorised to grant a limited sum to a suffering parishioner, and all such

WALTER ROSSIER.

Pope's
Walk. (continued)

sufferers were forbidden to beg. Some of these people were
impostors, feigning illness, whilst others soon became demoralized ; and even those who were honestly disposed,
after getting here, had no means of returning to their homes ;
and the result of all this was "the beggars of Bath".[1] The
streets for a century were infested . with these "beggars",
who were insolent, vociferous, and dangerous ; the evil, in
fact, was so great that in 1714 the Act referred to was
repealed.

About two years after (1716), Lady Elizabeth Hastings[2]
and Mr. Henry Hoare proposed the founding of a "Water
Hospital" for the benefit of proper objects of relief, Sir J.
Jekyl and Mr. Nash and the famous Dr. Oliver[3] being also
amongst its earlier supporters. Later, many others joined in the
laudable attempt to raise funds to promote the object. Many
difficulties had to be overcome, and in the year 1724 the
project was far from being regarded as a success. A sum
of £9,372 had been received ; but it was obvious that little
would be left out of this sum for an endowment fund after
the expenses of erecting a hospital had been met, and so it
proved. From this time until 1727 the scheme was in abey-
ance. In 1734 an Act of Parliament was obtained, when an
accession of gentlemen, including Ralph and Philip Allen,
joined the committee ; and then, besides the pecuniary diffi-

[1] The expression, "*Go to Bath*", arose from the reception of these
"beggars" at "*The Bath*". The importunate beggars in distant localities
were sometimes met with the unwelcome advice, "*Go to Bath*".—Fuller's
Worthies, co. Somerset; Mackay's *Journey through England*, Letter VIII,
p. 413.

[2] Lady Elizabeth was the younger daughter of the seventh Earl
of Huntingdon, and resided in Bath. She was devoted to charity
and acts of kindness ; and, what is more, she was a woman of great
judgment.

[3] He was famous as a physician, as a philanthropist, as a beloved
citizen ; and he was the inventor of "Oliver's Biscuits".

culty, that of obtaining a suitable site[1] proved a serious one. Two conditions were indispensable, namely, its comparative openness and its proximity to the springs. These obstacles frustrated the efforts of the committee until 1737. Wood, the eminent architect, then came to the rescue, and by his energy, business aptitude, and judgment every difficulty was obviated. At the corner of what is now Union Street, near the famous old "Bear Inn", immortalised by Smollett,[2] stood some old buildings, one of which had been used as a theatre, in which at this time plays could not legally be enacted. Wood purchased the whole of the ground

[1] Wood says : "Years were spent in this pursuit, in obtaining a suitable site, and several new designs, attended with great incidental expenses, were made by me to answer various situations and various purposes of the Trustees. At length the suppression of play-houses by the Act of Parliament, which took place the 24th of June 1737, and the death of Mr. Thayer the 9th of the following December, determined the matter in one week's time. For the Trustees, meeting on the 22nd of December to consider of a new Treasurer, after admitting Mr. Farquhar into their number, Dr. Oliver made them an offer of some land belonging to him, to build a hospital on, and it was accepted. But great opposition arising instantly against the Agreement, the Trustees at a 2nd meeting, on the 29th of December, declared it void ; and resolved to accept of a new offer that was made them of the theatre erected in the year 1705, as above, together with two dwelling-houses, some out-houses, and stable belonging to it, the estate of one Mrs. Carne, for £30 more than it stood engaged for to the above-mentioned Mr. Collibee."*

[2] "The communication (from Queen Square) with the Baths is through the yard of an inn, where the poor trembling valetudinarian is carried in a chair, betwixt the heels of a double row of horses, wincing under the curry-combs of grooms and postillions, over and above the hazard of being obstructed or overturned by the carriages which are continually making their exit or their entrance." The landlord was Phillott, one of whose sons was Rector of Bath ; another son was a banker, while another son was an officer in the Army.

---

* Mayor of Bath in 1785.

for £892 10s., with an annual ground-rent of £10 6s. 3d.;[1] and this ground was prepared for the great work.

The first stone of the building was laid on July 6th, 1738, by Sir William Pulteney (afterwards Earl of Bath), by whom the Bathwick estate had recently been acquired. It should be mentioned that, as the hospital was for the benefit of all patients throughout the country, *except Bath*,[2] suffering from certain disorders, a general appeal was made throughout the country for support, by Mr. Hoare, the treasurer and banker, and this appeal was fairly successful.

Almost the first *public* example of Allen's bounty, after he had successfully organized all his public undertakings, was in connection with this " National Institution". Wood prepared the designs free of cost ; and as soon as the site was cleared, Allen contributed and delivered all the freestone, wrought stone, paving stone, wall stone, and lime (valued at £1,000), to build and complete the walls; and afterwards he presented all that was needed for doorways and structural fittings of every kind, duly prepared under the care of Wood, each part ready for its place ; and to the capital account he added £1,000. Perhaps it should be stated that the building of his own mansion, at Prior Park, was proceeding at the same time.

From October 1724 to 1742, when the hospital was completed, £9,372 was received from all sources; the cost of building (not including Allen's material) was £7,330, thus leaving £2,042 for investment.

In May 1742, the institution was completed and opened for 130 patients.[3] In October, a sermon in further promotion of

---

[1] Since redeemed by the governors.

[2] An exception since abolished.

[3] To avoid the old evils of *making paupers* and leaving them in our city, the Governors in all cases received a deposit, which defrayed the travelling expenses each way of a patient, or covered the funeral expenses in case of death, This condition is still in force,

its interests was preached by Warburton[1] at the Abbey Church, from the text, "Let your light so shine before men, that they may see your good works, and glorify your Father which is in Heaven." The sermon was an admirable and effective explanation of the design and objects of the institution, the preacher dwelling with force upon the comprehensive character of its constitution. It was open to the nation, it appealed to the nation.

The list of contributors from 1724 to 1742 is an interesting one, and contains some well-known historic names ; Allen, in 1741, adding £500 to his previous donation, and becoming an annual contributor of £21.

In 1758 a sermon was again preached in the Abbey Church by the Rev. R. Olive, in promotion of the capital fund of the hospital, and resulted in the sum of £1,366 being collected generally. This and other sums, in addition to various endowments from time to time, if they have not altogether obviated the annual appeals for support, have preserved the hospital from that painful urgency which occasionally characterizes the appeals in support of similar institutions. From the first, there is little doubt that this valuable institution has been conducted with admirable firmness and prudence,[2] and with every regard to kindness and humanity.

Allen, doubtless, was deeply attached to and proud of this

---

[1] Besides this and the Thanksgiving Sermon preached in the chapel at Prior Park on the Suppression of the Scotch Rebellion, in 1746, Warburton preached a series of sermons at the Abbey, published in two small volumes at the cost of Allen. These and two small volumes of sermons preached in the chapel at Prior Park are all that he published in connection with Bath.

[2] Shortly after its establishment, a charge was made against a member of the medical staff. An inquiry, under the presidency of Philip Allen, showed an amount of care, combined with a judicial regard for truth and justice, which rendered the inquiry a model for all such painful investigations.

hospital, in the successful promotion of which he had borne his honourable share.   In a document now in our hands, written by Allen himself for his private use, he has noted down, apparently for personal reference, " An account of my money to be apply'd to good purposes, from Midr. 1744 to do. 1745 : The General Hospital, Bath, £450; St. Bartholomew's, London, £300." Then follow sums to parishes, to initials; one to the quarry surgeon, £50 ; one to Mrs. (Sarah) Fielding, £20, and so on ; the whole amounting to upwards of £1,500. The document is endorsed, " Mem. of the Application of Charity Money for the year ending with Midr. 1745. If I should Live so Long."[1]

From this time until his death there was the same quiet energy, the same business-like earnestness, and the same " doing good by stealth" for the gratification of his own heart and feelings, and the same steady open support for the sake of precept and example.

" Bath, July 8, 1842.

" Last Thursday being the Day appointed for laying the Foundation Stone of the intended General Hospital of this City, above twenty of the Trustees and Contributors met at the ' Rummer Tavern' and proceeded from thence to the Place appointed for erecting the Hospital, when the first stone was laid, on which was the following Inscription :

  " ' This Stone was the first which was laid in the Foundation ot the General Hospital at Bath, July 6, A.D. 1738. God prosper the Christian Undertaking.'

" When the Ceremony was completed, the Gentlemen return'd to the

---

[1] He lived for twenty-one years to witness the success of the hospital, and it may be confidently affirmed that from that period, 1764, until now, there has been no breach in that honourable record. If Allen could now look down upon the work of his own age he would see, on the site of what then was the Rectory House of Bath, the duplicate of the unique institution which he did so much to foster and establish, and which enables the hospital to receive 171 patients. It needs but one feature to render it complete, and that is the statue of Allen in the hall.

'Rummer', when His Majesty's Health, and that of the Prince and Princess of Wales, General Wade, and other absent Benefactors, were drunk, and all the Demonstrations of Joy possible shown on the Occasion, everyone appearing pleas'd with a Design so excellently well calculated for the good of Man in General and the Welfare and Happiness of the People, Wretched and Miserable, in particular. An handsome Present was made to the Workmen, and the Bells rang on this happy Occasion." —*London Evening Post.*

POSTAL ORGANIZATION.

During the period when he was building his noble palace, developing his vast stone quarries, and promoting the Water Hospital and other benevolent undertakings in and at a distance from his own city, Allen was at the same time devoting his energies to the discovery of all the weak points in the post-office, devising new safeguards, and constructing new, quicker, and permanent methods. Every obstacle was thrown in his way by the indifference of the Postmasters-General; and when his well-considered plans became irresistible, these *generous* and almost useless officials sanctioned and adopted them as their own.[1] Allen's knowledge of localities, trade, and manufactures was marvellous. He seems, however, almost to the close of his second contract, to have encountered more difficulty in dealing with and extirpating deliberate roguery and obstruction in certain districts, than in carrying out his practical schemes generally, and thus founding a system.

Of the character of the postal business in itself, at that time, we have now little conception. The non-stamping of letters, the difficulty of getting vouchers, and the ingenious methods adopted by the local postmasters for writing and sending sham letters, and then obtaining from the post-office a rebate of the postage of such letters—these, and similar evils, were no small difficulties to deal with. The great object, next to the

[1] See Mr. Herbert Joyce's valuable *History of the Post-Office*, pp. 136, 137, 138.

practical advantages of postal reform and its enormous importance to the country, was to purge the local post-offices of all
their corrupt, dishonest, and obstructive abuses, and transform
the officials into honest, rational men.[1] To this end Allen used
every means ; his patience, his forbearance, his simple but
impressive remonstrances, were in the end successful ; but it
should be especially observed that every rogue perceived that
he was "spotted", that he had been weighed in the balance
and found wanting, and that it rested with him by risking all
to lose all.   In a word, Ralph Allen achieved a twofold good ;
he successfully devised a great national reform, and transformed, ultimately, a whole department of rogues into honest
men ; and truly he could say, "Alone I did it."

The chapter on Allen in Mr. Joyce's book is by far the
most interesting in his valuable work.   It is the record of a

[1] "At this time, 1735, and for many years subsequently, the mails were
carried on horseback by post-boys, most of whom were sad rogues.   In
the year quoted a surveyor wrote : 'At this place (*Salisbury*) found the
post-boys to have carried on vile practices in taking the bye letters,
delivering them in this city, and taking back answer, especially the
Andover riders.   On the 15th found on Richard Kent, one of the Andover
riders, 5 bye letters, all for this city.   Upon examining the fellow, he
confessed he had made it a practice, *and persisted to continue in it*,
saying he had no wages from his master.   He was taken before the
magistrates, convicted, and *elected* to be whipped rather than imprisoned.
Inspector ordered him to be dismissed ; *without effect*.   Next day Post-
Office authorities sent same fellow post, who was insolent, took up letters,
resumed the postage charges, and then, with two other fellows, rode off
with three of the Government horses.'   The inspector had his revenge,
and Allen suffered no more from the delinquent, Richard Kent.   This
anecdote illustrates the general condition into which the Government
had allowed the department to drift.   Mr. Lewins says, in *Her Majesty's
Mails*, p. 110 : 'Mr. Allen not only reaped golden harvests, but deserved
to do so.   His energy and careful organizing powers are worthy of all
praise, and, inasmuch as he laid the foundation for the future improvement of the Post-Office, and carried out schemes over which officialdom
had failed, he deserved the gratitude of posterity.'"

new era, the working out of a new system, and the opening up by energy, indomitable pluck, and a rational intelligence, of a system of national communication, on which the future commercial supremacy as well as the social happiness of the nation were chiefly to depend.[1] The Government methods, as late as 1741, even with Allen's example before them, were vicious beyond description. When Allen showed these *statesmen* how to set the egg on its end, they thought it was too simple for men so transcendently perverse as they were to adopt.[2]

In 1741 began the fourth septennial period of Allen's contract. Mr. Joyce tells us that " in consideration of his contract being renewed there was an important condition, which Allen undertook to carry out. This was to convert the tri-weekly posts into posts *six* days a week, and to take the whole expense upon himself." Accordingly, in 1741, the post began to run every day of the week, except Sunday, between London and Bristol, between London and Norwich, and between London and Yarmouth, all the intervening towns participating in the benefit. When the distance (about 120 miles) is considered, which had to be accomplished on bad

---

[1] At the time Allen entered into his first septennial contract he was only 26 years of age, and when the first three years of that contract had expired he was a loser by the transaction of £270. That fact neither deterred him from persevering, nor in the least diminished his confidence in ultimate success.

[2] Lord Lovel and Mr. Carteret (afterwards Lord Carteret and Earl Granville) were men of great ability, but too indolent to grapple with a great practical question, involving endless details, on the carrying out of which the success of the whole system depended.

Mr. Joyce describes the cross-posts system as follows : " A bye or way letter would be a letter passing between any two towns on the Bath road and stopping short of London—as, for instance, between Bath and Hungerford, between Hungerford and Newbury and Reading, and so on."

roads on horseback, great weight having to be borne, with many stoppages, this was a great feat. Gradually this privilege was extended over the whole country.

It must here be observed that Allen had to encounter not simply the inherent difficulties of his own responsible duties, but he had to deal with the unpopularity and distrust resulting from the sins of the Government. There was scarcely an abuse, or any kind of espionage and treachery, of which the Government at this time was not guilty through the private office, which was independent of the Postmaster-General, for opening and inspecting letters. The head of this office was Willes, Dean of Lincoln, who, on this iniquitous office being abolished, was gazetted Bishop of St. David's, and in 1743 was translated to Bath and Wells. The office of a spy seems to have been a very strange training for the duties of a bishop. The House of Commons abolished this shameful office in 1742, but the Bishop continued to flourish from 1742 until his death in 1774.

It may be said that Allen's official duties consisted in the extension and perfecting the system which, under every conceivable disadvantage, he had established ; and in this arduous work he had to encounter, not simply the ordinary difficulties and complications of postal business in itself, but the perverse, obstructive, and reactionary tactics of the Government, out of which had sprung the evasion, the dishonesty, the delays, the trickery, and the rapacity of the officials employed, from the post-boys to the postmasters and the higher officials. These officials, it seems, had little to fear from detection, for they usually escaped with impunity, except in most glaring cases. Allen, on the contrary, never permitted a misdemeanant to escape—unless he chose to escape by becoming honest and amenable to authority and order. There was not an evil, not an abuse, of which successive Governments were not guilty. The Postmasters-General, from the earliest times down to the passing of the several Turnpike Acts, 1707, 1721, and 1739, seemed to be guided by no trustworthy computation of measurement. Bristol, which by road was 105 miles 3 furlongs, was reckoned by "vulgar computation" at 94 miles[1]; Bath, 103 miles, by "vulgar computation" 82 miles[2]; and these were only two examples of the many which generally prevailed. Out of this strange error, which involved the whole system of mileage, Allen of course had everywhere to bear the odium resulting from the alleged injustice to his *employés;* but the real injustice was to himself, the Government, having the most complete knowledge of the facts, denying him freedom of judgment and action. In this, as in other questions affecting the welfare of the people—commerce, literature, and art—the Government in relation to them had one aim and one alone, that was, to get as large a revenue as they could, without regard to increasing population, advancing civilisation, or political necessity.

Allen understood all this. He knew that unrestricted interchange of correspondence meant national progress in art, in literature, in commerce ; and of this policy he laid the foundations. Where officialdom had failed he succeeded, and we owe to him ungrudging thanks and gratitude. So far as we can judge, he was the only man of his time who possessed all the personal faculties and remarkable qualifications to deal with a question of this nature. First, by his perfect knowledge of the subject and his unique powers of organization ; next, by his personal sympathies and never-failing self-command and equable temper ; and lastly, by his indomitable courage,

---

[1] Ogilby's work, *Britannia; or, the Kingdom of England and the Dominion of Wales, actually Surveyed, etc.*, by John Ogilby, Esq., etc., 1728.

[2] The lines of road differed from the present, but the relative distances were identical. Bristol, for instance, was approached by way of Marshfield and by the road we now call Tog Hill.

combined with a never-failing courtesy which, amid all the difficult and complex nature of the system, secured to him the esteem and respectful co-operation of his vast staff scattered throughout the land. Allen it was who initiated the great postal reform ; he it was by whom the foundation was laid for future improvements, and to him and such as him we owe, in great measure, one of the greatest luxuries and blessings of modern times—a quick, a cheap, and an effective postal system.

SOCIAL AND PRIVATE LIFE OF RALPH ALLEN AT PRIOR PARK.

In dealing with the private and social life of Ralph Allen, we are bound to confess that we are wholly at a loss to tell our readers how he got through such a prodigious amount of difficult labour. There were two large stone quarries, involving not simply a close inspection and careful supervision, but all the trading details which of necessity followed. There were all the complicated details of the postal business, with its ramifications, extending over England and Scotland, with staffs of clerks and executives spread over the land.[1] There was a considerable home estate, much of which, having been neglected for a century, was denuded of its timber, its fencing destroyed, and its population demoralized. There were houses he was building in the city needing much care and supervision, besides the constant additions to, and alterations in, his large mansion ; and from first to last, on his plantations, Jones tells us he expended £55,000. Yet, withal, nothing escaped his observation or his careful inspection. He was always calm and collected, always finding time for works of kindness, whether in relation to institutions or individuals ; and at

---

[1] The staff in the Bath Office, under Allen's own direction, by whom the supreme orders were issued, consisted of only four or five clerks.

the head of his own hospitable and princely board not a
guest failed to receive his courteous notice and kindly smile.
We do not mean to say that Allen could work impossibilities ;
but, in all cases, he was able to accomplish so much by reason
of his clear and rapid perception of what was best to be done,
and by an equally clear and concise method of giving his directions, whether orally or in writing. Mr. Joyce quotes many
illustrations of this peculiar and valuable gift. Allen knew
his own mind ; and if he did at any time make mistakes, he
did not waste time by grieving over them, thus adding to the
loss. He never seemed to allow his mind to be oppressed,
and in all his intercourse with citizens or strangers, he left
the impression that the subject matter of conversation alone
occupied his mind.

When Ralph Allen, in 1742, entered into possession of Prior
Park there was no " society" in Bath ; none, as Burke has it,
amongst whom " the sentiments which beautify and soften
private *society* were to be found." There was no sympathy ;
no bond of union, amongst the various classes that then came
to Bath. Every person who visited Bath, from the highest to
the lowest rank, *i.e.*, from the wealthy aristocrat to the low-
born adventurer, cared nothing about society in the ordinary
sense of the word. The assemblies were characterized by
intrigue, libertinism, and vulgar gossip.

As Smollett wrote: "We have music in the pump-room every
morning, cotillions every forenoon in the rooms, balls twice a
week, and concerts every other night;" and later, he adds,
" this place, which Nature and Providence seems to have intended as a resource from distemper and disquiet, is become
the very centre of racket and dissipation . . . . Instead of that
peace, tranquillity, and ease, so necessary to those who labour
under bad health, weak nerves, and irregular spirits, we have
nothing but noise, tumult, and hurry, with the fatigue and
slavery of *maintaining a ceremonial, more stiff,* formal, and

oppressive than the etiquette of a German Elector." Here was the pith of the whole matter. This was the formality under the shadow of which the gambling was organised, the victims "spotted", and the *modus operandi* arranged. There was literally no such thing as social intercourse—the confidential intermingling of persons to cultivate the "exercise of those graces which adorn the sociable life", which was really the ideal at which Allen aimed at Prior Park for upwards of twenty years.

SOCIAL LIFE AT PRIOR PARK.

HE period from 1742 to 1763 in Bath abounds with an interest all its own. The social life at Prior Park was unique, giving to it a special and peculiar historical significance. Allen effaced all the stiff and preposterous barriers and conventionalities by which society was kept asunder. The gambler of the highest social rank of either sex would meet the most disreputable knave at Lady Hawley's or Wiltshire's Rooms, to lose a fortune; but they had not learned to tolerate the faintest distinction of social rank in ordinary life.[1] Allen brought together men and women of various ranks and grades—

> "And so, in grateful interchange
> Of teacher and of hearer,
> Their lives their true *distinctions* keep
> While daily drawing nearer."

In this, Allen displayed all his tact, and showed no little knowledge of mankind. At Prior Park he never lost or desired to lose touch with his old middle-class friends. Statesmen, lawyers, "lords and ladies of high degree", met members

[1] It may also be remarked that, in the Assemblies, the same absurd exclusiveness prevailed. There were benches for the duchesses, benches for ladies of lower rank, and benches for the commonalty.

of the corporation, and others, on all occasions ; and if, like
Philip Thicknesse, they fed from off Dresden china, they did not
afterwards, like that gentleman, vilify the master of the feast.
All Bath guests invited to Prior Park for concerts or to dine,
or for any other social purpose, were expected to sleep at
the mansion ; but in the winter, if for special reasons any of
them desired to return home, they were accompanied by
private watchmen and link-boys.   Allen was an early riser,
always ready to welcome his guests.   Fielding speaks of
him, " as walking forth on his terrace in the morning, when
the sun was rising in the full blaze of his majesty," than which,
he says, " one object in the lower creation could be more
glorious, and that Mr. Allworthy presented ; a human being
replete with benevolence, meditating in what manner he
might prove himself most acceptable to his Creator by doing
most good to his creatures."   The domain offered temptations
of pleasure and gratification to some ; the picture gallery to
others.   There was no stately, repelling, ostentation towards
guests, who saw and felt the hearty welcome of their host.

It was in 1728 that the Princess Amelia, when she was
quite a young woman, visited the city.   In 1752 she revisited
Bath, staying with the Duke and Duchess of Bedford in
Queen Square, and afterwards resumed her old quarters at
the Westgate House.   On this occasion she was accompanied
by her brother, the Duke of York.[1]   They, with the Duke of
Bedford, and many other distinguished guests, were entertained at Prior Park.   The visit ended by Allen offering his
mansion and establishment to the royal pair, which offer was
accepted, he and Mrs. Allen, Warburton, and Mrs. Warburton,
going for the time down to Weymouth, where Allen had a
house.

Gainsborough and Garrick often met at Prior Park ; and

[1] Princess Buildings (corrupted into Prince's Buildings), and York
House and Buildings, were respectively called after these two personages.

here it was that the famous artist painted one of the portraits of Garrick. It was at Allen's table that Quin (a frequent guest after the "old cock" came to Bath to "roost", first at Mrs. Simpson's,[1] in Pierrepont Street,[2] and then in the Abbey Yard, where he died), also met Gainsborough ;[3] and it was at Allen's table that the incident occurred between Quin and a noble lord. Quin, having uttered one of his irresistible witticisms, the nobleman observed : "What a pity 'tis, Quin, my boy, that a clever fellow like you should be a player !" "Why, my lord, what would you have me be, a lord ?"

Warburton was nearly always of the party, and he was wisely permitted to do as he pleased ; and what he pleased to do was usually acceptable to those present. He affected humility by selecting the stupidest person at the table by whom to sit, and with whom to converse, which may have been a way of manifesting his arrogance towards the more distinguished guests.

Charles Yorke, in his earlier manhood, was a frequent and most popular guest at Prior Park. He was the second son of the second Earl of Hardwicke, who occupied the house, No. 1, Wood Street, where Charles sometimes resided with his father. Charles Yorke was a lawyer of distinguished ability, marred sadly by habits of intemperance, but, withal, a man of charming manners, and much beloved at Prior Park. At the moment when (six years after Allen's death) he had attained to the Lord Chancellorship in 1770, he died by his own hand.

Thomas Potter (who was a close friend and adherent of Pitt, succeeding him as M.P. for Old Sarum, when the latter resigned the representation to accept that of Bath in 1757), second son

---

[1] He left Mrs. Simpson £100 at his death (see below).

[2] The house referred to in Pierrepont Street was, at a later period, the residence of Lord Chesterfield.

[3] He bequeathed Gainsborough £50.

of Archbishop Potter, was an ardent friend of Allen's, and a most popular visitor at Prior Park.[1] Potter was a tall, well-formed, courtier-like man ; and perhaps, in some measure, this fact gave rise to the rumour that Mrs. Warburton's admiration was not purely platonic. She was much younger than her husband, and was a woman of great beauty, witty, high-spirited, full of mirth, and very attractive.

William Pitt had been an occasional resident in Bath for some years before he was elected M.P. for the city in 1757, and before the Circus was built, in which he purchased No. 7, about 1760 (that side being first completed). He was sometimes the guest of a friend, and occasionally an independent visitor, and a constant attendant at the Baths. The incident which separated the political connection of Pitt with the city was a source of deep and painful regret to Allen, of which the details are fully given in another chapter. Apart from Allen's admiration for Pitt's splendid abilities and character, a great friendship and mutual affection existed between the two men. We have no doubt that Allen paid Pitt's election expenses, both in 1757 and 1761.

Writing from Prior Park to Mr. Pitt in 1756, Potter says : " The scenes at Prior Park change every hour, but the worthy owner has a heart that cannot change. The present joy at the birth of an heir [Ralph Allen Warburton, son of the bishop], does not respite the labours of the gardener. Half the summer will show the bridge ; the dairy opens to the lake [it is still standing, but sadly changed] ; vast woods have taken possession of the naked hills [already referred to], and the lawns slope uninterrupted to the valley."

---

[1] Potter was a firm adherent of Pitt, and evidently on most intimate and cordial terms with him. Potter was appointed Secretary to Frederick, Prince of Wales, which post he held until his death in 1751. He also held the appointment of Vice-Treasurer of Ireland, and died in 1759.

A constant guest at Allen's Bath residence, Prior Park, (before her brother knew Allen) was Sarah Fielding (the author of *David Simple*, etc.). This lady resided in a small house in Church Lane, Widcombe, called *Yew Cottage*, close to Widcombe House, and within sight of Prior Park. She was a handsome, well-bred lady, and the recipient of Allen's chivalrous attention, kindness, and bounty.[1] Allen daily passed her door on his way to and from the city, and cheered her somewhat dull existence by a kindly word. She was seldom omitted as a guest at his table, and was conveyed to Prior Park in his own carriage. She continued to live at the Cottage until the death of Allen in 1764, when she removed, for economy's sake, to the old village called *Wick* [now Bathwick Street] where she died in 1768. Her brother Henry, except during his brief residence at Twerton, lived with his sister at *Yew Cottage*, and was an honoured guest at Prior Park. Hurd, who met him only once there, described him physically as "a poor, emaciated, worn-out rake, whose gout and infirmities have got the better even of his buffoonery." Fielding, it appears, at this time was in an enfeebled state of health. He had lost none of his intellectual genius, but his strength and fire had departed, and perhaps he did not care about roasting a cold-blooded bishop. The impression still prevails that Fielding was a resident at Twerton. This belief arises from the fact that over the door of the cottage, in which he was only a lodger for, at most, ten days, there is a crest supposed to be that of the Fieldings. No man was less likely than Henry Fielding to have indulged in such a preposterous piece of vanity. The house, after Fielding's

---

[1] It would be impossible to tell, even approximately, the extent of Allen's pecuniary help and liberality either to Henry Fielding or to his excellent sister. No two writers agree, and not one quotes any trustworthy evidence. We have referred to Allen's private papers, and we give his Will *verbatim* [Appendix].

period, was occupied by a Mr. Williams, the founder of a large firm of brewers ; and he it may have been who put up the heraldic bearing in honour of the great novelist.

The Rev. Richard Graves, rector of Claverton, was, for fifty years or more, one of the best-known and most esteemed neighbours of our city. He was a wit, and a voluminous writer. His best-known work was the satire, entitled *The Spiritual Quixote*, in 3 vols. Graves was a peculiar-looking man, with a singular gait. He dressed in the clerical style of the period, *i.e., black-and-all-black*, even to the low-crowned, three-cornered black hat. Graves always carried a black, baggy umbrella, which he held before him, hanging on his open hand. His features, whilst pleasant and intellectual, wore an eager expression ; and he never walked, but trotted. He was a great favourite with Allen and all his guests. With his friend, the poet Shenstone, Graves visited Allen ; and he also tells us that he met Hoare, the painter, at Prior Park. Hoare painted Allen's portrait and that of Marshal Wade, Nash, and others. Hoare was an accomplished artist, a ripe scholar, and a very gracious man. Graves mentions also that "about the year 1752, I met Mr. Richardson,[1] in Mr. Leake's, the bookseller's, parlour

---

[1] ALLEN'S STONE YARD (BASIN). —*Tour in Great Britain*, 4 vols., 12mo, 1761. Written originally by Defoe, republished by Richardson, the novelist, in 1762, in which the following, written by him during this visit, first appeared :—

"The stone-yard of this great, because good, man, who may be styled the Genius of Bath, is on the banks of the Avon. In it is wrought the freestone dug from the quarries in Combe Down, which is another part of Odin's Down, purchased by him. He has likewise a wharf to embark the same stone in unwrought blocks, which are brought down from the quarry by an admirable tramway that runs upon a frame of timber of about a mile and a half in length, placed partly upon walls and partly upon the ground, like the waggon-ways belonging to the collieries in the North of England. Two horses draw one of these machines, generally loaded with two or three tons of stone, over the most easy part of the

(Richardson had married Leake's sister), the former telling me he was going to dine with Mr. Allen, at Prior Park. 'Twenty years ago,' Richardson said, 'I was the most obscure man in Great Britain, and now I am admitted to the company of the first characters in the Kingdom. I would have persuaded your cousin, Miss Chapone (who was then in Bath) to accompany me to Prior Park, but she said she should not like to go amongst strangers.' "

BISHOP WARBURTON.[1]

The most continuous visitor to Prior Park was William Warburton, who was introduced to Allen by Pope—as we have already shown. (See page 87.)

Warburton's friendly alliance with Pope was, to say the

descent, but afterwards its own velocity carries it down the rest, and with so much precipitation that the man who guides it is sometimes obliged to lock every wheel to stop it, which he can do with great ease by means of bolts applied to the front wheels, and levers to the back wheels. The freestone can be carried by the Avon into Bristol, whence it may be transmitted to any part of England, and the new works of St. Bartholomew's Hospital in London, as well as the Exchange of Bristol, are built with stone from Mr. Allen's quarry."

Miss Chandler, in the poetical *Description of Bath* written by her, thus mentions the machinery referred to :—

"Here is seen the new-made road and wonderful machine,
Self moving down from the mountain height
A Rock its burden of a mountain's weight."

Miss Chandler was a lady of good old Bath family, and having only a very small capital, she resolved to open a small milliner's shop at the entrance of *Wade's Passage*. Allen admired her independent spirit, and she was often a guest at his table.

[1] We desire to mention that in this article, on Warburton's relations with Prior Park, we have received very valuable assistance from a friend.

least, a curious coincidence, and had been brought about in a peculiar manner. Pope's *Essay on Man* had been published in 1733-4, and had raised a swarm of hornets about the poet's ears. Warburton himself had denounced *the rank atheism* of the Essay, which he declared to be *collected from the worst passages of the worst authors ;* but the most formidable attack came from Croussaz, a Swiss Professor, who had no difficulty in showing that the Essay was steeped in rationalism and fatalism, and that various parts of the Essay were inconsistent and self-contradictory—which was not surprising, seeing that the philosophical materials had been furnished by Boling-broke, and that Pope, without understanding them, had merely put them into verse, and supplied the poetical imagery. Pope must have felt the awkwardness of the situation and his inability to defend himself, in a case which he did not under-stand ; but at this moment Warburton, whom Pope has characterised as *the sneaking parson*, suddenly appeared upon the scene like a *deus ex machina*, much to Pope's surprise and delight, and rescued the poet from his helpless position by means of a skilful, but very sophistical, Commentary on the Essay, which he demonstrated to be free from the imputation of favouring fatalism and rejecting revelation. Pope's gratitude knew no bounds. Writing to Warburton in 1739, he says :—"You have made my system as clear as I ought to have done and could not. It is, indeed, the same system as mine, but illustrated with a ray of your own, as they say our natural body is the same still when it is glorified." What induced Warburton to step forth as the champion of Pope we can only conjecture. It may have been his love of paradox, which was almost a ruling passion with him ; or it may have been a cool calculation that he would glorify himself, as indeed he did considerably glorify himself, by an alliance with Pope. Warburton's literary vanity was gratified by an asso-ciation with Pope ; and it was through the influence of Pope's friend Murray, afterwards Lord Mansfield (to whom Pope addressed the fourth of his *Satires and Epistles*), that Warburton was appointed to the preachership of Lincoln's Inn, and afterwards to a prebend at Durham. Whatever may have been the motive, the *sneaking parson* and the writer of *rank atheism collected from the worst passages of the worst authors* forgot their differences and became fast friends. Warburton survived his friend by many years, and in 1751 honoured his memory by issuing an edition of the poet's works, in the frontispiece to which the artist—by Warburton's special instructions—made Warburton's bust larger and more prominent than Pope's, and represented light ascending from Warburton to Pope!

Having now said all that is necessary, for our purpose, of Warburton in relation to Pope, we will devote a few pages to the consideration of Warburton in relation to Allen. As we have said more than once, Warburton's visits to Prior Park commenced in 1741, at which time he was vicar at Brant-Broughton, near Newark; and there is no doubt that Allen's friendship was exceedingly valuable to Warburton. In 1745[1]

[1] In 1765 Warburton obtained the royal licence for his son, Ralph, to take the surname of Warburton-Allen. The youth died in 1771, in his twentieth year, and was buried at Gloucester.

"Near this place
lie the remains of
Ralph Allen Warburton,
the only son of
William Warburton, Lord Bishop of Gloucester,
and Gertrude his wife,
who died July 28, 1775,
aged 19 years.
He was a youth
eminently distinguished
for goodness of heart, elegance of manners,
and gracefulness of person.
How transient are human endowments!
How vain are human hopes!
Reader,
Prepare for eternity."

Warburton married Allen's favourite niece, Miss Gertrude Tucker, who remained childless until 1756, when she gave birth to her first and only child, Ralph Allen Warburton, with reference to whose paternity the finger of scandal pointed to a frequent visitor at Prior Park, the Archbishop of Canterbury's profligate second son, Thomas Potter, the boon companion of Wilkes,[1] and generally supposed to have had some share in Wilkes's filthy parody, entitled, *Essay on Woman*.[2]   In 1757 Allen's friend, Pitt, who was at that time member for Bath, procured the Deanery of Bristol for Warburton ; and three years later Warburton was, by the same influence, raised to the Bishopric of Gloucester.   From the time of his first introduction to Allen in 1741, and even after he became successively Dean of Bristol and Bishop of Gloucester Warburton lived mostly at Prior Park until Allen's death in 1764 ;[3] when Warburton and his wife came in for a legacy of £5,000 each and the rever-

[1] At this time the sister of Wilkes resided in Bath, and there is no doubt that in one of his visits to his sister he made the acquaintance of Allen.

[2] This parody on Pope's *Essay on Man* was a compound of lewdness and blasphemy. As the original was inscribed to Lord Bolingbroke, so the parody by Wilkes was inscribed to Lord Sandwich ; thus it began, "Awake, my Sandwich", instead of "Awake my St. John".   Thus, also, in ridicule of Warburton's well-known commentary, some burlesque notes were appended in Warburton's name.   Much scandal followed this vile production ; and when the question of Wilkes's breach of privilege was brought before the House of Lords, Warburton made a pompous speech, at the conclusion of which he exclaimed, that the blackest fiends in hell would disdain to keep company with Wilkes, and then asked pardon of Satan for comparing them together.   The composition was soon forgotten, and it was much regretted at the time that such ribaldry was made the subject of public animadversions, by which it received even temporary notoriety.

[3] Almost from his first introduction to Allen, Warburton preached occasionally in the private chapel at Prior Park. At Allen's request and at his cost, Warburton issued a volume of Sermons, 1745-6, preached in the chapel.

sion of the Prior Park and Claverton Estates was bequeathed
to Mrs. Warburton on Mrs. Allen's death—which took place
in 1766. It may excite surprise that a calm and unruffled
man like Allen, and a restless and explosive man like Warburton, should have maintained an unbroken friendship for
nearly a quarter of a century, but Allen was one

> " Whose sympathetic mind
> Exults in all the good of all mankind,"

and the last man in the world to pick a quarrel ; while merely
prudential considerations would be a sufficient guarantee for
the good behaviour of a self-regarding man like Warburton in
his conduct to Allen. That Warburton was supposed in some
quarters to have "sponged" on Allen is suggested by the
following anecdote. Quin the actor, in intercourse with
whom Warburton appears to have assumed patronising airs
and graces, was one evening asked by Warburton—" *the saucy
priest*" Quin calls him—to give a specimen of his dramatic
skill before the company which was assembled in Allen's
drawing-room. Quin excused himself, but offered to recite a
passage from Otway's *Venice Preserved;* and the application of the following lines was made perfectly and apprecia-
tively clear to the audience by the significant glances which
Quin cast at Allen and Warburton respectively as he dwelt
on the words " honest men" and " knaves" :—

> " Honest men
> Are the soft, easy cushions on which knaves
> Repose and fatten."

Warburton, however, was bound to Allen by something more
than by the tie of self-interest ; he was attracted to him by a
genuine admiration, amounting almost to reverence, for the
grandeur and nobility of his character, under the influence of
which " *the saucy priest* " seems to have been spell-bound. In
one of his letters he says :—" *He* (Allen) *is*, I verily believe,

the greatest character in any age of the world. You see his munificence to the Bath Hospital. This is but a small part of his charities, and charity but a small part of his virtues. I have studied his character even maliciously, to find where the weakness lies, but have studied in vain." Not only was Warburton unfaltering in his devotion to Allen, but he jealously resented even the remotest appearance of an attempt to belittle the great man; and, indeed, in this respect he was almost absurdly quick to discover offence, where an ordinary man would not suspect any. For instance, Dr. John Burton, an Oxford man and Fellow of Eton College, came to Bath with an introduction to Allen, took stock of men and things, and published his impressions in a brochure, entitled *Iter Bathoniense.* After playfully satirising the frivolities of Bath, and rather roughly—but in our opinion very justly—handling Beau Nash, whom he describes as " Master of follies, an effete, toothless, brazen-faced, shameless old man" [" *Magister ineptiarum, effœtus et edentulus senex . . . . . sine verecundia rubor immutabilis"*], Burton proceeds to exhaust on Allen the language of compliment and eulogy, contriving to perpetrate by the way a harmless, good-natured little pun, which most people would assuredly forgive. Here is the passage :—" Tandem inveni virum ; instar mille unum ; . . . . . virum inter Bathonienses suos facile principem; quem undequaque praesentem parietes ipsi . . . loquuntur ; quem illustrat gloriosa natalium obscuritas, fortunæ eundem et virtulis filium, ... virum quem non ego sane doctissimum, at certe omnium quotquot fere uspiam reperiuntur *literatissimum* appellare ausim, et *ex commercio suo literario* fructus pro merito suo uberrimos sine invidia consecutum."

[" I have at last found a man, one worth a thousand . . . . ; a man by far the chief among his fellow-citizens ; whose presence the very walls . . . everywhere proclaim ; a man whose notoriously humble birth renders the more illustrious, and shows

him to be at once the child of virtue and the favourite of fortune ; . . . . . a man whom I would not venture to call the most
learned, yet certainly of all men in the world *most conversant
with letters*, and one who, *by his connexion with letters*, has
deservedly acquired an ample and unenvied fortune."]

Of course, the words *literatissimum* (most conversant with
letters) and *ex commercio suo literario* (from his connexion with
letters) have reference to Allen's contract with the Post Office.
Few people would detect any offence in the allusion, but Warburton was furious with Burton, whom he characterises, in a
letter to Bishop Hurd, as a "*puppy*" for his "*saucy stupid joke*"
on the "man who received him so hospitably", and gibbeted
him in a note to a passage in the fourth book (lines 441-2)
of the *Dunciad*, where Dulness observes :—

> "The common Soul, of heaven's more frugal make,
> Serves but to keep fools pert and knaves awake," etc.

"Gentle Dulness ever loves a joke", Pope had said in a
previous book (ii, 34). Warburton, in his note, harks back to
this text, returns to the passage under consideration in the
fourth book, and improves the occasion at Burton's expense.[1]
Yet, if the citizens of Bath at the present day, realising Allen's
many-sided greatness as a postal reformer, as the creator of
the modern Bath stone trade, as the founder of the Bath
General Water Hospital, and as a magnet which attracted to
Bath all that was representative of the best and most interesting life of the country—in short, as a national benefactor, as a
benefactor to his city, and as the maker of Modern Bath ; if,
we say, the Bath citizens of to-day were to realise all this, and
were inspired with a desire to do honour to themselves and
tardy justice to Allen by erecting a statue to him in the most
conspicuous part of the city which he ennobled, we cannot

---

[1] On the intercession of Bishop Haytor this note was removed in
subsequent editions.

conceive more appropriate words for at least a part of the inscription than the words employed by Burton :—" *Virum inter Bathonienses suos facile principem, quem undequaque parietes ipsi loquuntur.*"

The opportunity of perpetuating Allen's memory in Bath by a monument in the Abbey and a statue in the city presented itself to Warburton on Allen's death ; but the Bishop went to work in his own wilful way. On the south side of Prior Park, in a large field, formerly the site of the ancient Grange and the Prior's farm and homestead, now popularly known as Monument Field, the proud prelate resolved to erect a monument to his friend—not in the city of Allen's labours and philanthropy, but away from the busy haunts of man in a spot unprotected from the mischief-loving wayfarer. Not only was the spot ill-chosen, but the monument itself—a circular tower enclosed in a triangle—is devoid of all merit and interest, and nothing could be colder and balder than the inscription (composed by Bishop Hurd) placed on a slab over the door :—

" Memoriæ sacrum
Optimi viri, Randulphii Allen.
Qui virtutem veram simplicemque colis,
Venerare hoc saxum."

The slab and the inscription have long since disappeared, and within thirty years after Allen's death the very purport of the monument was almost forgotten ; while at the present day there are scarcely twenty people in Bath who have the slightest idea what the fantastic edifice means. Allen, however, is not forgotten by us ; whereas Warburton, though he lived in Bath so many years, and was identified with her best known and most honoured citizens, is almost unknown, except to the curious few amongst us ; nor is there a single local tradition, or any event of local interest, popularly associated with his name.

MONUMENT ERECTED TO THE MEMORY OF RALPH ALLEN,
BY BISHOP WARBURTON,

We have now concluded our account of Warburton in his relations to Pope and Allen ; but a few words on Warburton, apart from those relations, may be of interest to the general reader, who is referred for fuller and more detailed information to the Reverend Selby Watson's interesting *Life of War-burton*, to which work we take this opportunity of acknowledging our obligations.

William Warburton was born in Newark towards the end of 1698, and received the greater part of his education at Oakham Grammar School. In 1714 he was articled to a solicitor for five years ; but at the expiration of his articles he renounced the law, and began to study for Holy Orders, which he entered in 1723, having received great assistance in the necessary preparation from his cousin, the Rev. William Warburton, Head Master of Newark Grammar School, who generously sacrificed to his youthful relative all the time that he could spare from scholastic duties. The future Bishop at once plunged into that career of authorship and controversy, for which he afterwards became so conspicuous. In 1728 he was presented by Sir Robert Sutton to the living of Brant-Broughton, near Newark, which he held till 1746 ; and it was in these eighteen years, during a life of seclusion and study little interrupted by parochial duties, that he laid the foundations of his vast knowledge and wide reading. How during this interval he became acquainted with Pope, who introduced him to Allen, and how Warburton was materially benefited by his associations with Pope and Allen, we have previously shown ; but Warburton had already established himself as an able writer and controversialist before contracting an alliance with these two powerful men.

We do not propose to detail or criticise Warburton's numerous works and pamphlets, but we cannot forbear a passing allusion to his *magnum opus*, generally known as *The Divine Legation of Moses.* The title of the book is familiar to every reader of English literature ; but most people have forgotten, or never knew, the object of the treatise and the arguments by which it was supported. The facts are very simple. The absence of the doctrine of a future state from the Mosaic Dispensation had been fastened on by the Deists as a decisive argument against the divine origin of the Jewish religion. At this point Warburton stepped in, and undertook to meet the Deists on their own ground, and from the facts alleged to deduce an opposite conclusion. Hence the full title of his work was "*The Divine Legation of Moses Demonstrated, on the Principles of a Religious Theist, from the Omission of the Doctrine of a Future State in the Jewish Dispensation.*" If it can be shown—and Warburton scarcely conceived the possibility of disputing the propositions—that (1) the doctrine of a future state of rewards and punishment has been accepted by all mankind as necessary to the well-being of society, and that (2) such a doctrine is not to be found in the Mosaic system, then, says Warburton, "one would think we might proceed to the conclusion :—*Therefore the Law of Moses is of divine origin.*"

Of course Warburton did not reach his conclusion in this simple way, or without first of all laboriously establishing his premises ; and in doing this he fetched a wide compass, being resolved—as he said—"to stretch the inquiry high and wide". Handling a great variety of topics, and covering a vast deal of ground, he presented a very extended front, of which the enemy was not slow to take advantage. Omitting all the numerous side-paths into which Warburton strayed, it is evident that his argument, as above stated, is exposed to all the attacks which can possibly be made against an argument, it being not difficult to plausibly dispute each premiss separately, and then—even assuming the validity of the premisses—to claim a *non sequitur.* To say nothing of the strained conclusion, which was vigorously attacked by Bayle,

L

Warburton had to face the strenuous opposition of classical scholars in his attempts to bolster up his first premiss by squeezing into all the ancient polities an implied belief in a future state ; nor did he fare better at the hands of theologians in his resolute efforts to establish his second premiss by stamping out of the Mosaic system all the supposed germs of a belief in a future state. *The Divine Legation*, however, made a stir, and found favour in some influential quarters ; and though the argument may not convince, and is now generally forgotten, it cannot fail to impress the curious reader with a sense of the author's powerful and versatile intellect. The strength and weakness of Warburton are traceable in this work, as in all his other numerous writings. Everywhere we see the vigorous understanding, the strong and retentive memory, and the wide reading of the author ; but it was considered that he read too much and too fast to assimilate all that he read ; hence Bentley's famous dictum : *"This man has a monstrous appetite, but a very bad digestion"*—a charge which Warburton seems indirectly to admit in one of his letters. The want also of a regular academic training often suggests itself, for Warburton left school before he was sixteen years of age, was then articled to the law for five years, and finally qualified for Orders without proceeding to a University.[1] Of Hebrew he knew practically nothing. With Greek writers his acquaintance was mostly second-hand, obtained (like Pope's knowledge of Greek) through the medium of French translations. A typical instance of this is given in the Rev. Selby Watson's *Life of Warburton*, p. 629. In a note on Shakespeare, Warburton quotes the following lines from the *Phœnissæ* of Euripides,

Ἐγὼ γὰρ οὐδέν, μᾶτερ, ἀποκρύψας ἐρῶ.
Ἄστρων ἀνέλθοιμ᾽ ἡλίου πρὸς ἀντολάς,
Καὶ γῆς ἔνερθε, δύνατος ὢν δράσαι τάδε,

[1] The honorary degree of D.D., which was refused by the Oxford University, was conferred upon him by Cambridge.

and then adds the English translation : " I will not, madam, disguise my thoughts. I could scale heaven, I could descend to the very entrails of the earth, if so be that by that price I could obtain a kingdom." This rendering was soon shown to have been taken bodily from Brumoy's French translation in the *Théâtre de Grecs :* " Je ne déguiserai point ici mes sentimens, Madame ; j'escalerois le ciel, et je descendrois aux entrails de la terre," etc., etc. Warburton's knowledge of Latin, though extensive, lacked all the higher attributes of fine scholarship. His knowledge of the language employed by the great Elizabethan writers was ludicrously defective, though he presumed to annotate Spenser and Shakespeare ; and this ignorance of Elizabethan English often implies ignorance of Latin. For instance, when Spenser says of " the tree of life " that God

> " Did it call
> The tree of life, the *crime* of our first father's fall."
>
> (*F. Q.,* xi, 46.)

Warburton observes in a note : " I apprehend Spenser did not call it by any such senseless designation, but that it is a mere blunder of the printer, and that the poet wrote :

> ' Did it call
> The tree of life, the *time* of our first father's fall ;'

i.e., he gave it that name at the *time* of our first father's fall. The particle *at* is frequently omitted by writers of that age." Yet Warburton ought to have known that *crime* is one of Spenser's numerous Latinisms, and that *crimen* in Latin may signify the *cause* of a crime as well as the crime itself. See Virgil, xii, 600—

> " Causam clamat *crimenque* caputque malorum."

Warburton's unfitness to edit Shakespeare is best illustrated by his tinkering with the line in *King Lear,*

> " I 'll speak a prophecy *or e'er* I go,"

L 2

where Warburton says that *or e'er* is not English, and for *or* substitutes *or two*, making the line run thus :—

"I 'll speak a proph'cy *or two*, e'er I go."

Yet the Elizabethan parallels for *or e'er* are not far to seek. Compare *Macbeth*: "dying *or e'er* they sicken." Also Psalm lviii : "*or ever* your pot be made hot with thorns."

In Warburton's controversial writings one feature stands out with unpleasant prominence—the merciless way he chastised his opponents with the valour of his tongue ; and there are probably few authors from whose writings may be gathered such a collection of bitter and abusive epithets. His vanity and arrogance could brook no contradiction, and woe betide the man who incurred his displeasure. We must remember, however, that Warburton, with his bold and fearless spirit, was essentially a fighting man, and that

"Men
Are as the time is ; to be tender-minded
Does not become a sword."

Moreover, the amenities of controversy were not so gentle as they are now. Hard words were the fashion, and it is quite possible for a man of vigorous intellect and strong feelings to express himself roughly without being hard-hearted. That Warburton had a warm corner in his heart is evident. His relations with his mother and his sister bring out very pleasantly his filial affection and brotherly love. He was a fond father, and doted on his promising son—*half his soul* he calls him—after whose premature death in 1775, the Bishop made a final settlement of his affairs, then ceased to take any interest in life, and gradually fell into a state of imbecility, in which he remained up to the time of his death in 1779. He was deeply attached to his "dear wife", whom he commends to Bishop Hurd's care in a note attached to his will in 1776. He appears to have been a good husband, for we are told that

Mrs. Warburton always seemed to feel a peculiar satisfaction, both during his life and after his death, in recounting his many excellencies. Above all, he was capable of gratitude. He never forgot the services of his cousin, the Head Master of Newark Grammar School, whose virtues he commemorated in a glowing epitaph. We have seen his generous, almost reverent, testimony to Allen's royalty of nature ; and he was equally steadfast to his first patron, Sir Robert Sutton. Pope, in his *Satires*, had pilloried Sir Robert ; but Warburton used his acquaintance with Pope to write a warm defence of Sutton, and succeeded in getting the name erased from the *Satires*. Lastly, if he was, like Cardinal Wolsey,

> " Lofty and sour to those that loved him not,"

he was, also, like that proud prelate,

> " To those men that sought him sweet as summer."

This we see in the case of Hurd, afterwards Bishop Hurd, who sought his friendship by extravagant compliments, maintained it by prudent subserviency, and finally wrote a life of his friend, which overflows with fulsome panegyric.

Warburton's death occurred in 1779, comparatively unnoticed ; and two years afterwards his widow married the Rev. Stafford Smith, the late Bishop's chaplain, who was presented by Hurd to the vicarage of Fladbury in Worcestershire. The epitaph to Warburton in Gloucester Cathedral is by Hurd.

> " To the Memory of
> William Warburton, D.D.,
> For more than Nineteen Years Bishop of this See :
> A Prelate
> Of the most sublime Genius and Exquisite Learning,
> Both which talents
> He employed, through a long life,
> in the support
> of what he firmly believed
> the Christian Religion,

and of what he esteemed the best Establishment of it,
the Church of England.
He was born at Newark-upon-Trent,
Dec. 24, 1698 ;
was consecrated Bishop of Gloucester, Jan. 20, 1760 ;
Died at his Palace, in this City, June 7, 1779,
and was buried near this place."

THE REVEREND RICHARD GRAVES AND WARBURTON.

In his *Diary*, Graves says :—

"At the first visit which I made at Prior Park [1757], I met Dr. Warburton for the first time, whom I ventured to pronounce one of the politest men I had ever seen. Those who only know him as engaged in controversy may be surprised at this. But I found him so attentive to everyone who spoke, particularly to myself, who am the worst of all possible speakers, setting everything that I said in the clearest light, and, in short, paying such deference to his *inferiors, as most of the company were* (for he was then Dean of Bristol), that he had certainly a claim to the character of a polite man, if destitute of superficial gentleness of manner. Indeed, when contradicted, or opposed, his antagonist would probably have no reason to triumph, as appeared on many occasions. It must be owned, likewise, that he treated some of his most respectable adversaries, as Dr. Stebbing, for instance, and Dr. Grey, with too much haughtiness and contempt. When Mr. Allen gave an entertainment to the Corporation [1757] on Mr. Pitt being chosen M.P. for Bath, Dr. Warburton sat at the head of the table. An old bencher of Lincoln's Inn, Mr. Keck, to whom I sat opposite, was telling a gentleman, who had asked him, whom they had got for a preacher now Dr. Warburton had resigned, 'Oh ! we have the finest preacher in England, Dr. Asheton.' 'Yes, sir,' said Warburton, who overheard him, 'I would have recommended a man of some learning to you, but you were determined to have a mob preacher.' Poor Keck drew in his horns, and made no reply."

Warburton was very deeply attached to Allen, but there must have been times when the good man could not help being tried by the arrogant, overbearing conduct of Warburton to Allen's guests. These defects of temper and disposition, if they were not due to some mental infirmity, might well expose him to the epigrammatic lines written upon him :—   ·

> "The first entitled to the place
> Of honour, both by gown and grace,
> Who never let occasion slip,
> To take right hand of fellowship ;
> And was so proud that should he meet
> The twelve apostles in the street,
> He 'd turn his nose up at them all,
> And shove his Saviour to the wall."

Warburton was unpopular in the city, his cold, haughty bearing repelling his equals and frightening his inferiors. At length he was very much avoided in the city, and was scarcely known by the citizens at large.

CLAVERTON MANOR.

Claverton, the old historic manor of the Estcourts, the Bassetts, the Holders, and the Skrines, as already mentioned, legally became Allen's property in 1752, by Equity of Redemption, but it was not until 1757 that he paid off the mortgage of £16,000 held upon the estate by William Skrine. The house, of which only the dairy now remains, was a beautiful mansion, standing on the eastern side of the terrace and steps.[1]

Tradition assigns the creation of this house to *John of Padua*, who is also said to have designed Kingston House at Bradford-on-Avon, and also Longleat. There was a good deal of romance mixed up with the Manor House. Estcourt represented Bath from 1695 to 1698, his town-house being in Broad Street, and a very worthy dignified old citizen he was. Bassett sat as the representative of Bath from 1640 to 1645, when, for no other alleged reason than his loyalty to the Crown, he was expelled. This same Bassett, entertaining Sir E. Hungerford and others

---

[1] The Claverton Estate is again in the possession of the Skrine family, the present owner being Henry Duncan Skrine, Esq., the owner also of the opposite estate of Warleigh Manor.

The Terrace, Claverton Manor.

in 1643, was fired at by a small force of Parliamentarians from the opposite hill. The ball entered the guest room, passed over the party, and lodged in the chimney wall. A skirmish in the valley on the Warleigh side took place a few days afterwards; three soldiers of the Parliamentarians and one Royalist were slain, and were afterwards buried in Claverton Churchyard.[1]

When Allen took possession of the estate, he was much pleased with the house, and brought down with him Warburton, Hurd, and Mason, the poet; to meet whom, Graves, the Rector, was invited. Allen usually brought his visitors once a week from Prior Park to dine and wander about the lovely domain, around and about which he had made excellent roads.

Allen had a very warm regard for Graves, who, being an excellent scholar, received pupils. Until Allen took possession of the Manor House, it was occupied by Graves, the rectory being too small. Allen, however, enlarged the rectory and built a school-room for his worthy friend. When Warburton's son was eight or nine years old he was sent to Graves to be educated, and remained there until he was ready for the university. About this time, or a little earlier, Potter introduced a gentleman at Prior Park named Strahan, who was, we believe, a clerk in the House of Commons, and who became a very regular visitor at Prior Park and Claverton. This gentleman conceived a great liking for Warburton's son, and became a regular correspondent of Allen's. Strahan wrote a very pretty hand, and conveyed much of the social and political gossip of the day to his Bath friend. Later on will be found an interesting account of John Wilkes and his trial in the House of Commons from the pen of Strahan.

[1] In the *Proceedings of the Bath Field Club*, vol. vi, p. 167, will be found a full account of this skirmish, by H. D. Skrine, Esquire, the present owner of Claverton and Warleigh.

Politics, Party, and Pitt.

We have already referred to the interest taken by Allen in politics, and the motives by which he was guided in his relations with Marshal Wade.[1] That Allen was an earnest Whig in all respects his later conduct shows. In every election subsequent to Wade's death there is no doubt the choice of candidates was to some extent determined by Allen's judgment. Nor can any blame be cast upon him in respect of this. Even the caricaturists of his day have no stronger censure to cast upon him than that he was permitted by his colleagues to have his own way ; but having regard to the standing, intelligence, and independence of many of those colleagues, we think the inference too broad, and that it is not too much to assume that one feeling of general confidence pervaded the whole body. There are two facts that stand out very prominently as marking the character of the Bath corporate body from the earliest part of the century to its close : (firstly) the absence of all deliberate jobbery and wrong-doing ; and (secondly) the men who were chosen, as will be seen by the following chapter, did honour to the city— they were men incapable of lending themselves to any of the corrupt and demoralizing practices only too common in that age of pocket boroughs, corrupt and complacent corporations.

The rupture with Pitt was, perhaps, the cause of more distress to Allen than any public event that ever concerned him ; and of this we shall have more to say in connection with the political squib—"The One-Headed Corporation"—and the correspondence with his illustrious friend, Pitt.

---

[1] Some years after Wade's death Allen erected an Obelisk, of triangular form, on the south side of the Prior Park mansion. There was on each face a handsome tablet, on which was engraved the civil and military achievements of the worthy Marshal. The obelisk was removed, we believe, by Mr. Thomas,

It was said by Thicknesse that Allen refused, from selfish motives, to become one of the representatives of Bath in Parliament, but that he took care to choose the members himself;[1] that is, he exercised unbounded influence over the Council. It may be well to see how he used his power. Allen was a warm adherent of the Hanoverian dynasty.[2] He was, as we have shown, attached to it by ties of interest, conviction, and by personal connection with Marshal Wade. The Marshal, as the representative of Bath from 1722 to 1748 (the year of his death), had little sympathy with any particular shade of politics which existed amongst the "Revolution party";[3] he cared chiefly for the dynasty. The Marshal was much more than the representative of the city in Parliament; he was its fast friend; he lived in it and loved it, and identified himself with its local institutions. So long as the Marshal lived, Allen seems to have contented himself with giving him and his colleague a steady and loyal support. The Jacobite and the High Tory party were relatively small and insignificant; but the great Whig party was split into two separate

---

[1] The fact that Allen was a Government contractor disqualified him.

[2] During the '45 Allen raised, clothed, drilled, officered, a company of volunteers, and provided drill-ground for them at his own cost of £2,000, during the two years of agitation. Richard Jones was the Lieutenant of the *corps;* and to this faithful *clerk of the works* was entrusted the building of Newton Bridge. On the Lower Bristol Road, opposite Newton Park, whence the brook flows, there was a sudden dip which frequently became impassable after a moderate downfall of rain. There was much grumbling, and certain proposals made to erect a bridge to span the hollow, which came to nothing. To obviate the great public inconvenience, in which he only suffered in common with the public at large, Allen undertook the cost and responsibility of building a good, substantial bridge, of which Lysons, the eminent antiquary, left a beautiful water-colour drawing, now in our possession. This is quoted as another example of Allen's public spirit.

[3] A term applied to the political party favourable to the Revolution of 1688, the Hanoverian dynasty, and Whig principles.

factions, and the conflicts in Parliament were almost limited to those two sections, Allen choosing the section which was led by William Pitt, in opposition to Walpole.

At the general election of 1747, Marshal Wade was again chosen a representative of the city, in conjunction with Robert Henley, who was descended from an ancient Somersetshire family. Henley's father was Anthony Henley, a man of great distinction, the friend of Dorset, Sunderland, Swift, Pope, and Arbuthnot. Generous and bounteous, learned and witty, he was one of the most popular men of his time. He represented Andover, and afterwards, till his death, Melcombe Regis. Considerable wealth came to him through his wife, who was sole heiress of the Hon. Penegrine Bertie, second son of Montague, Earl of Lindsey. Robert Henley, the second son of the marriage, was born in 1708, and ultimately succeeded to the family estate[1] on the death of his elder brother, Anthony. Educated at Westminster and Christ Church, he was entered at the Middle Temple, and called to the bar in 1732. Handsome in person, jovial in habits, he used to pass his vacations at Bath, and was one of the best known of the fashionable men at " The Bear." He was the gayest of the gay in the Pump-room in the morning, and amongst the most jovial of the topers in " The Bear" at night. His briefs at this time did not give him much trouble, but he cultivated the friendship of the Bath citizens, and was singularly popular. Lord Campbell relates the romantic story of his courtship and marriage, which is very similar to that previously told by Lord Henley,[2] in his *Life of the Earl oj Northington.*

[1] " The Grange," Hampshire. The original mansion was built by Inigo Jones. When the property passed into the possession of the first Lord Ashburton, he pulled down the old house and built the present magnificent mansion on the site.

[2] The Earl had eight children—three sons and five daughters. Only one son survived his father, and he seems to have been a man of unusual promise. His abilities were considerable, and his manners popular. In

There was at Bath, for the benefit of the waters, a very young girl of exquisite beauty, who from illness had lost the use of her limbs so completely that she was only able to appear in public wheeled about in a chair. She was the daughter and co-heiress of Sir Jno. Husband of Ipsley, in Warwickshire, who was the last male of a time-honoured race, whom Dugdale states to have been lords of that manor in lineal succession from the Conquest. Henley, struck by the charms of her face, contrived to be introduced to her, when he was still more fascinated by her conversation. His admiration soon ripened into a warm and tender attachment, which he had reason to hope was reciprocated. But it seemed as if he had fallen in love with a Peri, and that he must for ever be contented with sighing and worshipping at her shrine, when suddenly the waters produced so effectual and complete a cure that Miss Husband was enabled to comply with the custom of the place by hanging up her votive crutches to the nymph of the spring, and to dance the "Minuet de la Cœur" at the Lower Rooms with her lover. Soon after, with the full consent of her family, she gave her hand to the suitor who had so sedulously attended her. To the end of a long life she continued to enjoy a most perfect state of health, and their affection remaining unabated, she gave him that first of human blessings—a serene and happy home.

They were married by Henley's old schoolfellow, Bishop Newton, at the chapel in South Audley Street. After describing his settling in London and the family property descending to him, the memoir goes on :—

1783, he was appointed by the Coalition Ministry Lord-Lieutenant of Ireland. The daughters all formed high alliances, but they all died without issue, except the Lady Elizabeth, who married Sir Morton Eden, who was raised to the Irish Peerage by the title of Lord Henley. His son (who wrote his Grandfather's Life) married the sister of the second Sir R. Peel, and left by her a son, the present Lord Henley.

"After his marriage, Henley continued to go frequently to Bath, carrying his wife along with him.   He now led comparatively a sober life, but occasionally he would indulge in his old convivial habits, and, by his toasts and his stories and his very agreeable manners, he ingratiated himself so much with the Mayor and Common Council, forming a very small corporation, with the right of returning Members to Parliament exclusively vested in them, that they made him their Recorder, and agreed to elect him at the next vacancy one of their representatives ; being swayed, perhaps, not merely by his personal good qualities, but the prospect of his being now able to show his gratitude for their kindness to him.   Accordingly, on the dissolution of Parliament, which took place in the summer of the year 1747, he was elected a representative for Bath along with Field-Marshal Wade."

It is certain that he had ingratiated himself with the Marshal and Ralph Allen, and although he never distinguished himself as a speaker, he was a good lawyer and a fair debater. He was subsequently Solicitor-General to the Prince of Wales (afterwards George III).   In November 1756, he succeeded Murray as Attorney-General to the Crown, and on December 2 in the same year, on the issue of a new writ, was re-elected. In the following year he was made Lord Keeper by Pitt (by whom he was succeeded in the representation), an office which rendered his seat vacant and precluded him from sitting in the Commons, though it did not involve a peerage.   In 1760, the Lord Keeper Henley was elevated to the dignity of Lord Chancellor and the Earldom of Northington.   He held the Great Seal nine years, in two reigns (Geo. II and Geo. III), and during four administrations.

Marshal Wade died in 1748, and was succeeded in the representation by Sir John Ligonier, a distinguished military commander.   Sir John was re-elected at the general election in 1754.   In 1757 he was created an Irish Viscount ; at the following general election, in 1761, he was re-elected in conjunction with the same colleague, William Pitt ; and in 1763 he was made a Peer of the Realm as Earl Ligonier, when Sir John Sebright, Bart., was elected.

CORRESPONDENCE IN RELATION TO THE CONTEMPLATED VACANCY BY THE ADVANCEMENT OF HENLEY.

To Ralph Allen, Esquire.

" DEAR Sʀ,—Ever since I received your very friendly Letter, I have been endeavouring to acknowledge it. It is with the utmost Difficulty that I secure a moment for that Purpose now. All the Fatigues I ever underwent in Parliamᵗ were trifling to what we suffer now. We have sat six days upon the Enquiry into the Loss of Minorca. Sometimes we have sat 'till two in the morning, and never rose earlier than ten at Night. My Office on the Occasion confines me to a Chair the whole Time, so that it is with Difficulty I can by Exercise and Air lay in a sufficient stock of strength in the morning to undergo the Fatigues of the Evening. I I am afraid I do not keep the Accᵗˢ quite even, being obliged to spare a little from the Stock, wᶜʰ before was not abundant.

"Your kind congratulations on the complete Recovery of our Girl are but fresh marks of a friendship perfectly felt, and with the warmest Grati- tude. We have laid aside all Cares, but for her Beauty, and the Con- noisseurs in Faces say we need not suffer Apprehensions even on that Accᵗ.

"The Part you have taken in the Honours lately done to Mr. Pitt by the Corporation of Bath, is understood by him as it ought to be. He has been disabled from using a Pen by the Gout in his right Arm, wᶜʰ he is obliged to carry in a sling. He tells me he has made Shift to sign his Name to a Letter of Thanks, and he wishes that if that Letter shᵈ be printed, as probably it will in the Bath Papers, it shᵈ be done from a very correct Copy, as mankind are extremely alert in searching even for single Words to found some Accusation against him.

"When I shall be able to set out for Bath I cannot yet guess. After the Enquiry is over, I have some Business wᶜʰ will detain me a Day or two. But when the Enquiry will be finished, is a Question wᶜʰ no one can form the least Judgmᵗ of. As my Girl has been so long recovered, and as neither I nor my Servant will bring with us a single Garment wᶜʰ we have worn in London, I shall hope to come even without the Suspicion of Infection, of wᶜʰ the Dʳˢ· assure me there has been none this fortnight. When it was greatest there was not much, since the little Lad who attended upon me the whole Time my Girl was ill has not been fortunate enough to catch the Distemper. But I insist that Mʳˢ· Warburton shall tell me upon Honour whether Mrs. Allen or she shall have the least Apprehensions of me.

" Need I say how much I am bound to love and honour you and all Yours ?

" Yours most faithfull,

" Thursday, Apr. 27th, 1757.   "Tho. Potter."

————

To Thomas Potter, Esquire.

" Dear Sir,—I am very thankful to you for your last friendly Letter to me, and hope that we shall soon have the pleasure here which you are so good as to intend us.

" I was this morning much surpris'd, as well as concerned, to see an Address printed in the *Bath Journal*, from that Corporation to Mr. Pitt and Mr. Legge, that was never offered to their consideration. My great regard for them, as well as a due attention to my own character, obliges me publickly to advertize again'st this Imposition. Of which advertisement I have under this cover troubled you with a Copy, as well as a Letter wch Mr. Clutterbuck sent to me this morning on this subject.

" For your own and Mr. Pitt's private information, I beg Leave to supp'y you the few words wch I spoke on that occasion in the Town Hall.

" P.S.—The word *over-proud* in the Second paragraph of Mr. Pitt's answers to the Corporation must be a mistake, and if reprinted, will, I presume, be corrected."

" R. A."

The following correspondence also passed on the occasion:—

A Copy of Mr. Clutterbuck's Letter to R. Allen.

" Sir,—I have sent the Resolutions litterally as it is inserted in the Council book. I deliver'd your Message to the Mayor, who desires his Compliments to you, and says that as He thought something was necessary to be deliver'd, the Gentlemen with the Boxes, He sent the Address inserted in the News papers on the presumption it wou'd not give offence to an individual of the Corporation, and would have sent it Seperately to them for their perusal but the time would not permit.

" I am,

" Bath, 2nd May 1757.   " (Sign'd) Lewis Clutterbuck."

To Thomas Potter, Esquire.

"Bath, June 23, 1757.

"SIR,—Your obliging Favour, dated the 20th, came to Hand yesterday morning at eight : in it you hint at a conversation that pass'd between us in Regard to Mr. Pitt's being a Candidate for this City. I remember at that Time I set forth to you the Connections that were between Mr. Langton[1] and his Friends, and the Improbability of their desisting from the Intention of serving him till a generall Election.

"I immediately on the Receipt of your Letter conven'd my Friends on the Business express'd in it, which I apprehended was unknown to any other Persons. But at the first onset of Treaty with our Party I found the Town was canvassing in Favour of Mr. Pitt.

"Mr. Langton was sent to, and as his Resolutions are to offer himself a Candidate, his Friends are determined to serve him.[2]

"I should have given you an Answer sooner, but as the Affair was circumstanc'd possibly could not.

---

[1] Grandson of Sir Joseph Langton of Newton Park, who was one of the Representatives of Bath from 1690 to 1695. At this time there was no connection between the Langton and the Grenville (Temple) families. Earl Temple was created Marquis of Buckingham ; and his son assumed, by royal licence, 15th Nov. 1799, the additional surnames of *Brydges-Chandos*, and was created *Earl Temple, of Stowe*, with limitation, on failure of issue male under the *former* patent, to *Anne-Eliza-Mary*, his granddaughter. This lady married the late W. H. P. Gore-Langton, and her eldest son inherits the Earldom of Temple, of Stowe.

The Marquis above referred to was further elevated, 4th Feb. 1822, to the *Marquessate of Chandos* and *Dukedom of Buckingham and Chandos*. He married, 16th April 1796, Anna-Eliza, daughter and sole heir of James Brydges, 3rd and last Duke of Chandos of the family of Brydges, and by that lady (who died 15th May, 1836) left at his decease, 17th Jan. 1839, an only son, Richard-Plantagenet, the second duke, who left one son, Richard-Plantagenet-Campbell, third and last duke, who died in 1889 without male issue.

[2] It is clear from this letter and the preceding one by the Town Clerk, Clutterbuck, that, at this time, the writers did not desire "to serve Mr. Pitt."

M

"I and my Friends really have the same due Sense and Regard for Mr. Pitt as we have hitherto possess'd, and should be glad of testifying that Regard when we have an Opportunity of doing it.

"I am y^r most hum. Servt,

"EDWARD BUSHELL COLLIBEE.

" P.S.—Some of our Friends are absent, but when they return we shall have their Sentiments, which will resolve us how far we can serve Mr. Pitt. But you require such a speedy Answer that I cannot possibly say more than what I have as above.

" Deliver'd in at the Office 40 minutes after 12 in the morning."

[Collibee was Mayor of Bath on this and other occasions.]

To Ralph Allen, Esquire.

" Sunday night, near nine o'clock.

"DEAR SIR,—Your second xpress being this moment come in, I think it necessary to answer it in the same manner to prevent the Anxiety you may be under from a longer Delay. With Difficulty I have prevailed on Mr. Pitt to accept the Invitation sent by the Corporation, and without the Assistance of Ld Temple, whom I carried to give Weight to my Advice, perhaps I sh^d have failed in it. But an Answer in Form cannot be sent till to-morrow night, because, tho' I verily believe that every publick Promotion will be fixed tomorrow, yet at present it is not certain that Mr. Henley will vacate his seat till after the Parlm^t is prorogued, in w^h case it w^d be highly inconvenient for Mr. Pitt to be out of Parlm^t at the beginning of next Session. But this promotion being settled, and the Kg. being apprised of it, it is intended that Mr. Pitt sh^d take some office expressly to vacate his seat, which will be the highest complim^t that he can pay the Corporation. But I find it absolutely impracticable for him to think of getting down to the Election on acc^t of the arrear of business in the Secretary's office, not a stroke having been done in it since he quitted in April. But I shall certainly attend his Election in Bath, and the moment it is over proceed to my own at Oakhampton. Mr. Pitt is highly thankful for your invitation to P. Park, which he hopes to accept before the Winter. Sr Robert Henley has promised to resign the Recordership when we chuse he sh^d, and to keep it till then.

"He thinks it will be best to chuse a new Recorder while the Corporation is harmonious. He mentioned Mr. Pratt as a fit person, but, if you approve it, I have many reasons wch induce me to take it myself, having had an Education at the Bar, and being, I trust, qualified for it.

"Y^r faithfull and aff^t

"THO. POTTER.

" I propose returning from Oakhampton to drink the waters, and have taken the liberty to send to my wife to meet me at Prior Park, and to stay till you go to Weymouth."

To Edward Bushell Collibee, Esquire.

"Tuesday, June 28th, 1757.

"MR. MAYOR,—Give me leave to present to you, and thro' you to the Gentlemen of the Corporation of the City of Bath, my most respectfull and warmest acknowledgments for the high mark of their favour and Confidence in vouchsafeing to think of me for their Representative in Parliament. I have long ambition'd the honour of a Seat there, derived from a Body so independent, and so truely respectable as the City of Bath, and which can never fail to reflect Lustre and impart weight to whoever they shall be pleased to think not unworthy of so high and honourable a Trust. As soon as the necessity of affairs will permit me, on my return again to business, to be absent from my attendance on his Majesty's Commands, I propose to wait on the Corporation in Person, and to assure Them more particularly of the deep and warm Sentiments of Respect and Gratitude with which I am, and shall ever be, devoted to the City of Bath and to every member of the Corporation.

"I am, with the greatest consideration, Mr. Mayor and Gentlemen of the Corporation,

"Your most Obliged and most Obedient,

"humble Servant,

"W. PITT."

To Ralph Allen, Esquire.

"Tuesday, June 28th, 1757.

"DEAR SIR,—The repeated instances of your kind friendship, and too favourable opinion of your faithfull Servant, are such and so many, that thanks and acknowledgements are quite inadequate. Give me leave to present them to you, with a heart so truely yours as, on that account, makes me hope your goodness will accept them for something. I send open to you, for your perusal, two letters for Mr. Mayor, one private, in answer to his receiv'd yesterday, the other for the Corporation. If you will be so good to seal them, and order them to be delivered to Mr. Mayor, I shall be much obliged to you. You will please to observe I have prepared the Corporation for my not being able to attend them in person at my Election, the thing will be utterly impossible, and I trust the necessity of affairs and my indispensable attendance on His Majesty will excuse me. I shall be better able towards autumn to wait on the Corporation, and hope no impression of want of due respect will remain, when the peculiarity of my situation, at the present moment, is considered. I must in this, as in all the rest, rely on your goodness and friendship to help me out of my distress.

> " I am with my whole Heart,
> " Dear Sir,
> "Your ever obliged and Affectionate Servant,
> "W. PITT.

" My best respects to Mrs. Allen and Mrs. Warburton."

To Ralph Allen, Esquire.

" Tuesday, June 28th.

" DEAR SIR,—This is to go in an Express Mr. Pitt sends to Bath, in order to inform you, and likewise the Mayor, from whom in the name of Mr. Langton and his friends he has received a very polite Letter of Invitation, that matters are at last arranged in such a manner as will vacate Mr. Pitt's seat for Oakhampton, and enable him to be chosen at Bath. He tells the Mayor that he is determined, if he can obtain his Majestie's leave, and the publick business will permitt, to come down to Bath at the Election; but as we know the publick business will not permitt, it is agreed that I should attend and represent him. We are all to kiss hands to morrow, but no new Writs will issue till Tuesday, July 5th, when the Parl₁ meets for that purpose, and in order to be prorogued.

" As I must first attend Mr. Pitt's Election at Bath, and then go to my own at Oakhampton, it is necessary for me to precipitate the first and procrastinate the last. The writ issuing the 5th of July may be at Bath the 7th, and if Mr. Clutterbuck will get the Undersheriff to attend that day, he may make out immediately his precept to the Mayor, who may proclaim the Election the evening of the 7th, for Monday, the 11th. And I can manage as to defer that at Oakhampton to the 16th, whᵇ will give me time to visɪ the Electors of Bath and return Mr. Pitt's thanks before I set out for Oakhampton. But tho' the Writ for the new Election may not be in Bath till the 7th, it is not necessary that I sh^d stay from Prior Park so long. When I shall see it, I cannot now fix with certainty, but I know that till I do see it I shall be impatient. Sr Robert Henley is Ld Keeper, and now it seems Ld Halifax did not actually resign, but only threatened to do it.

"I am, with the kindest affection and regard,

"Dr Sir,

"Y^r most faithfull,

"THO. POTTER."

To the Right Hon. Mr. Pitt.

"Prior Park, June 29, 1757.

"DEAR SIR,—This morning, at nine o'clock, I received the obliging Letter which you honour'd me with, by an Express, with that which you was pleased to enclose for our Mayor, which, in obeydience to your commands, I immediately read, Seal'd, and Sent to Him.

"I have the Satisfaction to tell you that now every thing at Bath is just as you wish it, which makes me very happy ; for tis Impossible for any Expression, to shew you how much and how respectfully I am, Dear Sir,

"Your most hon'd and most obed' Serv't,

"R. A.

"My Wife and Mrs Warburton begs your acceptance of their hearty thanks and best wishes, and that Lady Hester[1] will permit them to send Her Ladyship their respectful Complm^{ts}."

To Ralph Allen, Esquire.

"Whitehall, June 30th, 1757.

"DEAR SIR,—The writ for Bath will be moved tomorrow, Sir Robert Henley having receiv'd the great seal this day.

"What I now beg leave to trouble you about is that you wou'd be so good to employ a person to be trusted to prepare the Under Sheriff and get the Precept ready, so that the election may be proclaimed time enough to fix the Election for Saturday, ye 9th of July. The writ will be in Somersetshire by the 3rd inst., and Tuesday is the latest day for the Proclamation, in order to go to Election on Saturday, as the day of Proclamation must be

---

[1] Sister of Earl Temple (*See* note, p. 161).

exclusive of the four days, the day of Election *inclusive*. I am more apprehensive that my attendance in Person on the Corporation will be utterly impossible, and I am very uneasy about it, lest I should appear to be wanting in that real regard I, with so much reason, feel for them ; may I again recommend this Distress to your friendly and kind offices, and hope you will add this to the many obligations I feel to you, and shall ever most gratefully acknowledge.

" I am, with all respects and affection,
" Dear Sir,
" Your most obliged and most faithfull Friend and Servant,
" W. PITT."

To the Right Hon. Mr. Pitt.
" Prior Park, July 2, 1757.

" DEAR SIR,—I have received the letter which you was pleased to honour me with the 30th of the last month, and in obedience to your Commands, a proper person, who can be confided in, is Imployed to prepare the Under Sheriff and get the Precept ready for your Election on Saturday, the 9th of this month.

" Your Presence at the Town Hall on that occation would be very pleasing to all your Electors if it had been consistent with His Majesty's Service, but Since it is not, I may safely venture to assure you that no bad consequences will attend your absence.

" When you receive an account from the Mayor of your unanimous Election, you, in your letter of thanks to Him and the Corporation, will, I presume, be pleased to mention with concern the cause of your necessary attendance in London on the National affairs, with your full intentions to make your Personal acknowledgmts for their distinguishing or rather peculiar regard to you, before the meeting of the Parliamt.

" Upon this pleasing occation permit me to say that you shall certainly find me to be with the truest Sincerity and the most affectionate Respect,
" Dear Sir,
" Yr most humble and most obed. Serv.,
" R. A."

To Ralph Allen, Esquire.
[Not dated, but obviously July 3rd, 1757.]

" DEAR SR,—I will say little to you in this Letter, because I will have the Pleasure of saying more to you when we meet. That I hope will be Tuesday or Wednesday next. Mr. Pitt writes to you and the Mayor by this Post. He certainly will not be able to attend the election, and, therefore, I am to represent him. In Order to enable me to attend at Oakhampton, wᶜʰ I must do ((for I have just now the Pleasure of hearing that tho' my Election there is safe I shall probably have a Competitor, and be obliged to let loose some Irish guineas), I have desired Mr. Pitt to recommend Saturday, the ninth of July, as the most convenient Day for the Election at Bath. Mr. Clutterbuck will, therefore, see that the Sheriff's Precept is delivered to the Mayor on Monday or Tuesday, so as to enable him to proclaim the Election before Sun set on Tuesday.

" I am just setting out for Bedfordshire.

" Yʳ most affecᵗ and obliged friend,

" THO. POTTER.

" Pall Mall, Thursday."

To the Right Hon. Mr. Pitt.

" Prior Park, July 12th, 1757.

" DEAR SIR,—Permit me upon my receipt of the obligeing Letter which you honour'd me with by the Express which you Yesterday sent to the Mayor and Corporation of Bath, just to say that it is Impossible for you to be more satisfied with the pleaseing Event which had been transacted in that City than I am with the honest and faithfull discharge of my Duty to my Country upon that occasion.

"And with the most Zealous and affectionate Respect you will allways find me to be,

" Dʳ Sir,

" (Sign'd)   Your most humble and most Obedᵗ Servᵗ,

"R. ALLEN.

" My ffamily begs your acceptance of their most respectfull Compliments."

William Pitt was a citizen,[1] and proud of the city which he now represented, and in which, from his early manhood,

---

[1] It is well known that the elder Wood designed the Circus, and that the execution of it was left to the younger. The house No. 7, with all its covenants and obligations, was conveyed to Pitt on the 3rd day of January 1755. The property was re-sold by Pitt in 1763, the year in which the breach between him and the Corporation occurred,

he had spent so much of his time, and from whose famous waters he had experienced such signal benefits during the terrible attacks of his constitutional malady.   We are unable to trace where Pitt lived during any of his occasional visits to Bath, but there is no doubt that on two of his visits he was entertained by Ralph Allen at his townhouse, and once, if not twice, at Prior Park.   He is said to have suggested the erection of the Palladian Bridge, of which mention is made, page 112.   We need not enter upon any historical or political disquisition, except so far as it may enable us to make clear the relations of Pitt with Bath, and to put into a more definite form some of the very interesting associations connected with him and with those other statesmen who either were the choice of Allen, or in the choice of whom Allen had, perhaps, the largest share.

In 1754, when Pelham died, Pitt was ill in this city, and on that occasion the Corporation paid him the most marked attention.   That body, with its most important member, Ralph Allen, showed the great Commoner almost regal honours.   His past and present conduct as a statesman deserved their warmest approbation, and they felt great resentment at the manner in which their distinguished fellow-citizen was treated by Newcastle in the construction of the new Administration.   They applauded his opposition to the subsidies to the German States.   They adopted an address to the king on the disasters which followed the war.[1] It is clear that they did not look for consistency in their idol.   If he opposed at one time what he afterwards supported, they probably thought that the capacity of the man

---

[1] In November 1755, Legge and Pitt were dismissed from office—the former (as Chancellor of the Exchequer) for refusing to sign the Treasury Warrants for the payment of the subsidies granted, and the latter (as Paymaster of the Forces) for his fierce denunciation of the principle of subsidies.

made all the difference between the soundness and the unsoundness of the policy pursued. In April 1757, he and his colleague, the Chancellor of the Exchequer, Legge, received each the freedom of the city in a gold box for "their services to the country during their late short administration."[1]

When a special vacancy occurred in the representation of the city, in 1757, by the elevation of Attorney-General Henley to be Lord Keeper, Pitt was unanimously chosen as his successor. [At the General Election of 1761, he was re-elected in conjunction with his former colleague, Viscount Ligonier. In 1763, this nobleman having been created a Peer of the Realm, a vacancy occurred, to supply which Sir John S. Sebright was elected, who thus became the colleague of Pitt.]

The disasters under the feeble ·administration of Newcastle had occasioned great national indignation, and the public voice proclaimed Pitt to be the man to "save the country". Up to this period, the Bath Corporation had enthusiastically supported their illustrious representative. After he entered upon the Administration—which lasted from June 17th, 1757, to October 1761, and in which he was practically all-powerful —he received the cordial approval and the repeated thanks of the Corporation, by whom he was elected, and of the citizens, who worshipped him. His conduct of the war, the policy of the war—indeed, every act of his public life—inspired his friends in Bath with exultant pride and commanded their unfaltering allegiance. In October 1760, the Mayor and Corporation unanimously adopted the following address to Mr. Pitt and his colleague, Lord Ligonier[2] :—

---

[1] Under the Duke of Devonshire. It began in November 1756, and ended in April 1757. It was during this Administration that Admiral Byng was tried, and Pitt used the noblest efforts, in vain, to save him.

[2] When the address was sent he was Sir John Ligonier.

To Lord Ligonier and Mr. Pitt.

"Bath, Oct. 6, 1760.

"SIRS,—We, the Mayor, Aldermen, and Common Council of this city, do transmit to you, our representatives in Parliament, our most grateful thanks, for exerting your great abilities with so much zeal and unwearied diligence in the service of his Majesty and our country, as hath reflected particular honour on our city. We are convinced we should not do justice to ourselves and brother citizens, if we did not pay that regard which is justly due to your distinguished merit, by taking the earliest opportunity of offering to you the same trust at the next general election ; and which we hereby beg the favour of your acceptance of, from,

"Gentlemen,

"Your much obliged and very humble Servants."

———

Mr. Pitt's Answer.

"St. James's Square, Oct. 9, 1760.

"MR. MAYOR AND GENTLEMEN OF THE CORPORATION,—I am this day honoured with your letter, and cannot defer a moment to express the sentiments of the warmest and most respectful gratitude for such a fresh mark of your condescension and goodness to me, after the many great and unmerited favours which you have already conferred upon me.

"Happy ! that my feeble endeavours for the king's service have, in your candid interpretation, stood in the place of more effectual deservings ; and that, actuated by the generous motives of zeal and steady attachment to his Majesty's Government, you are pleased again to think of committing to me the important and honourable trust of representing you at the next general election.

"Be assured, gentlemen, that I am justly proud of the title of servant of the city of Bath, and that I can never sufficiently manifest the deep sense I have of your distinguished and repeated favours ; nor express the respect, gratitude, and affection with which I remain,

"Mr. Mayor and Gentlemen of the Corporation,

"Your most faithful and most obliged humble Servant,

"W. PITT."

Lord Ligonier's Answer.

" *To the Worshipful the Mayor and the rest of the Corporation of the City of Bath.*

"North Audley Street ; Oct. 10, 1760.

" GENTLEMEN,—The very great honour done me by your letter of the 6th instant requires my earnest and most grateful thanks. Though your noble and generous way of acting is no new thing to me, who have had the honour to represent you in the two preceding Parliaments, and have experienced so often your goodness to me, nevertheless I must feel a very great satisfaction at the approbation you are pleased to express of my endeavours to serve my king and country as your representative. I accept with great gratitude this distinguished mark of your favour. The interest and honour of your city of Bath it will be ever my study to promote.

"I am, with the greatest regard and esteem,

"Gentlemen,

" Your most obliged and most faithful Servant,

" LIGONIER."

The following letter was written to Allen by Pitt after he had consented to renew his political connection with the city :—

To Ralph Allen, Esquire.

"St. James's Square, Dec. 16, 1760.

" DEAR SIR,—The very affecting token of esteem and affection which you put into my hands last night at parting, has left impressions on my heart which I can neither express nor conceal. If the approbation of the good and wise be our wish, how must I feel the sanction of applause and friendship accompany'd with such an endearing act of Kindness from the best of men ? True Gratitude is ever the justest of Sentiments, and Pride too, which I indulge on this occasion, may, I trust, not be disclaim'd by Virtue. May the gracious Heaven long continue to *lend* you to mankind and particularly to the happiness of him who is unceasingly, with the warmest gratitude, respect, and affection,

"My dear Sir,

" Your most faithfull Friend and

"most obliged humble Servant,

"W. PITT."

These cordial relations between the electors and the two representatives were creditable to both parties. There was neither servility on the one side nor arrogance on the other. Everything pointed to the continuance of those relations, which was indicated in the Address; and at the General Election in March 1761, the two members were unanimously re-elected. Pitt had steadily maintained his war policy; he was judged by it, and he was ready to stand or fall by it. The Corporation not only re-elected their members, but honoured them publicly at the Guildhall, and the citizens vied with each other in doing honour to the men, especially to Pitt, of whom they were justly proud. In October, Pitt was defeated in the cabinet on the question of war with Spain and left the Ministry. In December of the same year, the following *gushing* address was sent to Pitt by the Bath Corporation :—

"Bath ; Dec. 18th, 1761.

" SIR,—Had it not been for the particular relation in which we have the honour to stand towards you, we should, perhaps, have been still content, as others are, to enjoy in silence those fervours of gratitude which every true British heart must feel for the great, unparalleled services which you have done your king and country throughout the course of your late ministry.

" It is true that after so ample and honourable a testimony, borne to them by your royal master himself, it would be extremely vain in us to think that anything could be wanting to the glory of a character thus illustriously established. But though we can add nothing to you, we have ventured to employ this occasion to do credit to ourselves in that light, and are most ambitious to be seen of faithful and loyal subjects, for in these expressions of our great regard to you, we have only presumed to follow the gracious example of the best of kings.

" For the rest, there is no station where you can be found in which your country will not need and will not be sure to have your most effectual assistance.

" We have nothing, sir, further to offer but our ardent prayers for your health, a blessing so precious and so important to the public.

" We have the honour to be, Sir,
        " Your most humble and affectionate Servants."

Mr. Pitt's Answer.

"Hayes ; Dec. 22, 1761.

"MR. MAYOR,[1]—I have received the particular honour of a letter signed by you, sir, and by a great many other gentlemen of the Corporation, containing the most condescending and endearing remarks, marks of personal regard and favour towards me, and at the same time bestowing on such inconsiderable efforts as I have been able to exert in the service of my king and my country—testimonies of so distinguished and honourable a nature, that I only accept them with a confusion joined to unceasing gratitude.

" Allow me, Mr. Mayor, to entreat that you will please to communicate to the other gentlemen of the Corporation these my most unfeigned and respectful acknowledgments, and to assure them of my ardent and continual wishes for the prosperity of the City of Bath, and for the particular welfare and happiness of the several members of that ancient and considerable Corporation.

" I am, with the warmest sentiments of regard and respectful consideration, sir, your most obedient and most obliged humble Servant,

" W. PITT."

This correspondence, it must be remembered, followed the energetic councils given by the Minister to the King, as to the expediency of a declaration of war against Spain on account of the "Family Compact",[2] and her equivocal conduct

---

[1] At this time, Alderman John Chapman.

[2] The " Family Compact " was a secret alliance between France, Spain, and Naples, and stipulated that if England should be still at war with France on 1st May 1761, Spain would declare war against England ; and as return for this assistance, France was to restore Minorca to Spain.

With reference to which, as Lord Stanhope says, " the commencement of the War of Secession was never yet so fully vindicated as by the conclusion of the Family Compact."

In June 1761 there were fresh English successes, and France would probably have submitted to Pitt's terms, if Charles III, who had recently become King of Spain, had not renewed the " Family Compact", knowing that the vast colonial empire of Spain was endangered by the predominance of England in North America. Pitt, having secret intelligence of

towards those with whom we were at war, and it leaves no
doubt that the great minister felt that in resigning office he
had the sympathy and confidence of those from whom that
address came, whatever it was worth.

The war against Spain—which Pitt urged in vain in
October of 1761, and which his prescience had foreseen as
inevitable—was declared by Lord Bute, in January 1762,
three months after Pitt quitted office.   It seems probable that
this short delay and the retirement of the great minister had
encouraged Spain in the insolent and offensive course she had
taken against Great Britain.   Be this as it may, the attitude
of Spain, and her intrigues with France, if they justified war
in January, equally justified it in the previous October, when
Pitt "would have had the first blow, which is often half the
battle." "When once convinced of their hostile designs, why
allow them further time for preparation?"—which, indeed,
was just what the fatal delay accomplished.   The war was
declared on the 4th January 1762, and the Seven Years War,
of which the Spanish War was an episode, was concluded
early in 1763 by the Peace of Paris.   Bute resigned in
April.   The war had been carried on languidly by him, and
much against his inclination.   Pitt opposed the peace, because
he deemed it *inadequate;* it did not secure the objects for
which it was undertaken.   When Parliament met, he denounced the peace with vehement eloquence, but all to no purpose ; eloquence could not prevail against the corruption employed to buy over a majority of members in favour of peace.

There has been nothing to show that, as between Pitt and
the Corporation, either collectively or individually, there had
been any misunderstanding.[1]   When the peace was concluded

what had happened, urged the Cabinet to declare war on Spain at once.
The Cabinet, however, refused to follow him, and on October 5 Pitt
resigned.

[1] It would seem indeed that Pitt's resignation was regarded by the

which Pitt had so vehemently opposed, the Corporation, at a special meeting,[1] held in May 1763,[2] over which Ralph Allen presided, adopted the following Address.   It is printed in italics, because it will be observed that on the terms of the document hinged the whole future relations of Pitt with the Bath Corporation.   It is the more necessary to make this clear, because in the late Rev. F. Kilvert's paper on Ralph Allen he leaves the Address out of the Correspondence ; so in like manner Sir Jerom Murch omits it.   So that in each case the reader is left in a state of utter ignorance as to the character and wording of that document which gave Pitt so much offence, and led to the termination of his political connection with a city in which he had received so many proofs of the confidence and admiration of all classes.

TO THE KING'S MOST EXCELLENT MAJESTY.

" *We, the Mayor, Aldermen, and Common Council of the ancient and loyal city of Bath, do beg leave to congratulate, and most humbly to thank your Majesty for an* ADEQUATE *and advantageous peace, which you have graciously procured for your people, after a long and very expensive,*

---

citizens and the Corporation as a great public calamity.   It inspired Mr. T. Atwood, Burke's friend (who was Mayor, 1756-60-69), to write— well, a stanza, which, if it does not exhibit poetic genius, perhaps faithfully expresses the feelings of his colleague :—

> "Whence does the Gaul exult ?   Can *Broglie** boast
> At length one battle not entirely lost ?
> Or has the Spaniard their alliance joined ?
> Alas ! much worse—our Patriot has resigned !"

[1] Of which there is no record in the Journals.

[2] It should be mentioned here that in April of this year Viscount Ligonier (in the Irish Peerage) was created an English Earl.   His seat being thus vacated, two candidates were proposed—Mr. Long and Sir John Saunders Sebright, when the latter was elected.

---

* Duc de Broglie, who commanded a portion of the French Army.

though necessary and glorious war, which your Majesty, upon your acces-
sion to the throne, found your kingdoms engaged in.

" *And we take the liberty to assure your Majesty, that upon all occasions*
we shall be ready to give the most evident proofs of the truest zeal and
duty, which the most dutiful subjects can testify to the most gracious and
best of princes.

" *In testimony whereof we have hereunto affixed our*
    " *Common Seal, the* 28*th day of May* 1763."

———

To Ralph Allen, Esq.

" Hayes ; June 2, 1763.

" DEAR SIR,—Having declined accompanying Sir John Sebright in
presenting the address from Bath, transmitted to us jointly by the Town-
Clerk, I think it, on all accounts, indispensably necessary that I should
inform you of the reason of my conduct. The epithet of *adequate* given
to the peace contains a description of the conditions of it, so repugnant
to my unalterable opinion concerning many of them, and fully declared
by me in Parliament, that it was as impossible for me to obey the Corporation's commands in presenting their address, as it was unexpected to
receive such a commission. As to my opinion of the peace, I will only
say, that I formed it with sincerity according to such lights as my little
experience and small portion of understanding could afford me. This
conviction must remain to myself the constant rule of my conduct ; and
I leave to others, with much deference to their better information, to
follow their own judgment. Give me leave, my dear, good sir, to desire
to convey, through you, to Mr. Mayor and to the gentlemen of the
Corporation, these my free sentiments ; and with the justest sense of
their past goodness towards me, plainly to confess that I perceive I am
but ill qualified to form pretensions to the future favour of gentlemen, who
are come to think so differently from me, on matters of the highest importance to the national welfare.

" I am ever, with respectful and affectionate esteem, my dear sir,
    " Your faithful friend and obliged humble Servant,

" (Signed) W. PITT.

Lady Chatham joins with me in all compliments to the family of Prior
Park."

———

To the Right Hon. Mr. Pitt.

"Prior Park ; June 4, 1763.

" MY DEAREST SIR,—It is extremely painful to me to find by the letter which you was pleased to send to me the 2nd of this month, that the word *adequate*, in the Bath address, has been so very offensive to you, as to hinder the sincerest and most zealous of your friends in the Corporation from testifying for the future their great attachment to you.

" Upon this occasion, in justice to them, it is incumbent on me to acquaint you, that the unexceptionable word does not rest with them, but myself; who suddenly drew up that address, to prevent their sending of another, which the Mayor[1] brought to me, in terms that I could not concur in ; copies of the two forms I have taken the liberty to send to you in the enclosed paper, for your private perusal; and Sir John Sebright having, in his letter to Mr. Clutterbuck,[2] only acquainted him, that in your absence in the country he delivered the address, I shall decline executing of your commands to the Corporation on this delicate point, unless you renew them, upon your perusal of this letter, which for safety I have sent by a messenger, and I beg your answer to it by him, who has orders to wait for it.

" Permit me to say that I have not the least objection to, but the highest regard and even veneration for, your whole conduct ; neither have I any apology to make for the expression in which I am so unfortunate to differ from you. And with the utmost respect, affection, and gratitude, you will always find me to be, my dearest sir, your most humble and obedient servant,

"(Signed) R. ALLEN.

" The best wishes of this family always attend Lady Chatham.

"R. A."

To Ralph Allen, Esquire.

"Hayes, June 5, 1763.

" MY DEAR SIR,—I am sorry that my letter of the 2nd inst. should give you uneasiness, and occasion to you the trouble of sending a messenger to Hayes. I desire you to be assured, that few things can give me more real concern, than to find that my notions of the public good differ so widely from those of the man whose goodness of heart and

---

[1] Alderman Samuel Bush.
[2] Lewis Clutterbuck, the Town Clerk.

N

private virtues I shall ever respect and love. I am not insensible to your kind motives for wishing to interpose time for second thoughts; but knowing how much you approve an open and ingenuous proceeding, I trust that you will see the unfitness of my concealing from my constituents the insurmountable reasons which prevented my obeying their commands in presenting an address, containing a disavowal of my opinion delivered in Parliament relating to the peace. As their servant, I owe to these gentlemen an explanation of my conduct on this occasion, and as a man not forgetful of the distinguished honour of having been invited to represent them, I owe it, in gratitude, to them, not to think of embarrassing and encumbering, for the future, friends to whom I have such obligations; and who now view with approbation measures of an administration, founded on the subversion of that system which once procured me the countenance and favour of the city of Bath. On these plain grounds, very coolly weighed, I will venture to beg again that my equitable good friend will be so good to convey to Mr. Mayor and the gentlemen of the Corporation my sentiments, as contained in my letter of the 2nd instant.

" I am ever, with unchanging sentiments of respect and affection,

" My dear sir, most faithfully yours,

"W. PITT."

Letter to Mrs. Allen, accompanying the last addressed to Ralph Allen, June 5th, 1763.

"I cannot conclude my letter without expressing my sensible concern at Mr. Allen's uneasiness. No incidents can make the least change in the honour and love I bear him, or in the justice my heart does to his humane and benevolent virtues."

[The context of this letter to Mrs. Allen is missing.]

To the Right Hon. Mr. Pitt.

"Prior Park, June 9th.

"MY DEAREST SIR,—With the greatest anxiety and concern, I have in obedience to your positive and repeated commands executed the most painful commission that I ever received.

"Upon this disagreeable occasion, give me leave just to say that, however different our abilities may be, it is the duty of every honest man, after he has made the strictest enquiry, to act pursuant to the light which the Supreme Being has been pleased to dispense to him; and this being the rule that I am persuaded we both govern ourselves by, I shall take the liberty, not only to add, that it is impossible for any person to retain higher sentiments of your late glorious administration than I do, nor can be with truer fidelity, zeal, affection, and respect than I have been, still am, and always shall be, my dearest sir,

> " Your most humble and most obedient servant,
> " (Signed)   R. ALLEN.

" The best wishes of this family wait upon Lady Chatham."

Lord Stanhope thinks the word *adequate* slipped into the Address without design or the intention of conveying a meaning of especial significance. If it be so, it is singular that a word should have been used which, in itself, is so plenary in the sense it bears, and at the same time is the very converse of that which Pitt had used over and over again to characterize the peace—*inadequate*. It is not surprising that Pitt should have regarded the Address with scornful indignation, not simply as approving the peace, but as by implication reversing all the judgments the Corporation had passed upon his previous policy and conduct. The word was " untoward", and Pitt thought that not only the word, but the whole Address, was the artful work of Bishop Warburton.[1] Pitt

---

[1] Bishop Warburton had received his Bishopric from Pitt, and having promoted a similar Address from his own Chapter, the only Chapter in the Kingdom from which a similar Address was sent, it was natural that the Bishop should have been suspected of being "the power behind the throne" who had prompted Allen. The Bishop denied the accusation, but it is fair to presume that as he was constantly at Prior Park, he may have made known his intention of sending an Address and the sense of it, and thus unintentionally, or it may be too adroitly, influenced Allen's judgment. The Bishop wrote to Pitt, whose reply left a wound which troubled Warburton not a little :—" I will only venture to observe, my Lord, that the Cathedral of Gloucester, which certainly does not stand alone in true duty and wise zeal towards His Majesty, has, however, the fate not to be imitated by any other Episcopal See in the Kingdom, in this unaccustomed effusion of fervent congratulations on the Peace."

sold his house in the Circus at the close of the year, and, although he visited the city again in 1766 for the use of the waters, he does not seem to have renewed his intercourse with his former friends. He retained his seat until 1766, when he was created Earl of Chatham,[1] the dignity of Baroness Chatham having been already conferred upon his wife, Lady Hester Pitt (sister of the then Earl Temple).

THE ONE-HEADED CORPORATION CARICATURES.

In the first of these caricatures, dated 1763, the central figure is a large head—an admirable portrait—of Allen. Perched on it is a raven, who is croaking "Raafe, Raafe, poor Raafe." Allen is holding a scroll in his hands, on which the word "Adequate" is conspicuously written. A bishop (Warburton) in full canonicals is whispering into Allen's right ear, "'Tis I did this great work for you!" The devil, however, who is close upon the bishop's back, says: "No, no, friend, 'twas I, the father of political lies, that first thought of *Addressing!*" To which Coward replies, "Don't drive me, St. John,[2] I'll go graze on the Common or in Prior Park." In the right-hand upper corner is a portrait of Lord Ligonier, and in the left a portrait of Pitt. Around the figure of Allen are gathered the members of the Corporation, each in the character which symbolized his calling. The death's head and gallipots signified the

---

[1] In an amusing passage in *Barry Lyndon*, Thackeray puts some trenchant remarks into the mouth of his hero with regard to the Seven Years' War in which he had taken part, and concludes by a short reference to the "Marquis of Tiptoff" and Lord Chatham :—"Though a Whig, or, perhaps, because he was a Whig, the Marquis was one of the haughtiest men breathing, and treated commoners as his idol ; the great Earl used to treat them—after he came to a coronet himself—as so many low vassals who might be proud to lick his shoe-buckles."

[2] St. John was apparently a citizen who exercised some influence upon Coward ; there was no person of the name in the Council.

several medical men. The wagon—Walter Wiltshire, carrier ; the horse's head—John Glazier, coachman ; greyhound's head —Sir John S. Sebright, M.P. ; the ass's head—Leonard Coward ; the bishop—Bishop Warburton ; the double-faced head—Ald. Biggs, lawyer ; the clock-face — French Laurance, watchmaker ; the E. O. Tables—J. Leake, publisher ; the latticed window—Axford, glazier ; the lock—Hales, ironmonger ; the £500 and doll—Davis, jeweller and toyman ; the inkpot— Clutterbuck, the town-clerk, who is exclaiming, " What is all this *clutter* about" ; the soldering-irons—Atwood, glazier ; the hoop—Milsom, cooper. To the left stands the figure of Falstaff, whose identity is not so certain. He is very angry, and evidently was a man who thought he did well to be angry. From the part played by Thicknesse in Bath about this time, and from a close study of the character of the man, we feel almost certain that he it is who is intended to be represented by Falstaff. It is the more probable from the language he is made to use—" Dam ye for a set of poltroons, I'll drive you from hence with this dagger." The sturdy form, the attitude, and the true nature of Thicknesse's courage, are all so admirably depicted in the Falstaffian figure. It is difficult to conceive any " outsider" in Bath, at this period, who combined in himself so many unamiable qualities as Philip Thicknesse.

The caricature gave deep pain to Allen, because it imputed to him gross dissimulation—which was utterly foreign to his nature—and he was so little accustomed to be chidden by his Bath friends. Bishop Warburton thought it not beneath him to write to Pitt to vindicate himself from the implied charge of duplicity, or, what was worse, treachery, and complained of the character he is made to assume in the caricature.

Shortly after the first caricature appeared, a second was published—" A Sequel to the Knights of Baythe, or the One-headed Corporation." The Committee is here represented, the

A Sequel to the Knights of BAYTHE, or the One HEADED CORPORATION

members of which are most likely discussing Pitt's reply. Allen is presiding. After others have spoken, he is just saying, "An Adequate Peace merits an Adequate Address," when the curtain is drawn aside by a character whose identity we fail to recognise, who says, " I'll show them in their proper colours," and there stand Warburton, Pitt, Ligonier, and the redoubtable swash-buckler, Falstaff. The bishop says: " And I must have a stroke at 'em." Falstaff says : "They should drink the Waters, for the Body wants cleansing, by G—." Pitt exclaims, "Let who will represent such Wretches, I won't." Ligonier puts in, "Faith, Brother, they deserve to have no Members at all." Underneath the picture the following lines are printed :—

> " See *Liberty's* Champions still loyal and true,
> Displaying the tricks of poor R——h and his crew.
> Who thinking to show himself *courtly* and civil,
> Is eagerly riding *post-haste* to the *Devil.*

> "My friends (Hark ! he crys) of this wise *Corporation,*
> This *Adequate Peace* deserves *Congratulation.*
> His *Lordship* by me too his compliments sends,
> And promises shortly to make you amends.

> "Then to it they go, but, ye Gods ! such a Thing,
> Was never presented before to a ——
> For *Reason* her sentiments wisely expresses
> A Peace that is patch'd, should have patch'd up Addresses."

Allen for some time had experienced symptoms of internal disease, which proved to be cancer ; and there can be little doubt that the agitation caused him by the incident connected with Pitt, and the severe, not to say *savage*, reflections upon him in the caricatures, tended greatly to aggravate the disorder. Allen, however, bore himself with his usual calm and simple dignity. Whilst showing his deep and most heart-felt respect for, and deference to Pitt, and the regret at his resolution to give up his seat, Allen assumed the whole responsibility for the use of the offensive words, and adhered to them and the policy they implied.

The caricatures were as bitter as they were clever. The caricaturist, under the *nom de plume* of William O'Gaarth, had just previously published a work in two small volumes, entitled, *British Antidote to Caledonian Poison*, which consisted of a series of caricatures satirizing Lord Bute and glorifying Mr. Pitt. Each portrait in the work is drawn with the same characteristic skill, hits off with clever exaggeration the alleged foibles and political misdoings of Lord Bute and his adherents, whilst elevating Pitt to the highest pitch of heroism and virtue. It is not at all probable that Pitt was privy to the publication of these malicious prints, which, if Allen had been the meanest renegade, instead of the true and admiring friend, could scarcely have been justified. There was evidently a bitter political animus on the part of a small band of London politicians against all and any sort of opponents of Mr. Pitt.

ALLEN'S RETIREMENT FROM PUBLIC LIFE.

The following letter, written by Allen in the year of the political misunderstanding, indicates his consciousness that his local work had come to an end ; but even here there is a quiet, pathetic dignity. From first to last no attack, however unjust, ever extorted from him one word of complaint, remonstrance, or anger.

"Prior Park ; Oct. 18, 1763.

" SIR,—My weak state of health and growing Infirmities obliges me to beg that you and the other Gentlemen of the Corporation will permit me at their Hall to resign my Station of one of your Aldermen.

" Upon this occasion give me leave to make my most hearty acknowledgments for the great attention and distinguishing regard which you and they during a long course of years have been pleased to show to me, and to give the strongest assurance that in the remainder of my Life, one of my greatest pleasures on all proper occasion will be to testifie my utmost regard for the welfare of our City. and to show you and the other Gentlemen of the Community, every ffriendly act that may be in the power of them and of   " Sir,   ·

"Your most humble and obedient Servant,

"RALPH ALLEN."

"To Samuel Bush, Esq.,

"Mayor of Bath who is desired at the next Town Hall to lay this Letter before the Aldermen and Common Council of that City.

"P.S.—Upon this Resignation.   That the five hundred pounds which I sometime since desired your acceptance of towards the expence of Building a New Town Hall in our City shall be payed to any person for that purpose which you may be pleased to receive it whenever that useful and ornamental design shall be entered upon.

"R. ALLEN."

About the time this letter was written, or a little later, Allen removed to Claverton[1] for a few months while some

---

[1] [From the *Harvey Correspondence*, to show the difficulty of locomotion in those days.]

"Bath, May 13, 1723.

"LADY BRISTOL to LORD B.—I am (if possible) more dispirited to day after my bathing than I was last time, and that I believe you might see by my letter was enough, for I hardly knew what I writ, but think I told you I was to spend the evening with Mrs. Smith and Mrs. Paget, where they found me so bad that they held a consultation for me, and found it absolutely necessary I should be as much in the air as the weather would permit me to sit abroad ; (being not able to walk,) Mrs. Lewis was so kind as to desire I would try a coach, which I readily accepted of ; so she carryd Mrs. Smith, Betty and my self to vissit Mr. Skrine and his wife.   They have a very pretty place at Clarkendown [Claverton], but I not being able to see all the garden, lost (as they say) several beauties ; but it had need be as fine as Chatsworth, for the way to it (I think) is almost as bad ; I am sure my poor legs found it so ; that and being 4 in the coach made them in a sad condition, for which I cryd about an

alterations and painting of the rooms at Prior Park were going on ; but in the spring of the year 1764 he was prevailed on to undertake a journey to London, though he had laboured for some years under a complaint which made travelling irksome to him. He proceeded as far as Maidenhead Bridge, at the west end of which Allen had built the room with the bow window and the room over it. Here he found it necessary to halt for some days, when, finding his malady increase, he returned by short stages to Prior Park, where, on the 29th June 1764, his useful life terminated, in the seventy-first year of his age. He was buried in the church-yard of Claverton, where a pyramidal monument is erected over his remains, according to a plan which he left behind, with a short, plain epitaph expressive of his faith in the redemption and mediation of Christ.

" Beneath this monument lieth entomb'd the body of Ralph Allen, Esq., of Prior Park, who departed this life the 29th day of June 1764, in the 71st year of his age, in full hopes of ever-lasting happiness in another state, through the infinite merit and mediation of our blessed Redeemer, Jesus Christ. And of Elizabeth Holder, his second wife, who died 20th September 1766, aged 68."

---

hour after I came home, and as much this morning, though Mr. Skrine* tells me my Lady Rochester's legs were as bad as mine, when she came here last year, and that he quite cured her before she left the place with the same medicine he begins with me too night in a glass of the Bath water, and the same in the morning at the Pump. . . . But I think I have said enough of my self, unless I could tell you something better ; besides that I have chosen a very ill time to transgress the rules you laid down to me about writing, which I should never have been able to do, if your dear, kind prose had not been much more enlivening than your heroick verse."

---

* This was not the Claverton Skrine, but the local surgeon, who resided at *Hungerford House*, then called " Skrine's Lower House", and is now the " Abbey Church House."

On the occasion of her husband's death Mr. Pitt wrote to Mrs. Allen :—

"I fear not all the example of his virtues will have power to raise up to the world his like again."

CORRESPONDENCE WITH MR. STRAHAN.

HE following correspondence with Allen will tell its own story. The writer was, we believe, a clerk in the House of Commons and was much esteemed by Warburton and other friends of Allen.

"London, October 25, 1763.

"SIR,—I have sent by the machine which setts out tomorrow, the Reading·Glass you did me the Honour to desire me to procure for you. It cost £1 4s. od. If it does not suit your Eye, or is not otherwise precisely what you want, I can change it for another. Along with it I have sent the History Books I promised Master Warburton [*i.e.*, the Bishop's son], which, tho' of very small Value, have afforded much Entertainment to the Good People of England for some Centuries past. As they contain great Variety, and many of them deal in the Wonderful, it is likely some of them may attract his attention and allure him to read a little more than he might otherwise incline. A Boy of his lively Genius need but choose to learn anything to make himself Master of it.

"Every Eye is now turned towards this Opening of the Session. The Ministry, I am assured, do not propose to avail themselves of the Sanction given by Parliament to the late Peace ; but are determined to defend it, Article by Article, by clear and solid Argument, to the Conviction of every reasonable man in the Kingdom. The audacious Wilkes, it is thought, will be forthwith expelled. The Opposition are not supposed to exceed Ninety at most. In that case, the present Sett of Ministers, who, by-the-bye, act in conjunction with Lord Bute, whatever is pretended, if they have the Public Good really at heart, and do not fall by the Ears among themselves, will certainly stand their ground ; the Authority of Government will be re-established, and the great and important Business of the Nation will be at last attended to.

"I am very proud of your Approbation of the Paper you were pleased to take the trouble of Reading. All the merit I pretend to is that of Meaning well. It is a Misfortune which Great Men are peculiarly subject to, seldom or never to be approached by those who have Honesty enough to tell them the Truth.

"Permit me, Sir, to take this Opportunity of returning you my most grateful Acknowledgments for the very kind Reception you were pleased to give me at Prior Park. Nothing could possibly exceed the Pleasure I felt at seeing with my own Eyes what I had long been used to contemplate at a Distance with so much Esteem and Veneration. Such a Sight enlarges the mind, and enhanses the opinion of our very Nature. But I restrain myself for fear of offending you. Nothing is farther from my Intention than to give one Moment's Uneasiness to so respectable a Character, whose whole Existence deserves to be crowded with the choisest Blessings of Humanity.

"May you retain the undisturbed Enjoyment of your earthly Paradise till you are called to the Possession of another more permanent, better suited for the Abode of such enlarged Benevolence, where Ingratitude never enters, and where tried and pure Virtue can alone find an adequate Reward.

"I am, with the most perfect Esteem and Respect, Sir,

"Your most obedient and humble Servant,

"WILL. STRAHAN."

To Mr. Strahan.

"Prior Park, October 29, 1763.

"SIR,—I am very thankful to you for your obliging Letter and for the great Parcel of Books which you were pleased to send to our Dear Little Boy[1] for his Improvement, as well as for your Buying the reading Glass, which fits my Eyes, and I shall desire the Bishop to repay you for it. I truly am, Sir,

"Your obliged and most humbl Servt,

"Signed, R. ALLEN."

---

[1] Ralph Allen Warburton, who, dying in his 20th year, rests in Allen's tomb at Claverton, not at Gloucester, as inadvertently stated on p. 137.

To Ralph Allen, Esquire.

" London, Novr. 21, 1763.

" SIR,—I should have sooner acknowledged the Receipt of your Favour of the 29th ult., but that I was unwilling to give you any unnecessary Trouble, and waited till the Season arrived, when I might be able to write you something new.

" The Bishop of Gloucester (his Lordship tells me) has acquainted you with what passed in the Upper House in regard to Wilkes. The affair was happily kept so secret, that neither he nor his Friends were apprised of, or prepared for, the Blow, which most effectually reduced the seditious and profligate Fellow to that State of Insignificance and Contempt he so justly merits.

" As soon as the House of Commons met, Wilkes stood up in his Place, and read a short Account of his Imprisonment in the Tower, and complained of the Breach of Privilege. The Chancellor of the Exchequer acquainted them at the same time that he had a Message from the King relating to Privilege. Upon this a Debate arose, whether, previous to hearing either the Complaint or the Message, a Bill ought not to be read, agreeable to constant Practise, in order to open and constitute the Session. The complying with this Form, which could not take up above five Minutes, was opposed for some Hours by Mr. Pitt, in order to gain Time, and throw every Obstruction in the way of bringing the Affair in Question to a quickly Hearing. Mr. George Onslow, son of the late Speaker, cited the Case of one Mompesson, in whose behalf a Case of Privilege was heard, before the House entered upon any Business ; but as this regarded a Riot in the Lobby, and required immediate Redress, it was not to the Point. Mr. Pitt next attempted to unite the Resolution for reading the Bill to the hearing the Breach of Privilege ; that is, *Resolved, that the Bill be read before the hearing of the Complaint,* &c., with a view to postponing the receiving the King's Message, but without effect. Then Mr. Yorke stood up and observed, that as every Act they passed which had no special Commencement, had a Retrospection to the Beginning of the Session, and as a Session did not legally begin till they had done something in their Legislative Capacity, such as reading a Bill, it was therefore necessary, to prevent many Inconveniencies, to keep strictly to the antient Practise. Lord North then proposed an Amendment to the Resolution, viz., *Resolved that the Bill be read before receiving the King's Message, and hearing the Complaint,* &c. Upon which the House divided. For the Amendment 300, against it 111. Then the Bill was read. After this, the King's Message was received, and an Address voted upon it. Then the *North Briton*, No. 45, with the Examinations relating to it were read, when a Motion was made and seconded, that it was a false, scandalous, and seditious Libel, etc. Mr. Pitt still laboured to protract the Debate, by insisting that there was a wide Difference between a *seditious* and a *traiterous* Libel, and that these Terms ought never to be blended together; that the Actions which constituted Treason were very few, and all expressly mentioned in our Statutes ; and that he would call any Lawyer to the Bar who would avow that he had given it as his Opinion that this was a *traiterous* Libel. Mr. Norton (now Attorney-General) then stood up, and owned himself that Lawyer ; that he was not 'afraid to confess he gave that Opinion, that he was ready to support it, and dared that honourable Gentleman to call him to the Bar for so doing. Mr. Pitt only replied to this, by owning that the Gentleman had very well acquitted himself in his Reply to him, and complimented him on his abilities as a Lawyer. At length Mr. Pitt was obliged to give up the Point, and when Wilkes himself proposed the leaving out the Word *False*, would not second him ; so that [after a Division of 273 to 111 against leaving out these Words, *and to excite them to traiterous Insurrections against his Majesty's Government*] the Paper was voted, 'a false, scandalous, and seditious Libel, containing Expressions of the most unexampled Insolence and Contumely towards his Majesty, the grossest Aspersions upon both Houses of Parliament, and the most audacious Defiance of the Authority of the whole Legislature, and most manifestly tending to alienate the affections of the People from his Majesty, to withdraw them from their Obedience to the Laws of the Realm, and to excite them to traiterous Insurrections against his Majesty's Government'—and ordered it to be burnt by the Common Hangman. These are the precise Words of the Resolution, which I copied from the written Journal of the House, the Votes not being yet published.

" By the strenuous Opposition and Management of Mr. Pitt, as above narrated, the Debate was drawn out till past two in the morning.

"You, Sir, who, after the most diligent search into your own Heart, can find no Traces of Insincerity, or the least Inclination to a disingenuous Proceeding, will be very apt to wonder how a man of Mr. Pitt's great and acknowledged abilities, could submit to act a Part so truly unworthy of an honest mind. But so it happens, and a melancholy Truth it is, that Men, even of the greatest Talents, when once they deviate from that Rectitude of Conduct which every one ought above all Things to preserve, often suffer themselves to be seduced, by Pride, Ambition, Faction, or false Glory, to a Degree that highly disgraces Human Nature.

"The next Question to be debated in the House of Commons is, Whether the Author of a Seditious Libel is entitled to Privilege of Parliament. Upon this they were to have entered to day, but are again adjourned till Wednesday, occasioned by the Indisposition of the Speaker. The House of Lords meet to morrow, when they go upon the Breach of Privilege regarding the Bishop, who has acquired much Honour in this affair in that most impious Poem, of which they have proved Mr. Wilkes the Printer, and partly the Author.

"I shall not trouble you farther at this time, only I could not help observing from Mr. Pitt's Behaviour in the House last Thursday, in the Debate upon the Address in answer to his Majesty's Speech, wherein he made use of many Circumlocutions and Subterfuges (which a candid and honest Conduct had better spared him) that he means to drop his present Connexions as soon as he can, and once more slide into the Administration. How far I am right in this Conjecture time will discover.

"I purposed to have answered my dear young Correspondent's[1] Letter to-night, but must.defer it, it being now late. I sincerely hope this will find you in perfect Health. You have in truth added much to my Happiness. What I already know of your amiable Character gives me infinite Pleasure ; and it is so deeply impressed on my mind, that it is not in my Power to omit any Occasion, either Public or Private, of speaking my Sense of it. I must, therefore, intreat your Forgiveness for the Liberty I here take of assuring you that I am, with that perfect Esteem and Veneration which such singular Worth can alone inspire,

"Sir,

"Your most obedient and most humble Sert.,

"WILL. STRAHAN.

"If you have any Commands that I can execute here, you would make me very happy in employing me."

To Mr. Strahan.

"Prior Park, Nov. 24th, 1763.

"SIR,—I am very thankfull to you for the particular and clear representation which you was pleased to send to me of the Proceedings in the House of Commons.

---

[1] The young lad, Warburton.

O

" Little Ralph is thankfull for the kind Letter which you sent to him, and another nephew of mine[1] will soon repay you for the reading Glass that you lately bought for

"Sir,

Yr Obliged and most hum^ble Ser^t.,

"(Sign'd)   R. ALLEN."

To Ralph Allen, Esquire.

"London, Novr. 26, 1763.

" SIR, —I purposed to have sent you to night an Account of the Debates of last Wednesday and Thursday, when the Author of a Seditious Libel was voted not intitled to Privilege, 258 against 135. But my Business would not permit me to be at the House, and had I been able to attend, there was no room, almost the whole Lords being present. A Member, however, who attended the whole Debate, has promised me some Account of it to morrow, which, if I receive, I will send you by Monday's Post. Mr. Pitt was the only Person who mentioned Wilkes, and then he called him *a Blasphemer of his God, a Reviler of his King, and one who had endeavoured to subvert the Constitution of his Country.* This is somewhat particular, as he had all along endeavoured to serve him. Inclosed is an Account of the Poem,[2] published by one Kidgell, with an apparent View to his own Benefit ; for it serves no good Purpose to excite People's Curiosity to know the Contents of it. I was favoured with your Letter to day ; but I beg leave to observe, that tho' I intend to write you whenever I can send you any News, I do not expect that you should take the Trouble of acknowleging the Receit of mine. I know your Time is precious, and I would not wish to intrude upon it. I am, with the most perfect Esteem,

" Sir,

" Your most obedient and most humble Servant,

" WILL. STRAHAN."

---

[1] Ralph Allen, the younger son of Philip Allen.

[2] *An Essay on Woman, in Three Epistles.* The book was printed by Wilkes at his private press, 1763. It was one of the most lewd and disgusting books ever issued from any press. It was said at the time of its publication that Potter had a hand in this indecent "patchwork". In his intercourse with Bath, Potter concealed this "dirty" side of his character.

To Ralph Allen, Esquire.

"London, December 1, 1763.

" SIR,—The House of Lords, last Tuesday, agreed with the Commons in regard to the Affair of Privilege. The Speakers against the Vote were Lord Shelbourne, Lord Temple, the Duke of Newcastle, the Duke of Grafton, &c.—For it, the Chancellor, Lord Mansfield, &c. On the Side of Opposition Lord Shelborne spoke best ; but the Duke of Newcastle was not heard, and Lord Temple made a very poor Figure. He was told during the Debate, how very unbecoming it was for a Member of that House, who was indebted to the Crown for the most distinguishing Honours, to mix and associate with the Dregs of the People, to counte- nance and abett a Man who, with the most unprovoked Malice and the most unprecedented Effrontery, had endeavoured to calumniate Majesty itself ; to set at Defiance the Laws of his Country, and to stir up a Spirit of Discension between the two Parts of the United Kingdom. In answer to this, he declared (in direct Contradiction to all his late Conduct) that nobody had a greater Esteem for Lord Bute than he had, and that so far from being prejudiced against the Scots in general, or abetting those who had endeavourd to sow Discensions between them and us, he had always held that brave Nation in the highest Esteem ; that he had himself been an Eye-Witness of their gallant Behaviour during a former War, and had heard from good Authority of their intrepid Conduct in the most arduous Enterprises in this ; that he was not insensible how much this Kingdom owed to their Services, and thought this Country particularly happy in being united to so sensible, so hardy, and so industrious a People. The Lord Chancellor, in his honest, blunt, open Way, told them he had seen, with the utmost Concern, that Spirit of Licentiousness, which had spread of late to a most unsufferable Degree ; that the permitting this to pass with Impunity was really a Disgrace to all good Government ; that it essentially hurt the Reputation of the Kingdom with Foreigners ; that the rest of Europe could not fail to have a very contemptible Opinion of that Government that had not Power to secure itself from receiving such Insults, or to inflict upon the Authors of them the most examplary Punishment ; that he owned he had long ago in Council declared it as his Opinion, that this Evil ought to be stopt in its Progress, and that the King, by his just and legal Prerogative, had sufficient Power to do it ; and had his Advice been followed, Things would not probably have come to this Pass. Lord Mansfield, in a Speech of two Hours, with his usual Clearness, Precision, Accuracy, and Knowledge of the Law, treated the

O 2

Subject very fully, and shewed with irresistible Force of Argument, the Expediency, the Propriety, and the Equity of such a Resolution, so that it passed 155 against 33. Proxies included ; present 92 to 27.

" Thus hath this Opposition, which at the opening of the Session was thought to be so formidable, vanished into Smoke. The King's Servants will now have it in their Power to attend to the Business of the Nation without Interruption : and if they are honest, much public Good may yet be done this Season.

" Nothing is so true as that Honesty is the best Policy, and that all Wickedness is Misery. With what Pain must Mr. Pitt reflect on his late Conduct ; on the Baseness of cruelly sacrificing the best of Friends to his Ambition, and uniting himself with a Crew which he is already, for very Shame, obliged, in the most public manner, to disclaim any Connexion with. And yet I can hardly help droping a Tear to the Memory of his past Services, and lamenting, sincerely lamenting, that a Man of his rare and useful Talents should suffer himself, from mere want of Honesty, to sink into such universal and deserved Contempt.

" There is nothing left for me to wish you in this World, but an Allevia-tion of those Pains to which your bodily Infirmities subject you. This I most sincerely do. As for the mental Sources of Pleasure and Happiness, by much the most essential, those you have effectually secured by a long Life of Virtue and Beneficence, to which you can at all times look back with unspeakable Satisfaction.

" The *North Briton* is to be burnt at the Royal Exchange next Saturday by the Common Hangman ; and a loyal Address will be presented to the King by both Houses on the Occasion.

" I am, with the highest Respect,

" Sir,

" Your most obedient humble Servant,

"WILL. STRAHAN.

" I beg my most respectful Compliments to all the Family."

To Ralph Allen, Esquire.

" London, Decr. 8, 1763.

" SIR,—On Tuesday last the Tryal between Wilkes and the Under-Secretary Mr. Wood, as you will see by the Papers, came on before Lord Chief Justice Pratt, which lasted from Eight in the Morning till Eleven at Night, when the Jury, after retiring about a Quarter of an Hour, brought in a Verdict for the Plaintiff, with £1,000 Damages.

"The Defendant urged a double Plea : First, *Not Guilty,* and Secondly, *a Special Justification.* In order to which his Councel endeavoured to prove Wilkes the Author of the *North Briton,* No. 45, but this they did not do to the Satisfaction of the Court. In conclusion, after summing up the Evidence, which the Chief Justice did with great Candor and Impartiality, he observed, that he knew no Power the Secretaries of State were invested with superior to that of any other Magistrate ; that he was certain they had none, by any Law or Statute extant ; and that if the Secretaries could delegate to their Inferior Officers the Power of forcibly entering Houses, breaking up Bureaus, and seizing Papers without Limitation or Controul, there was an End of all Liberty, no man could be safe ; but, he added, that as this Power had been so long exercised without Interruption, that Circumstance ought to be considered, in favour of Mr. Wood, as a just Cause for the Mitigation of the Damages ; and, but for this, it is thought the Jury would have given their Verdict for a much larger Sum. A Bill of Exceptions was then offered for the Defendant, as to the Point of Law : Whether the Secretaries of State are or are not legally invested with the Power they have hitherto exercised ; so that the Affair will not be finally settled perhaps till it comes before the House of Lords. When the Trial was over, a vast mob, who had attended the whole Day (a large Posse of whom were evidently hired by Wilkes's Friends) made the Hall resound with their repeated Huzzas ; from whence they went to George Street to congratulate their Champion on his Success.

"The House of Lords have taken notice of the mob at the Exchange last Saturday, when the *North Briton* was burnt, but I really think not very properly ; for as the Disturbance was, by the best Information I can get, purely accidental, it was, of course, unworthy their Attention.

"It is just now reported (with what Truth I cannot say) that Lord Shelbourne is dismissed from his office of Aid de Camp to the King, and that Mr. Calcraft hath lost the Agency of all the Regiments he enjoyed.

"There is nothing else that I can recollect worth troubling you with. I hope our internal Peace will now be soon restored ; and am, with the highest Respect,

" Sir,

" Your most obedient, humble Servant,

" WILL. STRAHAN."

To Ralph Allen, Esquire.

" London, Janry. 2, 1764.

" SIR,—My Lord of Gloucester would bring you all the News from this Quarter.   This only serves to convey to you the Tender of my most fervent Wishes that you may be blest with many happy Returns of this Season ; that all you love may prosper, and that the Remainder of your Days may be as remarkably distinguished by Peace, Ease, and Tranquillity, as those which are past have been by the constant Exercise of every Virtue within the Reach of Humanity.   There is a Pleasure in contemplating your Character, which, tho' I am altogether unable to express, I yet most sensibly feel ; I cannot, therefore, help indulging myself in the Hope that you will yet be long preserved, the Delight and Happiness of your Friends, a bright Example of every Social Virtue, and the Ornament of your Native Country.

" I have presumed, through the Mediation of the Bishop of Gloucester, to prefer a Request in behalf of Mr. Leake,[1] which, if you think it at all proper, I know your Humanity will prompt you to comply with.   Of this you are the only Judge.   And I freely confess I have no Excuse for this Boldness, but that I do not think anything else could tempt me to be guilty of a Repetition of it.

" I pray for the Happiness of all under your Roof, and am, with the highest Deference and Esteem,

" Sir,

" Your most obedient and most humble Sert,

" WILL. STRAHAN."

————

" London, Febry. 20, 1764.

" SIR,—I was favoured with yours of the 24th past, and am extremely happy that you are not offended with my late Boldness.   The obliging Manner, also, in which you mention Mr. Leake, agreeable to your extensive and well-known Humanity, leaves me so much your Debtor, that I am truly afraid, tho' I shall never omit any Occasion, that it will never be in my Power to shew you the just Sense I have of your Kindness.

" I should have sooner done myself the Honour to write to you, but that I had nothing particular to trouble you with, and waited the Issue of the

————

[1] This "Request" was that Allen would place any available MSS. relating to himself and Prior Park at the disposal of Leake, the local publisher.

Debates in the House of Commons in regard to the Seizure of Wilkes's Person and Papers, by virtue of a Warrant from the Secretaries of State.

"On Monday this Debate was, opened by reading another Letter from Wilkes ; and then several Witnesses were examined as to the Behaviour of the Messengers at his House. Beardmore, his Attorney, in particular, gave a circumstantial (and evidently a partial) Detail of what happened on his Commitment to the Tower, and the steps taken to obtain a Habeas Corpus in order to his Release. After this, Mr. Webb, in his Place, gave a very full account of the whole Transaction, from which it appeared that Mr. Wilkes was treated with proper Respect and Decency, that his Papers were offered to be sealed up in presence of Lord Temple, who happened to be at his House when he was seized, or any other of his Friends, that on his Commitment to the Tower, tho' an Order was given that no Person should have access to him, that Order was reversed next morning ; and that no Obstruction whatever was given to his obtaining his Habeas Corpus. Mr. Wood next stood up, and in a very genteel manner acknowleged the Share he had in the affair, for which he had no Apology to make, as he imagined he was, in so doing, discharging the indispensable Duty of his Office. It was now near Eleven, when a Motion was made to adjourn, which passed in the negative, 379 to 31. They then proceeded to read authentic Copies from the Records of all the Warrants that had been issued by Secretaries of State for a Century past ; but this dry and unentertaining Business soon disposed the House to adjourn, which they did about twelve.

"From this night's Debate I plainly saw that the Ministry did not intend to bring the main Question to a Decision, and that the Opposition, on the other hand, meant nothing more than by pushing the matter as far as they were able, to make a Handle of it to raise a Cry against the Administration. This was so very obvious throughout the whole Altercation (for it deserves not the name of an honest Debate) that I own it hurt me exceedingly to see the Great Council of the Nation so uselessly and so factiously employed, whilst many of our most material and most urgent Concerns were suffered to be neglected. Mr. Pitt's Behaviour more particularly disgusted me. The Observations he made, and the Objections he raised during the Examinations, were apparently frivolous and insincere, and most unworthy of the high Character he once sustained with all honest men. I will not trouble you with Instances of this, tho' I could give you many, because I wish, in Gratitude for his former Services, they could be utterly forgotten. I will only say, I think his whole Conduct, since he gave up the Seals, is of a Piece ; exceedingly factious, with repeated, tho' unsuccessful, attempts to regain his Popularity, which I am now more than ever fully perswaded is irretrievably lost. 'Tis needless to observe to you, Sir, whose Love for your Country and for Human Kind is so notorious, how melancholy a Prospect it affords, to see Persons of the first Abilities in the Nation, and from whom we might expect every thing the Exigencies of the State requires, actuated by such unworthy Motives, instead of employing their Talents in the only way in which they can with true Glory exert them.

"Next Day (Tuesday) the House proceeded in hearing the Warrants read, among which was one issued by Mr. Pitt himself, when Secretary of State, ordering the Sailors and Passengers of a certain Ship to be brought before him to answer to the *Premisses*, tho' no Charge whatever was mentioned in the Warrant. To this Mr. Pitt readily pleaded Guilty, and with much affected Contrition and Submission, threw himself upon his Country. He insisted likewise that Mr. Wood (of whose Honour and Fidelity he had had, he said, repeated Experience whilst in Office) stood there his Fellow Criminal, and that they ought both to submit to the Justice of their Country. Mr. Wood replied to this, that he did by no means look upon himself in the Light of a Criminal ; that what he had done he thought it his indispensable Duty to do ; and that he only waited the Sentence of the House upon his Conduct, from whence he would not depart till they had pronounced it. It was now near two in the morning, when it was proposed to put this Question : *That a General Warrant for apprehending and seizing the Authors, Printers and Publishers of a Seditious Libel, together with their Papers, is not warranted by Law.* This gave rise to a fresh Debate ; after which another Question was put, viz., *That this Debate, and the further Consideration of the matter of this Complaint, be adjourned till this Day at twelve o'Clock;* which was carried in the negative, 207 to 197. Then this last Question, amended by inserting the Words, *Friday morning next* instead of *this Day at twelve o'clock*, was agreed to without a Division. It was then moved, *That the Complaint against Robert Wood, Esq., a Member of this House, for a Breach of Privilege of this House be discharged.* Upon which it was again moved to adjourn; which, upon a Division, passed in the Negative, 208 to 184. And then the Motion for discharging the Complaint against Mr. Wood, Mr. Webb, and the Messengers, was agreed to without a Division. Then the House adjourned till Friday, it being now half an Hour after Seven in the Morning. The Speakers of chief note this Day were, the Attorney General, Mr. Grenville, Mr. Wilbraham, Mr. Wedderburn—Mr. Pitt,

Sir William Meredith, Sergeant Huett, Thos. Townsend, CoL Onslow, Mr. Beckford, and Mr. Mawbey—Mr. Pitt spoke 10 or 12 times.

"On Friday they accordingly resumed the further Consideration of this Matter, when both Sides exerted themselves to the utmost in mustering their whole Forces, so that the House was very full. Many excellent Speeches were delivered, which did more Honour to some People's Talents than to their Candor and Integrity. At length the Question was proposed : *That a General Warrant for apprehending and seizing the Authors, Printers, and Publishers of a seditious and treasonable Libel, together with their Papers, is not warranted by Law, although such Warrant hath been issued according to the Usage of Office, and hath been frequently produced to, and so far as appears to this House, the Validity thereof hath never been debated in the Court of King's Bench, but the Parties thereupon have been frequently bailed by the said Court.* Upon this a very warm Debate arose, which terminated in putting the previous Question, *That this Debate be adjourned till this Day four Months;* which, upon a Division, was carried by a very narrow majority, 232 to 218. The Reasons for dismissing the Question in this manner are sufficiently obvious. Many and great Inconveniences would attend the explaining the *precise* Power of a Secretary of State. In all Governments there is lodged *somewhere* Powers not warranted by Law, to be exercised upon great and critical Occasions, such as times of open Rebellion or dangerous and secret Conspiracies ; and as under our Constitution, which admits of greater Liberties to the Subject than the best Republic that ever existed, every Minister exercises this Power at his Peril, we have nothing, in my humble Opinion, to apprehend from the Abuse of it. This I am fully perswaded every Member in the Opposition were duly sensible of, notwithstanding their violent Declamations to the contrary. Those who spoke this Day, in the Order in which they spoke, are as follows :—

Attorney General.
Mr. York.
Attorney General.
Lord North.
Lord George Sackville.
Colonel Burgoyne.
Mr. Nugent.
General Conway.
Mr. Stanley.
Mr. Hussey.

Lord Frederic Campbell.
Mr. Shelly.
Lord Granby.
Mr. Charles Townsend.
Dr. Hay.
Mr. Richmond Webb.
Mr. Dowdeswell.
General Townsend.
Mr. Fuller.
Lord Barington.

Charles Townesend.	Mr. Thos. Townsend.
Lord Barington.	Mr. Eliot.
Mr. Wilbraham.	Mr. Thos. Townsend.
Sir Francis Delaval.	Lord North.
Mr. Pitt.	Mr. Barré.
Mr. Grenville.	Mr. Shiffner.

"In this manner hath this important Affair been composed for the present ; and I hope the Remainder of yᵉ Session will go on pretty smoothly ; at least, I see not any new Matter for the Opposition to take up that will answer their Purpose. 'Tis high time, you will doubtless think, that the Legislature should seriously set about settling our new Conquests, and improving by all other means the late Peace, which, bad as it may by some people be represented, appears more and more every Day to be a very great and seasonable Blessing to this King-dom.

"To morrow, Mr. Wilkes's Trial for being the Author and Publisher of yᵉ *North Briton* comes on before Lord Mansfield at Westminster, the Issue of which I am in little Pain about, as the Jury is Special, and the Proof strong and clear. The same Day the House of Lords are to take into Consideration an inflammatory Pamphlet entitled, *Droit le Roy*, in which the Prerogative of the Crown is pretended to exceed whatever was exercised in the most arbitrary Reign. This Publication is another Effort to disturb the Peace of Government, and divert the Attention of the Administration from the real Business of the Nation.

"I shall endeavour to transmitt to you any thing that comes to my Knowlege during the Course of these Distractions. In the mean time permitt me to turn my Thoughts to a much more agreeable Subject, which I shall mention with that Openness and Freedom so natural to me, and which your known Candor emboldens me to use, even when I address myself to you.

"From the most feeling Sense of your excellent and uncommon Character, which hath inspired me with a Veneration that gives me in-expressible Pleasure, and which I shall ever glory to avow, I am extremely solicitous for the Increase and Preservation of your honest Fame. With this View I have often observed to the Bishop of Gloucester how very desirous I was that the Influences of your Virtues might be per-petuated beyond the Period (long as I hope that will be) of your own Life, and that you could be prevailed with to put such Materials into his Lord-ship's Hands, as might serve to illustrate many Parts of your Conduct, which from your singular Delicacy and Modesty you have ever been most careful to conceal.[1] This I am the more strongly impelled to solicit from a full Conviction, that an authentic Detail of a Life so pregnant with Instances of public Spirit and private Benevolence will be of the most general and lasting Utility, not only as it will do honour to this Country and to human Nature, but as it may prove a strong Inducement with many to *endeavour* at least to follow your Example. I have many other arguments to offer in support of the Propriety of my Request, which I could easily enumerate to any other Person. To yourself I will mention no other than the above, as it is the only one that is likely to weigh with you. I leave it, therefore, to your Consideration, and am, with the highest Esteem, and the most ardent Wishes for the Continuance and Increase of your Happiness,

" Sir,

" Your most obliged and most obedient Servant,

" WILL. STRAHAN.

" I past two very agreeable Hours last night with the Bishop, whom I found in good Health and Spirits."

To Mr. Strahan.

" Prior Park, Feb^ry. 29th, 1761.

" SIR,—My thanks attend you for your Clear Representation of the late Important debate, and I am not Insensible of the too favourable Sentiments that you retain of

" Sir,

" Your obliged most hum^ble Servant,

"(Signed)   RALPH ALLEN."

LOCAL POSTAL ARRANGEMENTS FOLLOWING ALLEN'S DEATH.

No doubt Philip Allen (Ralph Allen's elder brother) was an able coadjutor with Ralph in the practical working of the postal operations, although it does not appear that he held any

---

[1] It is to be seen that the writer was not unobservant of Allen's characteristic modesty and reserve with regard to himself and his personal actions.

recognised official position under the Government. It seems
certain, however, that after Ralph Allen's death, Philip discharged the duties of local post-master until his death, which
occurred on Wednesday, December 4th, 1765, and is thus
officially noticed :—

"Ordered.—That Mr. Thomas Foley be appointed Deputy Postmaster
at Bath, in the stead of the late Philip Allen, Esq., deceased, to commence
the 5th of Jany. next."

After Ralph Allen's death, all his post-office work (that of
Postmaster excepted) was transferred to London, and the
office, which was created for its performance, the " Bye and
Cross Road Letter Office", as it was called, consisted of only
eight persons. In London, without Ralph Allen to superin-
tend, more persons may have been employed upon the work
than at Bath, but it is very unlikely there were fewer.

A Copy of the official Minute, making appointments to this
office may be interesting, if only because it shows that there
was a second Philip Allen, the elder son of Ralph's brother,
Philip.

"Wednesday, Oct. 24, 1764.

"Ordered,— That Philip Allen, Esq., be appointed Comptroller and
Resident Surveyor[1] of the Bye and Cross Road Letter Office, and that
Mr. William Weaver be appointed the Comptroller's Clerk.

"That Mr. Thomas Hyett be appointed Accomptant of the said Office,
and that Mr. Ambrose Serle be appointed Clerk to the Accomptant.

"That Mr. William Ward be appointed Collector to the said Office, and
that Mr. John Atkinson be appointed the Collector's Clerk.

"That Mr. John Spicer be appointed Clerk of the Dead and Refused
Letters in the said Office ; and

"That Mr. Thomas Gibbons be appointed Office and Storekeeper in
the said Office—all to commence from the 10th of Oct. 1764."

The salary of Philip Allen (Ralph's nephew) was: as
Comptroller, £300, and as Resident Surveyor, £200, or £500

---

[1] This official is now called " District Surveyor".

altogether. In 1783, the Postmasters-General proposed that his salary should be raised from £500 to £600, and the reason they gave for the proposal, with their accompanying remarks, has a not unimportant bearing on the point in question.

" We have proposed," they say, " an addition of £100 a year to Mr. Allen during his continuance, as he enjoyed a salary of £900 a year under his late uncle at Bath, who projected and formed this Branch. We have also proposed an addition of £50 a year each to the Accomptant and Collector, and of £20 a year to the Clerk to the Comptroller, who were all brought up from Bath at the same time with Mr. Allen on the establishment of the Bye and Cross Road Letter Office in London in 1764."

PEDIGREE

BENNET FAMILY.

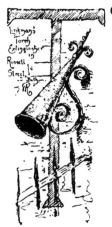

TO deal with Prior Park and the Allen family without referring to WIDCOMBE HOUSE and the Chapman and Bennet families, would be difficult. At the same time, having in *Historic Houses in Bath*, and *Bath, Old and New*, entered largely into the subject, we content ourselves with giving a clear and tolerably full table of genealogy, which, with a few brief notes, will afford all the information likely to be of interest; it will, moreover, show the connection between the Bennet and the Allen families.

Philip Bennet was the best known member of the family in Bath, having represented the city in Parliament from 1741 to 1747. The youngest sister of this gentleman became the second wife of Philip Allen, who died in the same year as her husband, 1767.

PEDIGREE

OF

THE FAMILY OF BENNET, OF WIDCOMBE, MAPERTON, AND SOUTH BREWHAM IN THE COUNTY OF SOMERSET; AND OF TOLLESBURY, CO. ESSEX; ROUGHAM, CO. SUFFOLK; AND CHEVELEY, CO. CAMBRIDGE.

ROBERT BENET, Keeper of the King's Seal in England, 1180.

William Benet FitzRobert, Co. Wilts.

Peter Benet FitzRobert, one of the chief citizens of Winchester, 1208.

Ascelin Bennet, Clerk of the King's Exchequer, an Archdeacon, Commissary of Ramsey Abbey (*Litt.*, 7 *Johan.*, *Rot. Chart* I, f. 103), 1195-1205.

Henry Benet, holds certain manors and lands in Wilts, Suffolk, and Cambridge. 1279 (7 *Edw. I, Rot. Fund.*).

....Benet, miles, holds lands near Southampton under the Abbey of Bec-Herlewyn (*Plac. de quo Warr.*).

Adam Benet of Churiblunterdon, Co. Wilts, 1271.

John Benet, heir to his father's lands in Wilts and Cambridge, 7 Edw. I, High Sheriff of Wilts, 1266 (*Plac. de quo Warr. Rot.* 54).

Galfred Benet of Suwicke, Co. Wilts, 1274 (*Test. de Nevill*).

Adam Benet of Churiblunterdon, 1327.

John Benet of Wilts, appointed by the King Governor of Monmouth Castle, 1327 (Hoare's *Hist. Wilts.*).

Galfrid Benet of Telesford juxta Suwicke, Co. Wilts.

John Benet, M.P. for Bridgwater, 1319. Living at Endford, Co. Wilts, 1338.

William Benet of Malnesbury, 1338. Collector and Keeper of the King's Wool Customs for Ireland, 1322.

Walter Benet of New Sarum (*Abb. Rot.*, 274).

William Benet, in Holy Orders. 1364 (*Inq. p.m.*, 38 E. III).

Peter Benet of Bereford, =Christiana, dau. and heir of Somenour of Byrmerton.

| a

Thomas Benet of Lopene Magna.

John Benet of Norton Bavent, son and heir, Lord of West Harnham, Co. Wilts (*Lansd. MS.* 306).

John Benet of Norton Bavent ; bur. there October 13th, 1467.

Thomas Benet of Norton Bavent, eldest son=......, daughter and heir of .. Page of the Devizes, Co. Wilts. (*Harl. MS.* 5185, 45).

John Benet of Norton Bavent, only son=Agnes, daughter of ...... Forwarde. (*Harl. MS.* 1092, 61).

William Benett of Norton Bavent, from whom the Benetts of Norton Bavent.

John Benett, fourth son (*Harl. MS.* 1092, 61).

At about this time the family of Bennet, Earls of Arlington and of Tankerville, said by Morant to have descended from the Wiltshire stock, may probably have taken their descent. William Bennet of Newbury, father of Henry Bennet of Newbury (will proved London, Jan. 10th, 1485), may well have been son or brother of John, buried at Norton in 1467. It may be remembered that Norton and Newbury are scarcely forty miles apart. And from the Newbury stock the London Branch undoubtedly comes.

William Benett, D.C.L., Precentor of Sarum ; bur. Sarum 1558.

John Bennet of Heytesbury, M.P. for Heytesbury (*MS. Fam. Reg.*) ; bur. at Heytesbury. Eldest son (*Harl. MS.* 1092, 61).

Edward Benett, or Bennet, M.P. (*MS. Fam. Reg.*), only son of=Cicely, daughter and heir of ... Franklyn (*Fam. Reg.*). (See her John Benett, M.P. for Heytesbury ; buried at arms in Sam. Benett's Commonplace Book, 1660.) Heytesbury.

Philip Benett, b. Heytesbury, 1548 : bur. Brewham, Feb. 11th, 1632. Marr. 14th Nov. 1586 to Elizabeth, dau. of John Turner of Middleton in Norton Bavent.

Edward Benett, Lord of the Manor of S. Brewham, b. Heytesbury, Oct. 26th, 1567 ; bur. Brewham, Nov. 14th, 1626. Marr. 1605, Susanna, dau. of Thomas Churchey of Wincanton.

Emlyn, b. 1551.
Margaret Benett, b. 1553.
Faith, 1562.
Joane, 1564.
Cicely, 1566.
Mary, 1570.
Dorothy, 1574.
(*Fam. Reg.*)

Thomas Benett, eldest son, b. 1542 ; bur. at Heytesbury, Sept. 5th, 1612.

John Benett, Bart., Heytesbury, 1545. M.P. for Heytesbury, 1586, and buried there (*Lansd. MS.* 1218 ; *MS.*)

a

b

c

| a | | | b | | c |

William of Heytesbury ..., 24, 1603; bur. Heytesbury (*Fam. Reg.*).

- William of S. Brewham, m. Margaret Lewis.
- Edward of Chorlington, m. 1, Elis Tyning; 2, Agatha Burden; 3, Agnis Norman.
- Thomas of Brewham, m. Mary ......
- John, m. Margaret Longman.

Philip Benet of Bayford and S. Brewham, Col. Denzil Holles' Regt., 1642; born Brewham, May 10th, 1610; bur. Brewham, Sept. 25th, 1690. = **Mary, dau. of Rich. Shute of Bayford; b. Bayford, March 2nd, 1611; marr. 1634 or 1635; bur. Brewham, Dec. 14th, 1691.**

- Edward, Capt., and bur. Brewham, 1613.
- Cycely, ... Parson, died at St. Christopher's, Susanna, m. John Collens, and died in New England. Elizabeth, mar. Thomas Creech, and died at Barbn.

Philip Bennet, only son and heir; bapt. Stoke Rister, March 4th, 1637; died Wincanton, April 1725, Lord of the Manors of Maperton and South Brewham. = **Anne, dau. and co-heir of Thomas Strode of Maperton; b. 1655; mar. Maperton, 1677; bur. Wincanton, 1735.**

- Mary Bennet, born Bayford, 1635; bur. West Pennard, 1693. Mar. John Walter, issue four sons and three daughters.
- Martha Bennet, b. Brewham; mar. 1666, John Clements of Meere, who died Jan. 5th, 1691, issue John and Martha.

Philip Bennet, b. Maperton, Sept. 2nd, 1678; d. March 15th, 1722; bur. at Maperton. = **Jane, only child of Scarborough Chapman of Widcombe House, Co. Som.; b. Widcombe, April 23rd, 1672; mar. Widcombe, Aug. 29th, 1702; bur. Maperton, May 2nd, 1772.**

- Abigail, b. Nov. 20th, 1682; mar. 1722, Saml. lhurges. Anne, b. March 18th, 1680; d. unmar., Oct. 17th, 1705. Mary, *ob. inf.*, 1688. Martha, *ob. inf.*, 1699.
- Mary, b. Mapleton, 1694; m. William Burleton of East Knoyle, from whom the family of Burleton Bennet.
- James, b. 1681; bur. Mapleton, 1683. Strode, b. 1691; bur. Wincanton, 1711, unmar. Sarah, b. March 5th, 1694; living unmar. 1736.

Anne, dau. of .... Estcourt of Co. Gloucester, sister of Thomas Estcourt; bur. Widcombe, April 11th, 1730, aged 24, *s. p.* = **Philip Bennet, eldest son, M.P. for Shaftesbury 1734, for Bath 1741. Lord of Brewham, Widcombe, Maperton, and Tollesbury; where bur. Dec. 9, 1761.** = **Mary, dau. and sole heir of Thomas Hallam of Tollesbury and Clackton; bur. Widcombe, Aug. 14th, 1739.**

- Robert Bennet of Shaftesbury; bur. Widcombe, Aug. 14th, 1750, *s. p.*
- Thomas Bennet of Lascelles' Regt. of Foot. Admon. granted to his brother Philip, May 7th, 1748.
- ..... bur. Bathampton. Susan, bur. Bathampton. Mary, mar. ..., Doddington, M.P.
- Jane, b. 1704, died April 14th, 1767; mar. Philip Allen, brother of Ralph Allen; d. 1767, leaving issue, Mary, mar. Cornwallis, Lord Hawarden;[2] Philip and Ralph.[3]

P

[1] Lord Hawarden resided at Prior Park for some years, until his death in 1704. He was succeeded by his son, the only issue of this marriage, at whose death, in 1707, the connection of the Maudes with Prior Park ceased.
[2] Philip succeeded his uncle, Ralph, as Post-master, in 1764; died 1787.

| a

Philip Bennet of Widcombe=Mary, dau. of Rev. Chris. Hard of Aller, and
and Tollesbury; bapt. Wid- co-heir of her brother Christopher and
combe, April 11th, 1734; James Hand of Cheveley, Co. Cambs.
bur. Widcombe, 1774.

Thomas, b. Widcombe, Jan. 31st, 1736; bur. Widcombe, Sept. 22nd, 1737.

Mary, b. Widcombe, 1735; *ob.* Will dated March 5th, 1784.

Philip Bennet, only child and heir, b. Widcombe, April 14th, 1771; bur. Rougham,=Jane Judith, only child and heir of Roger
May 1853. Lord of Rougham, Tollesbury, Widcombe, and Cheveley Green.   of Rougham Hall. Co. Suffolk.

Philip Bennet of=Anne, dau. and
Rougham Hall, co-heir of Sir
b. May 9th, 1795; Thomas Pilk-
M.P. for West ington, Bart.,
Suffolk 1845-54; of . . . . Yorks.
d. 1866.

James Thomas=Henrietta
Bennet, Rector Eliza, dau.
of Cheveley; of James
b. 1796; bur. . . . . .
Cheveley, 1868. of Dor.

Edward=Bennet
of
Copdock
Lodge.

Christopher, *ob. s. p.,* 1853.

Ralph, *ob. s. p.,* 1875.

William, *ob. s. p.,* 18 . . .

Jane Fenny, mar. Rev. S. H. Alderson, and left issue.

Two sons and two daughters.

Philip Bennet, =Barbara,
R.H.G.; dau. of
b. 1837, Edgar
d. 1875; Disney.
only child and
heir.

James Thomas=
Hand Bennet,
b. 1832.

Edward Keding-=Frances Caroline,
ton Bennet, dau. and co-heir
b. 1834, D.C.L., of William Thos.
F.S.A., Rector of Adams Reilly.
Burwell.

Mary, mar. W. G. Blake and . . .
Edith Anne.

James Philip, *ob. s. p.,* 1849.
Henry Bower Butts, *ob. s. p.,* 1849.

Four sons and one daughter.

One son and one daughter.

One son and one daughter.

One son and two daughters.

One son and two daughters.

" Philip Bennet of the Parish of Lyncombe and Widcombe, Bachelor, and Mary Hand, of the Parish of Aller, in the County of Somerset, were married in this Church by licence this fourteenth day of December, in the year One Thousand Seven Hundred and Sixty-nine, by me.

" John Chapman, Rector.

" This Marriage was solemnized } Philip Bennet.
between us in the presence } Mary Hand.
of Ralph Allen.[1]
Robt. Fleetwood.

" N.B.—The Parish Church of Lyncombe and Widcombe by the late Marriage Act deemed Extra Parochial, and the Parish of St. James is rebuilding.

" I do hereby Certify the above to be a true Copy from the Marriage Register of the Parish of St. Peter and Paul, in the city of Bath, extracted from the register this 9th day Nov. 1813.

" Signed, JAMES PHILLOTT, Rector of Bath."

In the Widcombe valley, opposite Prior Park, there stood, and still stand, the ancient and picturesque little Church and

---

[1] This Ralph Allen was the younger son of Philip Allen and nephew of Ralph Allen, and is the same mentioned as witness also in the following :—

" No. 572.

" Cornwallis Maude, Esqre, of the Parish of Laugharne, in the County of Caermarthen, Widower, and Miss Mary Allen, in their Parish, Spinster, were married in this Church by Licence, this tenth day of June, in the Year One Thousand Seven Hundred and Sixty-six, by me, Duel Taylor, Rector of Bath.

" This Marriage was solemnised ⌉ Cornwallis Maude.*
between Us. ⌊ Mary Allen.

" In the presence of Ralph Allen and Philip Bennet.

" I certify ye above to be a true copy from ye Marriage Register of ye Parish of St. James, City of Bath, extracted this 3rd Day June 1830.

" CHARLES CROOKE, Rector."

---

* Afterwards Lord Hawarden. Mary Allen was the daughter of Philip Allen, by his marriage with Jane Bennet.

Widcombe
Old Church
and House.

Walter Rossi Esq

Manor House, with their lovely surroundings, forming one of the most beautiful groups near the city.

The Church was built in 1502, and is dedicated to St. Thomas á Becket. The Manor House stands upon the site of a pre-Reformation mansion, which was standing long before the first Richard Chapman, by subtlety, acquired the estate at the Reformation (*vide* p. 40). In 1656 Walter Chapman employed Inigo Jones to design a new mansion.[1] This Chapman family, to whom reference has already been made, figure throughout Bath history for three and a-half centuries. The race has presented various types in almost every profession and trade. There is scarcely a public office of any consideration which has not been filled by a Chapman, sometimes with credit, and occasionally the reverse. The elder branch, of whom the representative lived from the Reformation, down to 1702, in affluence and dignity, became extinct by the death of Scarborough Chapman, when began the reign of Philip Bennet, who married Chapman's only child in the year of her father's death. Besides Philip and other issue, she had a daughter, Jane, who became the wife of Philip Allen, and she died in 1767. It was in 1736 that the last-named Philip Bennet restored the south front of Widcombe House, on which are his arms and those of his two wives ; he also made the present entrance, and erected the two handsome pillars, each being surmounted by the Bennet crest. He added the pretty group of offices in the south garden, close to the Church. It is strange that this gentleman, so reserved and circumspect up to middle age, entered about 1747 upon a career of wild dissipation, squandering his fortune with reckless prodigality.

---

[1] *Dictionary of Architecture*, article " Inigo Jones".

BEAU NASH.

[" There are things we do and know perfectly well, though we never speak of them—the moral world has, perhaps, no particular objection to vice, but an insuperable objection to having it called by its proper name. The Ahrimanians worship the devil, but don't mention him, and a polite public will no more bear to read an authentic description of vice than a refined English or American will permit the word *teacher* to be pronounced in her presence."—*Thackeray.*]

T would be difficult to write of Ralph Allen and his Times without touching upon the subject of Beau Nash. Of Nash we have ventured to make some brief but emphatic observations in *Rambles about Bath, Historic Houses*, and *Bath, Old and New*. We believe we were the first local writer by whom any unfavourable criticisms were published on the life and character of the notorious beau. For some reasons, or for no reasons, we are expected to receive the charming romance by Goldsmith as a trustworthy account of Nash ; that is, we are expected to accept his inferences, despite his facts. We may say that Goldsmith's biography of Nash has been the quarry from which all succeeding biographies of Nash have been hewn. It is true that a few writers, aiming at novelty, have manufactured a few dull anecdotes for our edification. We accept Goldsmith's dictum expressed in the opening paragraph : " History," he says (he should also have

said Biography), "owes its excellence more to the writer's manner than the materials of which it is composed." We freely admit that Nash, in succeeding the coarse and vulgar Webster, about 1706, perceived that any attempt on his part to "organize" society, must be made in a different spirit and with a higher aim than had ever entered the mind of his predecessor. Moreover it is clear that, at the outset, Nash really aimed at purifying the curious, not to say motley, and promiscuous admixture of people with whom he had to deal ; and we frankly allow that for nearly fifteen years he performed his self-assumed functions with decision and prudence.[1] The assemblies were conducted with propriety and success. Again, Nash's private life, if not beyond impeachment, was fairly good. Sobriety was always one of his virtues, and so far he was an example to the by no means exemplary youth of the period who ranged themselves under his banner, and, in a sense, were subject to his sway.

After this all was changed. The first assembly-rooms were

---

[1] Nash possessed no private fortune, and as he gradually lapsed into luxurious and extravagant habits, he became reckless and unscrupulous as to the methods of gratifying them. This mode of life, doubtless, was largely encouraged by the snobs and fashionable cads of the day. There was literally no moral restraint exercised by the society from whom Nash received his principal support. And it must again be admitted that illiterate and ignorant as Nash was, yet in natural shrewdness, general intelligence, and insight into the sort of human nature with which he had chiefly to do, and in the audacity and the assumption of a plausible and factitious authority, he did exercise a unique and irresistible influence upon the persons with whom he had to deal.

The life and character of Nash are excused—nay justified—on the ground of the unrestrained licentiousness of the age. This is the very essence of our indictment. We say that whilst he "curbed the young bloods" of the day and repressed the coarse and vulgar vices which had previously prevailed, Nash erected his own policy—more dangerous because less manifest and revolting—into a system, carried on in secret with all the subtlety and cunning of which Nash was a consummate master·

erected in 1708 by Harrison,[1] the central room of which still

[1] [In the *Hervey Correspondence* just published, there is a characteristic illustration of even the earlier and better habits of Bath society and Nash's conduct in relation thereto.]

"Bath, Sept. 20, 1721.

"LADY BRISTOL TO LORD BRISTOL.—Notwithstanding all the regularity I boasted of, I can send you nothing but complaints ; for I have been very bad again with my hysterick disorder after I writ my last letter, which I believe you will not wonder at, when you see by it the distraction of mind I was then in, and am likely to continue so, if to-morrow's post does not bring me some comfort ; pray God send it for both our sakes, that I may be easd in my mind, and you in your body, which sure if you are, you will not loose a moment to bless me with your dear and much longd for presence ; so much longd for that sure I shall die with joy once more to behold you. O what would I not give this were the happy minute ; for I do love you beyond expression farr more than ever (if that be possible) ; I was made sensible this morning in a dream what I might suffer by to-morrow's post ; for I dreamd you were worse, and putt myself into such a passion of crying that I have not been able to recover it all the day, tho' I have had a good deal of company to dine with me, which I believe you will think pretty necessary, (tho' I have a bad cook,) when I tell you I have eat but one meal at home before this this week, so very charitable and kind to me are the most agreeable people in this place ; and as the greatest compliment can be made to me, your health is constantly drank. I wish I could tell you any news to entertain you, but really I can't tho' the town is as full as possible, but such a mixture as was never got together at the building of Babel ; yet one piece of news I must not forgett, which is that I threw fifteen mains yesterday morning, and I got but fivety pound by it ; Mr. Nash said he had a great mind to write you word of it ; here is very deep play ; Mr. Stanup [Stanhope] has improved it since he came ; Nash lost fivety pound a Saturday at Harrison's, and as they say broke all the windows according to custom. There is several parties of ladys and gentlemen gone to Bristol to see a review, and General Whiteman is to give a ball there ; I had the honour to be invited, but I neither likd my company, nor was fitt for such an expedition, if I had. To-morrow I am to begin pumping by Doctor Friend's directions, which I shall follow in that particular, tho' not in his orders to continue in this cursed place longer than till I can gett a conveyance to carry me off, which I am sure you will not lett me be long

forms the Lecture Room of the Literary and Philosophical
Institution, close to the North Parade. After Harrison's
death the rooms were leased, in 1737, by Miss Hayes, who was
herself a gambler and married the notorious Lord Hawley.
In 1720 Thayer employed Wood to build the rival rooms,
almost opposite, the first lessee of which was Mrs., or, as
she was called, *Dame Lindsay;* and, although the Assemblies
were held at the rival rooms alternately, it was at the
Dame's rooms in the thirties that Nash became a confederate
with this bad woman, and afterwards with her successor,
Catherine Lovelace ; then with Walter Wiltshire, and lastly
with Walter's son, Walter ; and, in a word, Nash found the
victims, and the gamesters successively plundered them.
Rigorous laws were made by the Government to suppress
the gambling, but without success. The monster was
scotched, not killed, the laws being evaded by the invention
of new games. The result, therefore, so far as the victims
were concerned, was "heads I win, tails you lose." This
system was carried on for many years ; and when Nash
departed from his original simple habits, it was only by the
plunder which, for the time, he shared with his confederates,
that he was enabled to sustain the large expenditure in which
he indulged. The system came to an end by a wrong move
of Nash's.

After the repressive laws referred to were passed, it became
necessary to evade their provisions by the invention of a new
game. This was devised by A——e in conjunction with one

without, if you feel half the torments I endure by my stay ; either come
or send for me, for I am not able to bear it any longer ; I am wretched
beyond expression, and shall not have an eye left in a little while to make
my complaints to you ; I can bear no more : adieu, my life.—My Lord
Radner bids me tell you that these waters will certainly cure you as he
knows by experience ; therefore hopes you will come for your own sake
as well as mine, else I shall make them loose their creditt."

C——k, who having quarrelled, as thieves sometimes do, the former, with Nash and Wiltshire (lessee of the Rooms) and a man named J——e, formed a quadruple alliance, the chief provisions of which were that the operations should be carried on at any and all times except during the ordinary assemblies. This alliance meant, further, that whilst Nash was not to be seen in it, he was to provide the victims, take the lion's share of the plunder, whilst his colleagues were to work the machinery, conduct the bank, and to meet all legal risks and responsibilities. Then came the *dénoûment.*

Wiltshire refused to pay over to Nash a large sum which he claimed as his share of plunder. Nash brought an action to recover it, and was at once non-suited on legal grounds ; but the matter received additional notoriety by the Vestry of St. Peter and St. Paul (Abbey) suing Wiltshire and recovering the fine of £500 for keeping a gambling house. This, occurring about 1745, was a death-blow to Nash's usefulness and influence. Every public transaction after it was accompanied by an accusation against his gambling confederates, and a tedious printed apology for and an attempted justification of himself. In a word, his reputation was gone ; and all the "charming writing" and the specious gloss of Goldsmith, in the Life, fails to rehabilitate him.

The admirable projects to which Nash had in his better days set his hand, even with great forbearance and help of former colleagues, came to nought. The Mineral-Water Hospital lingered for years before it was brought to a successful issue by Wood, Allen, and others.

When the late John Forster undertook to write the *Life of Goldsmith,* it is doubtful whether, previously, he had been acquainted with *The Life of Nash.* Forster, indeed, must have been surprised to find that a subject such as Nash should, for any reason, have engaged the attention and the pen of the author of *The Vicar of Wakefield* and *The Citizen of the World.* Forster thinks Goldsmith must have seen and known Nash. We think not. Goldsmith was never in Bath before 1771, when, according to Forster himself, he paid a visit to Lord Clare[1] on the North Parade. Nash died ten years previous to that, and some years before his death he had become a helpless invalid. The fact, perhaps, makes little difference. Forster, as might be expected, makes the best of the case. Goldsmith, no doubt, was led to write the *Life of Nash* by some eccentric instinct—some feeling of blended sympathy and romance. Forster saw, as most other careful readers who read between the lines now see, namely, that Goldsmith was concealing more than he was relating, and relating only such half-truths as answered his purpose. Forster says the "book appears quite a surprising perform-ance for fourteen guineas." We should say it would have been a more "surprising performance" if Goldsmith had undertaken it for mere pay.

The age truly was a vicious one, and the worst of its vices culminated in Bath ; but it was an age, as we have shown, not altogether incompatible with public and private virtue, difficult, perhaps, as its exercise may have been, amidst so much profligacy and so many shameless vices.

Goldsmith apparently did not or would not see that if Nash joined a quadruple alliance for an immoral, an unlawful, and in every sense, an unjustifiable purpose, he shared the odium and blame of that alliance. The rogues fell out, and

---

[1] The Earl of Cork and Burlington on this occasion was residing at No. 9, North Parade, his neighbour at No. 10 being the Duke of Northumberland. On returning home one day Goldsmith entered No. 10 instead of No. 9, and making his way into the drawing-room, the Duke and Duchess being absent, he "cuddled" himself up on the sofa, went fast to sleep, and in that condition was found by their Graces when they returned. The surprise of Goldsmith was great, but the Duke and Duchess, knowing who he was, were very kind, made him stay to dinner, and were ever after his fast friends.

Goldsmith writes as if he thought that the violation of the axiom "honour amongst thieves" rendered Nash a martyr to virtue, instead of exhibiting him as the leader of a nest of robbers, whose study it was to plunder a public who had trusted him as an honest leader and "king".

To sum up Nash's character, we say that if he had followed out the original lines he had marked out for himself he might have been a benefactor to the city. He departed from those lines. The successes of his earlier days did not satisfy his vanity. What was good and lawful in itself and for the advantage of the community at large, was to be made subservient to other ends—evil, base, and demoralizing. The primary duty of Nash was a simple and praiseworthy one. It was simply to protect society in the exercise of a charming —and indeed what had become an almost indispensable— amusement—the "condenced step and rythmic movement"; to blend the various elements of society into something like a harmonious whole. This task Nash had partly succeeded in accomplishing; that success assured him a moderate competence. Nash's vulgar nature could not submit to simple honesty and exemplary habits. Licentiousness, equipages, and even mock dignity were costly luxuries, and they must be paid for. But how? Here was the test of Nash's principles. The transactions afford a curious psychological study. Nash conceived a comprehensive plan for plundering in private the community that trusted him in public. The Assemblies he conducted with propriety and regularity, and his rigid adherence to the hour of closing, really facilitated the proceedings of his wily agents in seducing their victims from the innocent to the guilty work that followed.

Goldsmith, in relating the guilty transactions which led to the legal proceedings (*Life of Nash*, pp. 68, 69, 70, 71), quotes from the Psalms, "For the Lord hateth lying and deceitful lips." That is to say, the Lord hated the subordinate sharpers, but loved the sharper-in-chief simply because he was outwitted. The game was carried on in Wiltshire's Rooms, and the chances to the players were literally hopeless. Nash organized, directed, controlled. He found he had been out-witted, that his creatures had "defrauded" him. "I," he says, "taking them to be honest, never enquired what was won or what was lost ; and thought they paid me honestly, till it was discovered that they had defrauded me of 2,000 guineas!"[1] of which, with his concurrence, they had first "defrauded" the public.

Goldsmith never mentions the trusting public, hundreds of whom were ruined by trusting Nash. Nash suing Wilt-shire (the lessee of the rooms) to recover his winnings, and being non-suited, and Wiltshire[2] being then sued by a local

---

[1] Smollett in his earlier visit to Bath saw a good deal of the life, after Nash had given himself up to the gambling and gamblers, to enable him to keep up the large expenditure which his later expensive and immoral habits entailed. The fact is indisputable that the state of society in Bath was rotten to the very core. There was not a vice that did not pre-vail. It varied in degree rather than in kind, according to the social status and position of the various sections into which society was divided. Every form of gambling then prevailed, until the Legislature, almost in vain, attempted to cope with the evil. No sooner was it attacked in one form than, Proteus-like, it assumed new forms and presented new diffi-culties. It was an evil age, of which Smollett has given us a striking picture. "About a dozen years ago, many decent families, restricted to small fortunes, besides those that came hither on the score of health, were tempted to settle in Bath, where they could then live comfortably, and even make a genteel appearance, at a small expense. But the madness of the times has made the place too hot for them, and they are now obliged to think of other migrations. Some have already fled to the mountains of Wales, and others have retired to Exeter. Thither, no doubt, they will be followed by the flood of luxury and extravagance, which will drive them from place to place to the very Land's End ; and then, I suppose, they will be obliged to 'ship them'."

[2] Lessee of what are now spoken of as Wiltshire's Rooms, which were erected opposite Harrison's by Humphrey Thayer in 1720.

public body for keeping a gaming house, and being mulcted in a fine of £500, Goldsmith does not refer to.

There is a curious and pathetic story told by the architect, Wood. A young lady who was known as *Madame Sylvia* occupied apartments in his house. Her habits were singular, not to say mysterious, but Wood never suspected her of immoral habits. On the contrary, she was refined in speech and manner, and unusually affectionate towards Wood's children. One night, returning home late, after entering the children's room, and kissing them in their sleep, she went into her own apartment and hanged herself with her own garters. Neither Goldsmith nor Wood ever knew who she was, nor has her name ever been revealed by any local annalist, even if it were known. We are indebted for the following fact to a private note made by the famous Dr. Henry Harington in a copy of Wood's *Description of Bath*. The unfortunate General Braddock had two daughters, to the elder of whom he left £15,000, and to the younger a small annuity, which she eked out by becoming a governess. This younger daughter, then, was the *Madame Sylvia*. On the death of the elder sister, Sylvia inherited her fortune, came to Bath, got into the clutches of "Dame" Lindsay and others, who, like Nash, inherited the blessed assurance of the Psalmist that lying and deceit could not be imputed to them. Dame Lindsay,[1] like Nash, did not touch the unholy things herself. Her "simplicity", like that of Nash, never degenerated into the weakness of running needless risks by doing a dirty or a dangerous thing so long as it could be done by deputy. True, Goldsmith assures us, by implication, that Nash and Dame Lindsay had not erred from "the sacred dictates of the Psalmist"!

Some years ago, during the visit of the British Archæological

---

[1] Lessee of Harrison's Rooms, on the site of the Royal Literary Institution, the old assembly room still forming the public *Lecture Room*.

Association to Bath, public attention was called to the anachronism involved in the epigram on Nash's statue in the Pump Room. The late Mr. Ezra Hunt had (with ourselves) called attention to the fact that the thing referred to was a picture, not a statue.

The lines have been generally attributed to the pen of Chesterfield, and constantly quoted as his in the several works descriptive of Bath ; it is clear, however, that Chesterfield has no claim to their authorship. The original lines referred to a "picture", not a "statue". The verses from which the couplet is quoted may be found in the first volume of Southey's *Specimens of the Later English Poets*, page 392, and were written by Jane Brereton, who died in 1740. The poem is inscribed "On Mr. Nash's picture at full length, between the busts of Sir Isaac Newton and Mr. Pope", and is as follows :—

> " The old Egyptians hid their wit
>   In Hieroglyphick dress
> To give men pains to search for it,
>   And please themselves with guess.

> " Moderns, to tread the self-same path,
>   And exercise our parts,
> Place figures in a room at Bath,
>   Forgive them, God of Arts.

> " Newton, if I can judge aright,
>   All wisdom doth express,
> His knowledge gives mankind new light,
>   Adds to their happiness.

> " Pope is the emblem of true wit,
>   The sunshine of the mind ;
> Read o'er his works for proof of it,
>   You'll endless pleasure find.

> " Nash represents man in the mass,
>   Made up of wrong and right ;
> Sometimes a knave, sometimes an ass,
>   Now blunt, and now polite.

> " The picture, placed the busts between,
>   Adds to the thought much strength ;
> Wisdom and wit are little seen,
>   But folly at full length."

It may also be added that the *statue* which is constantly referred to as the supposed picture between the busts of Newton and Pope, was not in existence until many years after the verses were written.   Whose is that picture ?   It could not have been either Hoare's or Hudson's.

After Nash's fall, his means diminished and his reputation gone, he was obliged to economise.   For some years, he lived in the large house[1] in St. John's Court, the Saw-close front of which is now obscured by the atrium of the Theatre going through the first storey.   After Nash left the house many celebrities lived in it, Mrs. Delany being one of them.   Nash removed to the smaller house on the north of his former one, the handsome door entrance being at the gable, or south end of it, and is still to be seen.   Here, it is to be feared, that Nash no longer deserved the immunity from the fate of the gamester, for he did his gambling in person, and not by deputy !

The private life of Nash from his early manhood was never very good, but age did not improve his habits.   The latest victim of his unrestrained lust was a good-looking girl named Juliana Popjoy, a dressmaker.   During her early connection with Nash she rode about the streets of Bath on a dapple-grey horse ; in her hand she carried a many-thonged whip, and hence she was known as " Lady Betty Besom".   Nash died in 1761, and at this time " Lady Betty" was about 30 years of age.   During the last five years of his life, Nash was a poor helpless invalid, and this young woman tended him with exemplary fidelity and kindness, ultimately to find herself helpless, homeless, and characterless.

[1] The " Doctor Johnson" Public-house

" At Bishopstrow, her native place, near Warminster in Wilts, the cele-brated Juliana Popjoy, in the 67th year of her age. In her youth, being very handsome and genteel, she was taken notice of by the late celebrated Beau Nash, a gentleman noted for his gallantry, dress, and generosity ; when he soon prevailed on her to tread the flowery paths of pleasure with him ; she was accordingly ushered into the blaze of the world, was mounted on a fine horse, and had a servant to attend her. This seem-ingly happy state continued some time ; but at last, Mr. Nash's finances being low, a separation took place, when poor Juliana experienced a sad reverse of fortune, and was driven to almost the lowest ebb of misery. However, she did not, like too many of her sisterhood, take to parading the streets for a livelihood, but to a very uncommon way of life. Her principal residence she took up in a large hollow tree, now standing within a mile of Warminster, on a lock of straw, resolving never more to lie in a bed ; and she was as good as her word, for she made that tree her habitation for between thirty and forty years, unless when she made her short peregrinations to Bath, Bristol, and the gentlemen's houses adjacent ; and she then lay in some barn or outhouse. In the summer time she went a simpling, and occasionally carried messages. At last, worn out with age and inquietude, she determined to die in the house where she was born ; accordingly, a day before her exit, she reached the destined habitation, where she laid herself on some straw, and finished her mortal pilgrimage."—*Contemporary Account.*

APPENDIX.

WILL OF RALPH ALLEN.

Extracted from the Register of the Prerogative Court of Canterbury

I, RALPH ALLEN, of Prior Park, in the Parish of Lyncomb and Wid-comb, in the county of Somerset, Esquire, being of a sound disposing mind, memory, and understanding (Praised be God), do make and declare this my last will and testament in manner following (that is to say) :—

Principally I recommend my soul to Almighty God in full hopes of everlasting life, through the merits and intercession of our only redeemer and saviour Jesus Christ, and my body I remit to the earth to be decently buried in the Church of Claverton in the said county, and as to the disposition of my worldly estates, wherewith it hath pleased God to bless me, I give and dispose of the same as follows, that is to say, I give my wife one annuity, or clear yearly rent of thirteen hundred pounds, for and during the term of her natural life, and chargeable on and made payable as hereinafter mentioned. Then I give and devise to my said wife all that my capital messuages called Prior Park, wherein I now live, with all my Dove houses, coach-houses, stables, outhouses, buildings, gardens, courts, barns, yards and offices thereto belonging. And all the messuages, lands, and tenements which I purchased from Pool (since deceased), and all and every the messuages, lands, and tenements I lately bought and purchased of and from Simon Collet and the trustees of John

Marchant, clothier, deceased, and all that my estate called Comb Down, with all houses and buildings. To hold the said Capital messuage with its appurtenances, and the said estates before mentioned, to her my said wife, and her assigns, for one hundred years,[1] commencing from the day of my death if she my said wife shall so long live, she repairing and keeping the premises in good and sufficient repair. And I also give my said wife and her assigns, from time to time, full and free Ingress, Egress, and Regress at all times, either on foot or with coaches, chariots, and other carriages of passing and repassing in, by and through and over all or any the new roads by me made from Dole Mead Gate to Combe Down, and of all other ways, drives, and other Roads by me made or to be made or used into, upon, through, and over any of my lands, tenements, or hereditaments in the parishes of Lyncomb and Widcomb, Monkton Comb, Bathampton, and Claverton, or either of them, in the said county of Somerset, and also all my messuage or tenement, with the appurtenances at Weymouth, in the county of Dorset, I give and devise to my said wife and her assigns, for and during the term of her natural life. Item, I give and devise to my said wife and her assigns, for and during the term of her natural life, the free use of my plate, china, and household goods of my said house at Weymouth. Item, I give and bequeath to my said wife all her jewels, rings, watches, seals, trinkets, and all other the Ornaments of her person, absolutely as her own, and I also give her, my said wife, the use of all my household goods, Pictures, plate, china, Linen, implements and utensils of household, which shall be in or belonging to the house wherein I now live at the time of my decease. But in case may said wife shall happen to die without making any compleat or full disposition of her jewels, rings, watches, seals, trinkets, and other ornaments of her person in her lifetime, or in writing by will or otherwise, Item, I do hereby give the said Jewels, Rings, Watches, Seals, Trinkets, or such other part or parts as shall not be by my said wife given away or disposed of as aforesaid, unto my nieces, Gertrude

---

[1] A legal fiction, as covering all questions of time and limitations. Mrs. Allen died two years after her husband.

Warburton, wife of the Reverend Lord Bishop of Gloucester, and Mary Allen.[1] Spinster, equally between them, share and share alike, and all my household goods, pictures, plates, china, Linen, implements and utensils of household I will and direct, shall be and remain in my dwelling house at Prior Park, and be held and enjoyed by such person and persons to whom I have hereinafter given and devised the said house, in the nature of and as Heirs Loom, except such parts thereof as my wife shall in her life time, or by her will in writing or otherwise give away and dispose, and which gift and disposition I do hereby empower her to make. And I hereby direct that the said jewels, household goods, china, plate, and other things, both in my house at Prior Park and in my house at Weymouth, shall not be liable or subject to pay any of my debts. I give my said wife six of my coach-horeses or geldings, and such harness for such six horeses, and also such two of my saddle horeses or geldings, with two such saddles and bridles as my said wife shall choose. Item, I give my said wife my Coach and Post Chaise, with all appurtenancies belonging. Item, I do hereby charge and make liable all and every my manors, messuages, lands, and tenements, and real estate whatsoever (except what I have before given my said wife for her life), with the payment of my wife's annuity hereinbefore given to her, and direct the same to be paid at four quarterly payments, Christmas Day, Lady Day, Midsummer Day, and St. Michael the Archangel, by equal portions, the first payment to be made on such of the said feasts as shall next happen after my death, and to be free of all taxes and deductions whatever. And I do hereby invest my said wife with all other powers and remedies for recovering my said annuity by entry and distress, or by receiving the rents and profits of my said estates as fully as if the same was repeated here at large. And I do hereby declare said annuity to be in lieu and discharge of any dower of thirds which she, my said wife, can or may claim out of any my Estates, and whereas by the Articles made on my brother Philip Allen's marriage with his present wife I am obliged to pay him two annuities of one hundred pounds per annum, each at such times as therein mentioned, and the same is chargeable on all or some parts of my Estates in the parish of

---

[1] Whom Allen sometimes called Molly. After Allen's death she married Cornwallis Maude. See page 211.

Lyncomb and Widcomb, I do hereby exonerate such estates from the payment of the said annuities, and do will and direct the same to be charged and chargeable on my Estate and lands in the Parish of Bathampton, during so long as my said wife shall happen to live. Item, all my and every my manors, messuages, lands, tenements, and hereditaments whatsoever, which are of freehold tenure (subject to my wife's Estate for life in those particular Estates I have before given to her) I give, devise, and bequeath unto John Chapman, one of the Aldermen of the City of Bath, and James Sparrow of the same city, Clerk, To hold to them and their heirs and assigns In trust, that they, my said trustees, or the survivor of them, and the heirs and assigns of such survivor, do and shall from time to time, and at all times hereafter during my wife's life, receive the rents, issues, and profits thereof and (after paying taxes, Repairs, and all other outgoings) do in the next place pay and discharge my said wife's annuity, and do out of the rents and profits of my Bathampton Estate, pay my brother, Philip Allen, annuity or annuities, and do pay and apply the overplus of the nett Profits of all the said Estates (which are not given my said wife for her life) if any be, after such deductions as aforesaid, to my niece, Gertrude Warburton, wife of the Rt. Rev. William, Lord Bishop of Gloucester, for her own sole and separate use, separate and apart from her present or any after taken husband, and her receipt alone to be a sufficient discharge for the same. And from and after my wife's decease I will my said Trustees, and the survivor of them, and the heirs and assigns of such survivor shall stand seized of all and every my manors, messuages, lands, tenements and hereditaments of freehold tenure, to, for, and upon the following uses (that is to say) As, to, for, and concerning, all that my Manor, with all lands and hereditaments thereto belonging, situate and being in the parish of Bathampton aforesaid, with all Courts, Royalties, Jurisdictions, and Rights whatsoever thereto appertaining (except the Warren), and also all that my Estate and interest of and in the Lands and Estate I purchased of His Grace the Duke of Kingston, and now out upon the lives of William Skrine, Esq. and his sister, To the use of my brother Philip and his heirs for ever in lieu of the £200 per annum I am obliged to pay him by his said Marriage articles. And I will and direct that my said brother and his heirs do, within

six months after he or they become entitled to the said Estate here
bequeathed him, release, acquit, and discharge all other my estate
and lands of and from the payment of the said annuities for ever
after, but in case my said brother shall refuse to accept of such
devise and bequest in lieu and satisfaction of such annuity (the same
being of much greater value), I then direct the said devise and bequest shall become void, and that they, my said Trustees, do pay him,
my said brother, the sum of £5,000 as a purchase for said annuities,
which purchase I am empowered to make by the said marriage
articles ; and as to all other my manors and messuages, lands, tenements and hereditaments of freehold tenure (including the Warren
I have excepted before), and also including all my estate and lands
before given to my brother Philip and his heirs, in case my said
brother refuses to accept thereof upon the terms aforesaid, to the use
of and in trust that they, my said trustees, and the survivor of them,
and the heirs and assigns of such survivor, do and shall with all convenient speed after my wife's decease, by sale or mortgage of all or
any part thereof, raise and levy the sum or sums of money as shall be
sufficient to pay and satisfy all my just debts and legacies hereinafter
given, in case my personal estate shall not be sufficient for that purpose, and to this further use, intent, and purpose that they, my said
trustees, and the Survivor of them, and the heirs and assigns of such
survivor, shall stand and be seized of all and every the same last-
mentioned manors, messuages, lands, tenements, and hereditaments,
or such part thereof as shall remain unsold for the purposes aforesaid,
To and for the several uses, intents, and purposes hereinafter
mentioned (that is to say) In trust, that they and the survivor of
them, and the heirs and assigns of such survivor, do and shall receive
the rents, issues, and profits thereof, and every part thereof, and after
paying taxes, repairs, and other outgoings, do and shall, from time to
time, pay and apply the neat produce of the said rents, issues, and
profits to my said Niece, Gertrude, for so long as she shall happen to
live, to her own sole and peculiar use, separate and distinct from her
present or any other husband, and her receipt alone shall be a
sufficient discharge for the same.   And I will my said Trustees, and
the survivor of them, and the heirs and assigns of such survivor shall,

during the life of my said niece, be seized of the same lands, messuages, and tenements and hereditaments In trust, to support and
preserve the contingent uses and estates hereinafter limited from
being defeated and destroyed, but nevertheless to permit and suffer
my said niece, Gertrude, to hold and enjoy the rents, issues, and
profits of the same premises as I have hereinbefore directed, and
from before and after the decease of my said niece, Gertrude Warburton, In trust for the 1st, 2nd, 3rd, and all and every other the
son and sons of the body of my said niece lawfully begotten or to be
begotten, severally, successively, and in remainder one after another,
as they and every of them shall be in seniority of age and priority of
birth, and the several and respective heirs male of the body and
bodies of all and every such son and sons lawfully issuing, the elder
of such sons and the heirs male of his body, to be always preferred,
and to take before the younger of such son and sons, and the heirs
male of his and their body and bodies issuing, And in default of
such issue, In trust for all and every the daughter and daughters of
the body of my said niece, Gertrude Warburton, lawfully begotten or
to be begotten, to be equally divided between them if more than one,
share and share alike, to take as Tenant in common, and not as joint
tenants, and the several and respective heirs of the bodies of all and
every such daughter and daughters lawfully issuing.   And in case
one or more daughters shall happen to die without issue of her or
their body or bodies, Then as to the share or shares of her or them so
dying without issue, In trust for the survivors or survivor, and others
or other of them, to be equally divided between or among them (if more
than one) share and share alike, to take as Tenant in Common, and not
as joint tenant, and the several and respective heirs of the bodies of
such survivors or survivor, and others or other of them, and if all such
daughters but one shall happen to dye without issue of their bodies,
or if there shall be but one such daughter, In trust for such surviving
or only daughter and the heirs of her body, And in default of such
issue, Then in trust for my nephew, Captain William Tucker,[1] and
his assigns, for and during the term of his natural life, without im-

---

[1] Nephew of Allen and brother of Mrs. Warburton.

peachment of waste, except wast. in pulling down houses and buildings, and from and after the determination of that estate to the use
of the said John Chapman and James Sparrow, and their heirs,
during the life of my said nephew, Captain William Tucker, In trust
to support and preserve the contingent uses and Estates hereinafter
limited from being defeated and destroyed, and for that purpose to make
entries and bring actions as the case shall require, yet nevertheless
to permit and suffer the said William Tucker and his assigns, during his
life, to receive and take the rents and profits thereof, and of every part
thereof, to and for his and their own use and benefit, and from and after
his decease, In trust for the 1st, 2nd, 3rd and all and every other,
the son and sons of the body of the said William Tucker lawfully to
be begotten, severally, successively and in remainder one after
another as they and every of them shall be in seniority of age and
priority of birth, and the several and respective heirs male of the
body and bodies of all and every such son and sons lawfully issuing,
the elder of such sons and the heirs male of his body to be always
preferred, and take before the younger of such son and sons and the
heirs male of his or their body and bodies issuing.   And in default of
such issue In trust for all and every the daughter and daughters of
my said nephew, William Tucker, lawfully forgotten or to be begotten, to be equally divided between them (if more than one)
share and share alike, to take as Tenants in common and not as
joint Tenants, and the several and respective heirs of all and every
such daughters and daughter lawfully issuing, and in case one or
more of such daughters shall happen to die without issue of her or
their body or bodies, then as to the share or shares of her or them
so dying without issue, In trust for the survivors or survivor and
others or other of them to be equally divided between or among
them (if more than one) share and share alike, to take as tenants in
common and not as joint tenants and the several and respective
heirs of the body of such survivors or survivor and others or other of
them.   And if all such daughters but one shall happen to dye
without issue of their bodies, or if there shall be but 1 such daughter,
In trust for such surviving or only daughter and the heirs of her
body lawfully issuing, And in default of such issue then in trust for

my niece, Mary Allen, and her assigns for and during the term of her natural life without impeachment of waste, except wast. in pulling down houses and buildings, and from and after the deter- mination of that estate to the use of the said John Chapman and James Sparrow and their heirs during the life of my said niece, Mary Allen,[1] In trust to support and preserve the contingent uses and estates hereinafter limited from being defeated or destroyed, and for that purpose to make entries and bring actions as the case shall require, yet nevertheless to permit and suffer the said Mary Allen and her assigns during her life to receive and take the rents and profits thereof and of every part thereof to and for her and their own use and benefit, and from and after her decease, In trust for the 1st, 2nd, 3rd and all and every other the son and sons of the body of the said Mary Allen lawfully to be begotten severally and succes- sively and in remainder one after another as they and every of them shall be in seniority of age and priority of birth and the several and respective heirs male of the body and bodies of all and every such son and sons lawfully begotten issuing, the elder of such sons and the heirs male of his body always to be preferred and take before the younger of such son and sons and the heirs male of his and their body and bodies issuing, and in default of such issue, In trust for all and every the daughter and daughters of the body of my said niece, Mary Allen, lawfully begotten or to be begotten, to be equally divided between them, if more than one, share and share alike, to take as Tenants in common and not as joint Tenants, and the several and respective heirs of the bodies of all and every such daughter and daughters lawfully issuing, and in case one or more of such daughters shall happen to die without issue of her or their body or bodies, Then as to the share or shares of her or them so dying without issue, In trust for the survivors or survivor and others or other of them to be equally divided between or among them, if more than one, share and share alike, to take as tenant in

---

[1] Mary Allen was the only daughter of Philip Allen, by his second marriage with Jane Bennet of Widcombe House. In 1766 she became the second wife of the first Viscount Hawarden. See pp. 211, 228.

common and not as joint tenant, and the several and respective heirs of the body of such survivors and survivor and others or other of them, and if all such daughters but one should happen to dye without issue of their bodys, or if there shall be but one such daughter in trust for such surviving or only daughter and the heirs of her body lawfully issuing and for want or in default of such issue to the use and behoof of my own right heirs forever. Provided, nevertheless, and it is my express wish and desire that it shall and may be lawful to and for them my said Trustees and the survivor of them and the heirs and assigns of such survivor in my wife's lifetime to make sale or mortgage of all and every my freehold manors, messuages, lands, tenements, and hereditaments, except my Manor and Estate at Bathampton, and my estate and Interest in the lands purchased of the Duke of Kingston as aforesaid for the purposes of paying my debts and legacies, and I do hereby empower them to make such sale or mortgage as aforesaid, in case the party or parties for the time being who shall become intitled thereto by the limitations and bequests aforesaid shall request the same, and in case also that the same is not to be in prejudice to my wife's estate for her life or the annuity I have hereby given her.   Item, All my leasehold messuages, lands, and tenements whatsoever, subject to my wife's Interest therein for her life, I give, devise, and bequeath to them my said trustees upon the following trusts, that is to say, in trust that they my said trustees and the survivor of them, and the Executors and Administrators of such survivors do and shall pay and apply the neat rents and profits thereof to my said niece, Gertrude, and her assigns for and during her natural life, separate and apart from her present or any other husband, and her receipt alone to be sufficient discharge, and after her decease I give the same leasehold estates to her son Ralph Warburton and executors and assigns for all the residue and remainder of the several terms that shall be thereon to come at his mother's death, But in case the said Ralph Warburton shall die before he arrives to the age of 21 years, then I give the same leasehold estates to my nephew, Captain William Tucker, and his executors and assigns, for all the residue of the several terms that shall be thereon to come in case my said nephew be living at the death of the said Ralph Warburton, but if he be then dead, I give the same leasehold estates and premises to my niece, Mary Allen, and her executors and assigns for all the Estate and Interest that shall be thereon respectively to come. Item, I give and bequeath unto my loving wife the sum of £500 to be paid within one week after my death. Item, I give to the said Lord Bishop of Gloucester my whole library of books, and whereas upon the marriage of the said Lord Bishop with my niece Gertrude his wife, I did by certain Articles of Agreement, dated on or about 25 Mar. 1745, and made between me the said Ralph Allen on the one part, and the said Lord Bishop on the other part, covenant and agree to pay unto one or more trustee or trustees to be named and approved by the said Lord Bishop and Gertrude his wife or the Survivor of them, or the executors or admors. of such survivor, within the space of one yr. after the death of my now wife the sum of £5,000 in part of a fortune with my said niece. Now, in case I should happen to die in the lifetime of my said wife, I do hereby order and direct to such trustee or trustees to be nominated and approved of as aforesaid the sum £5,000 instead of the said sum of £5,000 so by me covenanted to be paid after my said wife's death as aforesaid, and to be upon the same trusts as are mentioned and declared in and by the said marriage articles and to be paid in 6 months after my death. Item, I give and bequeath to my wife the sum of £1,000 to be by her paid and applied to and for such charities as she shall see proper. Item, I give my brother, Phillip Allen, the sum of £2,000 to be paid him in 6 months aft. my death. Item, I give and bequeath to my said niece, Gertrude, the sum of £5,000 to be paid her within 6 months aft. my death, and to be separate and apart from her present husband and not subject to his debts, control, or management, but to do therewith as she shall think proper. I give my nephew, Phillip Allen, the sum of £1,000.[1] I give my nephew, Ralph Allen,[2] the sum of £5,000, to be paid them respectively within 12 months next aft. my death. I give my niece, Mary Allen,

---

[1] Elder son of his brother, Philip.
[2] Younger son of Philip Allen. See p. 211.

the sum of £10,000 to be paid her in 12 months next after my death. Item, I give to my nephew, Captain Wm. Tucker, the sum of £10,000 to be paid him in 12 months next after my death. I give to my sister, Gertrude Elliott,[1] the sum of £3,000 to be paid in six months after my death. Item, I give to my nephew, Phillip Elliott, the sum of £1,000, to be paid him in 6 months after the death of my wife if he my said nephew be then living. And I give to my grand nephew, Ralph Elliott, the sum of £1,000, to be paid 6 months after my said wife's decease if he my said grand nephew be then living. Item, I give to my nephew, Captain William Tucker, the additional legacy of £5,000, to be paid him in 6 months after my said wife's decease, and to my niece, Mary Allen, I give the additional sum of £5,000, to be paid her in 6 months after my wife's death. Item, I give and bequeath unto the Reverend James Sparrow the sum of £5,000, and to his son, James Sparrow, I give the sum of £100, and to Mrs. Ann Bennett the sum of £100, which said 3 last mentioned legacies I will be paid within twelve months aft. my decease. Item, I give to my grt. nephew, Ralph Warburton, the annuity of £40 a yr. I purchased for his life in the Government security for his own use and benefit. Item, I give to Docr. Wm. Oliver Jerry Peirce, Mr. Jno. Knipe, Clerk, the Reverend Mr. Hurd, of Shurkaston, and Aldn. Chapman, Wm. Hoare, Lewis Clutterbuck, Gent., Jos. Lobb and Ralph Mould £100 each, which said last mentioned legacies I will be paid in twelve months after my death. Item, I give to the 3 children of Henry Fielding, Esqre., deceased, the sum of £100 each, and to their Aunt, Sarah Fielding, I give the sum of £100, which said 4 last named legacies I will be paid in 12 months after my decease. Item, I give to my servants William Ward and Isaac Doddesly the sum of £100 each, And I give to my servant Saml. Mellard the sum of £50. I give to Richd. Jones,[2] each of my menial servants, except Wm. Ward, Lamb Prym, Is. Doddesley and Saml. Mellard, 1 yr.'s wages over and above what shall be due to them at my

---

[1] The wife of Richard Elliott, Esquire, of St. Austell, to whom she was married May 20, 1732.

[2] Richard Jones was Allen's Clerk of the Works, and after Allen's death he was appointed City Surveyor of Works.

decease. I give my clerk, Saml. Prynn, the sum of £400, and to his wife £100 for her extordiny. care of my wife in her great illness, to be paid in 12 months after my death, and it is my express will and meaning that if by any unforeseen accidents and misfortunes my real and personal estates shall prove insufficient to pay the whole of my wife's annuity, debts and money legacies, Then and in such case I do hereby direct that all and every the Legatee and Legatees herein named whose respective legacy and legacys shall amount to the sum of one thousand pounds and upwards, shall abate in proportion to their legacies, and such legatee and legatees to have and receive Interest for such abated sums at the rate of £4 per cent. per annum, to be computed from the day of my death to the day of my said wife's decease, and then such legatee and legatees to be entitled to have and receive their respective abated sums if my Estate will admit thereof. Item, all the residue of my goods, chattels and personal estate, whatsoever and wheresoever not hereinbefore disposed of, I give unto the said John Chapman and James Sparrow, my said Trustees, in trust to pay all my debts, funeral expences, legacies, and charges of proving this my will. Then my will is, And I do hereby give and bequeath such neat estate as shall be so remaining after the above ends and purposes are fully satisfied to my said Trustees to place the same out at Interest, and to pay such Interest to my niece, Gertrude Warburton, for and during her natural life, separate and apart from her present or any after-taken husband, and her receipt to be a sufficient discharge for the same, first allowing thereout to my Great Nephew, Ralph Warburton, the sum of £200 yearly towards his education until he arrives at the age of 21 yrs., and after allowing him, the said Ralph Warburton, £400 per annum instead of the said £200 per annum during the joint lives of his mother and my said wife, and after the death of my wife his mother surviving allowing him £600 per annum for his life instead of the said £400 per annum, And I give the said Ralph Warburton the said annuities accordingly, and to be clear of all deductions and over and above the £40 per annum I have hereinbefore given him, and the said annuities to be paid by two half-yearly payments, (to wit) the nativity of Our Lord Jesus Christ and St. John the Baptist, by even and equal portions. And I will the said allowances or annuities shall be deducted by my said trustees out of what real and personal Estates and Incomes I have herein-before given to his said Mother, if the yearly produce of the neat produce of my residuary Estate shall not be sufficient for that pur-pose. And from and after the decease of my said niece, Gertrude Warburton, I give the said neat principal of my residuary Estate so as aforesaid directed, to be placed out at Interest, unto the said Ralph Warburton, his executors and administrators, for his and their own use and benefit, if he shall happen to survive his said mother, but if he dies in his mother's lifetime, then I give and bequeath the same to my Nephew, Capt. Wm. Tucker, and my niece, Mary Allen, and their respective executors and administrators, not as joint Tenants, but as Tenants in Common, but if only one of them shall be living at the death of my said Niece, Gertrude Warburton, her said son being then dead, I give the same principal Estate to such One so surviving, and his or her executors or administrators, but if it shall so happen that neither of them, my said nephew and niece, Capt. Wm. Tucker and Mary Allen, shall live to be entitled to the said principal Estate, I then give the same to such person and persons, and in such parts and proportions, as my niece, Gertrude Warburton, shall, by any deed or deeds, writing or writings, to be by her executed in the presence of and attested by two or more credible witnesses, or by her last Will and Testament so executed and attested as aforesaid limit, direct, or appoint, give or bequeath, and in default of such limitation or ap-pointment, gift, or bequest, then in trust to pay the same principal Estate to the Executors, Administrators, or assigns of my said Niece, Gertrude Warburton, and I give the same accordingly, and I will that my said trustees shall deduct and detain out of the trust moneys and Estates, all cost, damages, and expences they shall sustain or be put unto in the execution of the trusts hereby in them reposed, and that they shall not be chargeable with or accountable for any more moneys than he or they shall actually receive, and shall not be accountable one for the other of them, or for the acts, receipts, or defaults of the other of them, but each for his own act, receipt, and default only, and I do hereby make, constitute, and appoint them, my said Trustees, the said John Chapman and James Sparrow, joint Executors In trust of this my last will and Testament, and do hereby revoke all former wills and Testaments by me made. In witness whereof I have to this, my Last Will and Testament, contained in 3 skins of parchment, to the 2 first skins thereof set my hand, and to this third and last skin set both my hand and seal, this 28th day of June, one thousand seven hundred and sixty three.

Ralph Allen.

Signed, sealed, published, and declared, by the said Ralph Allen, the Testator, as and for his last Will and Testament, in the presence of us who have subscribed our names as witnesses thereto at his request, in his presence and in the presence of each other—Richard Rogers—James Mullins—Robt. Foreman.

1.

I, Ralph Allen of Prior Park, in the Parish of Lyncomb and Widcomb, in the County of Somerset, Esquire, do declare the following bequests to be a codicil, and as part of my last will and testament of this day's date, that is to say, I give my servant, Francis Breed, for his great care of me in my severe illness, the sum of £300. I give to Mrs. Moore, late Nurse to my Grt. Nephew, Ralph Warburton, for her great care of him in his infancy, the sum of £200. I give to Mrs. Mary Poyntz the sum of £100. I give to Alderman John Chapman the additional sum of £100 in case he takes upon him the execution of the trust of this my will. And I give to the Lord Bishop of Gloucester the sum of £500, all said legacies to be paid in 12 months aft. my death. Witness my hand and seal this twenty-eighth day of June, one thousand seven hundred and sixty three.

Ralph Allen.

Signed and Sealed by the said Ralph Allen as a Codicil to his last will in the presence of us—Richard Rogers—James Mullins—Robt. Foreman.

2.

I do hereby confirm the legacy of £1,000 given to Mr. Pitt on the other side of this paper, by deeming that gift to be the second

Codicil to my last will, dated yesterday at Prior Park, June 29th, 1763. RALPH ALLEN.

The former Codicil was in the following terms :—

" For the last instance of my friendship and grateful regard for the best of friends, as well as the most upright and ablest of Ministers that has adorned our Country, I give to the Right Honble. William Pitt the sum of £1,000, to be disposed of by him to any one of his children that he may be pleased to appoint for it. And I hereby declare this to be a Codicil to my last Will and Testament, dated the first day of last August, Prior Park, November 10th, 1760.

R. ALLEN."

3.

Prior Park, June 29, 1763.

I do hereby declare that it is my will and intention that if Capt. Tucker[1] should, upon the death of his sister Warburton and her child Ralph, or other children that she may hereafter have, come into the possession of my Estates of inheritance, and my niece, Mary Allen, should then be living, In such case do give at that time to Molly the additional fortune of £15,000 over and above her other legacies, and I do deem this to be a 3rd Codicil to my last will dated yesterday. RALPH ALLEN.

4.

I, Ralph Allen of Prior Park, in the County of Somerset, do give to Retkiren Allen, of St. Columbe, in Cornwall, the annual annuity of £20 during his natural life, to be quarterly paid to him by my Executors without any deduction and out of the £1,000 which, in my will dated the 28th day of last month, I have given to my wife for she to dispose of at her discretion to charitable uses; it is my desire that she will £200 of that money to James Donnell, who was my servant in the Stables and is now blind, and that in the disposal of the remainder of the £1,000 above mentioned, it is my desire

---

[1] Capt. Tucker predeceased his sister, Mrs. Warburton, and in 1797 Mrs. Warburton (then Mrs. Stafford Smith) died—her son had long predeceased her. At her death the only son of Lord Hawarden, Thomas-Ralph, succeeded to Prior Park, and died without issue in 1807.

that Richard Gibbs and other old labourers now employed by me, or old servants passed their labour and not particularly taken notice of by me in my last will, may be considered and taken care of out of that money by my wife, And I declare this paper to be a 4th Codicil to my will, July 6th, 1763.   RALPH ALLEN.

5.

Wednesday, June 27th, 1764.

40 minutes after 7 a.m.

Mr. Allen desires to be buried as privately and decently as possible, without pomp, in the Churchyard at Claverton, in a Vault made to hold eight. The inscription for, and draught of the Tomb, which is to be of stone, are both made, and are in one of the Drawers in the room in which he now lies. His will is in the second drawer of the Chest nearest his bed. He dies in perfect good will towards Mr. Pitt concerning whom there is a codicil added to his will; he wishes happiness to all, desires that a part of a Will not yet signed relative to his nephew Mr. Phillip Allen's marriage may stand good in the manner intended by that writing, of which Mr. Clutterbuck (and, I think he said) Mr. Phillip Allen, Senr., were acquainted; he also desires that all those who have attended him in his illness may be rewarded, and that I may be taken care of; is very thankful to God for his present ease, and chearfully submitts to his decrees. He enquired tenderly for Mrs. Allen, desires that Mr. Mears may be paid a full year's allowance as if he had lived, without any deduction for what has already been paid of the year. 20 minutes aft. 8 o'clock— Tho. West—Thomas Hyett—Hugh Frazer—Francis Breedon.

Proved at London with five codicils, 11 August 1764, before the Judge, by the Oaths of John Chapman, Esqre., and Rev. James Sparrow, Clerk, the Executors to whom Admon. was granted, having been first sworn by Comon. duly to administer.

CHAS. DINELY. ⎫
JOHN IGGULDEN. ⎬ Deputy
W. F. GOSTLING. ⎭ Registers.

294 *Simpson,* 74 *B.P.*

R

PRIOR PARK AT THE PRESENT DAY.

AFTER the death of Lord Hawarden[1] in 1807, Prior Park was sold to a rich Bristol merchant, Mr. Thomas, a member of the Society of Friends. This gentleman felled as much timber as paid the greater part, if not the whole, of the purchase-money.

In 1829, the property again changed hands, passing into the possession of the late Bishop Baines, for the purposes of a Roman Catholic Seminary ; and with the exception of a few years' interval, during which it was occupied by a Mr. Thomas Thompson, it has been occupied and used for the same purpose. Bishop Baines was a man of pre-eminent ability, and held in great honour and esteem, not simply for his great learning, but for the dignity of his character and the gentle beneficence and kindness of his disposition.

Anyone looking at the view of the vast sweep of the original mansion and offices as given (p. 109), and comparing it with the present, will perceive several changes. The Palladian steps in front of the mansion were constructed by Bishop Baines ; the original stables are raised a storey and used for purposes of the college ; whilst on the site of the pigeon-house and *port-cochere* a handsome chapel stands. But, considerable as are these changes, the great deterioration in this beautiful estate is in the grounds, especially in the rear. It is deplorable to see the roads and fences and the surroundings generally. But when it is remembered what pecuniary resources would be required to keep such an estate in handsome condition—in their beauteous original condition—we can only avert our face, and cry, "*Alas ! alas !*"

Prior Park is now passing into the hands of that vigorous and enterprising educational body, the *Christian Brothers*, a Roman Catholic community, under whom the establishment is to be carried on with ample capital and a competent staff of masters and pro-fessors. We look forward to the revival of those external beauties which, in former times, were the lories of the glocality and the city.

---

[1] See pp. 211, 228, marriage of Cornwallis Maude with Mary, daughter of Philip Allen, and niece of Ralph.

INDEX.

At Batheaston.

LONDON :
PRINTED AT THE BEDFORD PRESS, 20 AND 21, BEDFORDBURY, W.C.